LOGAN

LIGHTHOUSE SECURITY INVESTIGATIONS MONTANA

MARYANN JORDAN

Logan (Lighthouse Security Investigation Montana) Copyright 2024

All rights reserved. No part of this book may be reproduced or transmitted in any form or by any means, electronic or mechanical, including photocopying, recording, or by any information storage and retrieval system without the written permission of the author, except where permitted by law.

If you are reading this book and did not purchase it, then you are reading an illegal pirated copy. If you would be concerned about working for no pay, then please respect the author's work! Make sure that you are only reading a copy that has been officially released by the author.

This book is a work of fiction. Names, characters, places, and incidents are either products of the author's imagination or are used fictitiously. Any resemblance to actual persons, living or dead, events, or locales is entirely coincidental.

Cover by: Graphics by Stacy

Cover photograph: Eric McKinney 612Covered Photography

ISBN ebook: 978-1-956588-68-2

ISBN print: 978-1-956588-69-9

❦ Created with Vellum

ABOUT THE AUTHOR

I am an avid reader of romance novels, often joking that I cut my teeth on historical romances. I have been reading and reviewing for years. In 2013, I finally gave in to the characters in my head, screaming for their story to be told. From these musings, my first novel, Emma's Home, The Fairfield Series, was born.

I was a high school counselor, having worked in education for thirty years. I live in Virginia, having also lived in four states and two foreign countries. I have been married to a wonderfully patient man for forty-two years. When writing, my dog or one of my cats can generally be found in the same room if not on my lap.

Please take the time to leave a review of this book. Feel free to contact me, especially if you enjoyed my book. I love to hear from readers!

Facebook

Join my Facebook group: Maryann Jordan's Protector Fans

Sign up for my emails by visiting my Website!

Website

AUTHOR NOTES

Logan and Vivian's story was first released as a novel, *Thin Ice*, part of a multiauthor series (Sleeper SEALs). When I wrote their story, I knew that Logan would make an incredible leader of a security firm. Since I was writing my Saints Protection Investigation series, I made sure to involve his character near the end. I have also kept Logan "alive" as he occasionally popped up in my Lighthouse Security Investigations and Lighthouse Security Investigations West Coast series.

The time is finally right to bring Logan back to the forefront. *Thin Ice* is no longer available. I have completely rewritten the book... different protagonists, different reasons for his mission to Alaska, where he meets Vivian, and a completely different experience as he begins the process of building a Lighthouse Security Investigations Montana.

And for those of you who say, "But there are no lighthouses in Montana!" You will discover how it all works out as you read this story!

When writing fiction, I research topics so the reader can enjoy the story and feel as though it is as real as possible. I often change the names of cities and places. Choosing to do so allows me creative license to write the places as I see them and not become bogged down in trying to re-create a real place.

In this story, I have taken that one step further. Our heroine is a scientist and is asked to utilize her skills in order to help our hero. I ask, dear readers, that you follow the story, accepting that not all laboratory procedures and methods are completely accurate. This is fiction—enjoy!

the landing pad outside Cut Bank, Montana, circling over the small town right on the edge of a steep bank leading down to a river. He had knocked off about fifteen minutes on their tour but figured it was due to him for having to listen to their bickering.

Although Cut Bank's population was only about three thousand people, tourists looking for wildlife photo opportunities came to the town this time of year. The three small hotels in the town and three in nearby Shelby filled up quickly.

After assisting Dorothy down and silently nodding toward both of them, he pivoted away, deftly extinguishing any further requests to see the natural Montana vista from his helicopter. After refueling, he waved to Gus, the owner of the small airfield, and climbed back in the cockpit, soon lifting off the ground.

In quiet solitude, he traversed the landscape below, a slow hum of satisfaction moving through him as he surveyed what was his. When he came to Montana, he'd initially planned on buying a small spread. But the right price for a family trying to sell off a large estate acreage was too good to pass up. Loneliness occasionally gnawed at him, but he tried to tamp those feelings down. *Who'd want to live way out here, and where would I meet them?* With no answer to those questions, he just enjoyed the peace.

Five minutes later, he touched down once more, this time with an air of contentment on his own property. Guiding his craft into the metal, dome-topped hangar, he parked his bird next to his Lakota—a huge, military-grade helicopter used for mountain rescues of skiers or stranded hikers.

Climbing out, he stretched the kinks out of his back before beginning his routine maintenance. Qualified as a mechanic and a pilot, he alone handled his birds until the annual inspection was due. With a final pat on its side, he walked to the hangar door and pulled it shut, sliding it along the channel until it closed securely. Locking it, he activated the security he had installed before trudging over the hardened ground toward his low-slung ranch house.

His acreage included flat, scruffy land with trees and hills leading to the mountains in the background. The one-story house with a basement was on the land when he bought it, and he added the helicopter hangar. The house was plain but functional, large enough for him, and sturdy enough for the winters. A porch gave it a homier appeal but was added to cut down on the direct sunlight blasting through the front windows.

Stepping into the neat interior, he walked straight to the kitchen, threw open the refrigerator door, and reached inside to grab a beer. None. *Fuck.* He knew he had been getting low but dreaded making the trip to the grocery in town. It wasn't the act of shopping that irked him, but rather the prospect of social interaction. *Nah, that's not true.* It was just hard being around people who didn't really know him or would never be able to understand him. He rubbed his aching knee and wondered if he even knew himself nowadays. This wasn't the future he'd envisioned for himself.

Sighing, he debated for a moment but decided he

also needed milk, bread, soup, vegetables, and a few other staples.

"Meow."

At the same time he heard the meow, he felt the tabby feline rubbing against his legs. Looking down, he grinned. "Hey, Poncho. You need something to eat, too?" Even if he ran low on his own supplies, he always stocked the dog and cat food well. Reaching into the cabinet, he grabbed a can of cat food and dumped a measured portion into the dish on the counter. Placing it on the floor, he watched as Poncho quickly scarfed every morsel and then looked up at him in expectation.

"You know what the vet said. No more kitty treats. You have about two more pounds to lose to be as svelte as you need to be." He squatted and rubbed the cat's fur, hearing the purring begin immediately. Poncho had come with the ranch and was skinny when Logan first moved in. Feeling sorry for the scrawny fella, he overfed him, not realizing how quickly Poncho would pack on the weight. Now, on a diet, Poncho protested mightily at feeding time but never passed up a chance to sleep next to Logan, whether on the sofa or the bed.

"Okay, you've eaten. Now, I need to get some things for me." Grabbing the keys to his truck, he headed out the door.

Fifteen minutes later, he drove into Cut Bank, stopping at the little grocery store on the outskirts. A larger one had opened on the other side of the tiny town, but he preferred the quiet, comfortable feeling in the older one, run by a couple who didn't have a predilection for talking everyone's ear off or asking too many personal questions.

Moving through the glass door, he nodded politely to the woman behind the cash register. "Marge." His voice sounded rough even to his ears.

"Logan," she replied, her smile firmly in place as her tight gray curls bounced about her head before she looked back down at the magazine opened in front of her.

Walking through the aisles, he quickly loaded his cart with the necessities, calculating they would last him several weeks. He preferred to stock up at one time so he didn't have to make too many trips. Avoiding the few other shoppers, he pushed his cart toward the counter and waited patiently as the woman in front of him balanced a toddler on her hip and tried to contain a small child interested in the candy.

The little boy fingered a candy bar longingly, and Logan could see the wheels turning in his head, wondering if his mother would notice if he took it. Clearing his throat, Logan gained the little boy's attention. His wide eyes looked up at the large man standing next to him. He snatched his fingers back to his sides before looking down at his shoes.

As the mother paid and placed the toddler back into the cart, she turned to take her little boy's hand, who glanced back at Logan as they left the store. Logan didn't mean to scare him, but he knew his grumpy persona probably terrified the kid.

Sighing, he placed his items on the counter, and as they were rung up, he grabbed the candy bar at the last one to beat around the bush, he asked, "What the fuck are you two doing out here? Did I miss the memo for some meeting, or did you get lost?" He remained in place, still stunned at his visitors.

"You going to invite us in, Bishop?" the first man asked, grinning.

Stepping back, he still couldn't believe who was walking into his house. Jack *fuckin'* Bryant and, if he wasn't mistaken, Mace *where-the-hell-did-he-go* Hanover.

2

Logan was still shocked at his company and surprised that the two men had traveled all the way to Montana without letting him know they were coming. Not that he minded, but with some of the trips he made, it was always a gamble whether he was home. He stepped away from the door, setting the safety on his weapon and waving his arm to welcome his visitors inside.

Jack moved toward him with his hand outstretched. Logan reached out, clasping it, his handshake firm. One of his former SEAL teammates now worked for Jack's Saints Protection Investigation business in Virginia, and that was how Logan had met the stoic former Army Special Forces soldier.

"Bishop, you're looking good," Jack stated, his eyes roving over Logan from head to toe and back again. "Have you met Mace Hanover?"

Logan turned to the other iconic man and shook his hand. "Never met but heard a lot about. Mace, it's nice to meet you." Mace had also been former Army Special

Forces with Jack, but Mace had gone off the grid and the rumor was he had been recruited for CIA special operations.

The large, dark-haired, olive-skinned man held his gaze and smiled. "I've been looking forward to this for a long time."

Logan led them into his living space and inclined his head toward the sofa. "Make yourself at home. I was just at the store. You want a beer?"

Jack nodded, and Mace replied, "Wouldn't turn one down."

Logan walked into the kitchen, rotely grabbing three bottles from the refrigerator while his mind raced. It was obvious by their visit something was happening, but what? He couldn't imagine. Letting out a long breath, he returned to the living room, handed each a bottle, and then settled on the chair facing the two men on the sofa. Considering he never had company, he glanced around, wondering what the other men thought of his place.

The small living room was furnished simply with a comfortable sofa and easy chair facing a corner stone fireplace and a flat-screen TV on the wall. Warm paneling covered the walls, decorated with a few framed photographs of Montana vistas in various seasons. A Native American handmade blanket in reds and browns graced the back of the chair. A handwoven rug of the same colors covered the center of the wooden plank floor.

To the right was a table, mostly scattered with papers and a laptop. A map of the area was tacked to the been enough for Mace to notice as he offered a chin lift, then leaned forward, his forearms resting on his knees.

"I retired some years before your knee gave out. I heard about it... how your mission ended with success but with an injury that cut your career short."

Logan grimaced, hating the reminder of why he had no choice but to retire. One last mission—successful but devastating. When he went back to get a fallen team member, his knee took the brunt of a fall, tearing it to shreds. He'd saved a life and gave up his career all in the same minute. But if he had to do it over again, no question—he would have made the same decision.

Mace continued as though he hadn't noticed Logan's expression change. But Logan had a feeling that very little got past Mace.

"My own career path had gone sideways at one point, but I had the opportunity to lead a team for the CIA that included special op personnel from SEALs, Deltas, Rangers, Air Force... hell, it was a dream come true. All egos were checked at the door, and the experience let me know that I wanted to replicate that when I got out. No more military or governmental bullshit... just me taking on the missions I wanted."

Interest flared... or maybe it was more curiosity. With a short nod, he indicated for Mace to continue.

"Anyway, I had some money come my way, and then it seemed the government was willing to pay for me to go private. Built Lighthouse Security Investigations. Based in Maine."

Logan continued to nod but couldn't imagine why

Mace was here 'cause there was no way he'd consider moving to Maine to work for someone else.

"So now I have a team, a special compound that holds our company, and since we're right on the coast, we can deploy boats when needed. And the government I used to serve that would then put restrictions on me now sends jobs my way to handle how I see fit. And I only take the jobs I want. We have other contacts and even do our own missions to assist the local area."

Jack snorted, drawing Logan's attention. "That's how Mace met his wife."

Logan's brows lifted. He knew Jack and most of his Saints had met their significant others, but it was hard to imagine the hard-edged man in front of him as married. Then Mace's face gentled into a softer smile, and Logan could have sworn he'd just witnessed a personality change right in front of him.

Getting his mind back to the reason his visitors showed up, he said, "I admire what both of you have done, but forgive me if I don't see what it has to do with me."

Mace nodded slowly, but his gaze never wavered. Logan's confidence always gave him the upper hand in situations, but he fought the urge to squirm under Mace's perusal.

"Makes sense," Mace said. "Why the fuck would I come all the way out to Montana to tell someone I'd never met what the fuck I've been doing?" He chuckled. "No, I don't want to ask you to give up all this and come work for me. What I want is for you to consider a business proposition."

Logan's brows lifted to his hairline. *A business proposition?* His mind blanked, uncertainty now taking precedence over any ideas he thought might have brought the two to his door.

"I enlisted Carson Dyer to start work on a Lighthouse Security Investigation on the West Coast in California. He and I now work together as business partners, and he's started taking assignments after hiring the best employees."

Logan worked to keep his breathing steady. Mace's revelation was fascinating, but Logan was still in the dark as to how it pertained to him.

Mace leaned back and took another swig of his beer. "I'd like you to consider doing the same."

Logan's mouth opened, then he narrowed his eyes. "You want me to do the same what, exactly?"

"Consider being a business partner of LSI as an owner. You'd be the leader, the one calling the shots, and the person the others would report to."

"And where would this proposed LSI business be located?"

"Right here."

"Here?"

Mace and Jack looked at each other, and both men smiled. Mace turned back to Logan. "I don't figure you plan on moving. You have a great location, and it seems you do a lot more here than anyone knows."

Logan's eyes narrowed again, but he remembered Jack telling him that Mace had checked him out. Nodding, he said, "Got some land—"

"You've got almost two hundred acres that extend

from here to the base of the closest mountain," Mace interjected.

"Okay... and I have a couple of birds—"

"You've got more than just two helicopters in your hangars."

Logan snapped his mouth shut. He hated to be interrupted, but Mace wasn't just shooting at the target, hoping to randomly hit something. Mace had his facts right. Heaving a sigh, he said, "What about this place? Not exactly like your setups, is it?"

"Plenty of time to work on that. You'd get the money necessary to build the kind of place that would work for you and the business."

The three men sat in silence for several long minutes, all finishing their beer as Logan pondered the bizarre situation. He finally said, "This proposition is interesting, but I've only worked alone since getting out."

"And not just flying tourists around," Jack said, re-entering the conversation.

Logan looked over at Jack, knowing he'd only come on the visit to be the familiar face to connect him with Mace.

"You're not the only former SEAL trying to settle into a life that isn't very rewarding," Mace said. "I find the men and women who I think are right for the job and make an offer. Carson is starting this process, too. A lot of former special operators out there... but not everyone is right to work for LSI. It takes someone special." He cocked his head to the side, his gaze never leaving Logan. "Bet you know of a few yourself who would fit the description of a Keeper."

Logan's first thought slid to some people he'd worked with and lost touch with. The idea that they might work with him again lit a tiny spark. The second thought had his chin rear back. "Keeper?"

"The idea of the lighthouse keepers of old. My base is underneath the ground in the caves of the Maine coastline, directly under an old decommissioned lighthouse. Carson is near one. Keepers guide people to safety. They protect and rescue when necessary."

Logan barked out a rough laugh, evidence that he rarely laughed aloud. "I hate to be the one to point it out, Mace, but there are no lighthouses in Montana."

Mace turned and looked out the window toward the mountains close by. "What's that?"

Logan bent slightly to see what Mace was indicating. "That's a light tower. Keeps aircraft from slamming into the mountainside in the dark. It can also be used for rescues, giving someone a directional point."

Mace turned back, his lips curving slightly. "You're a pilot. You know how necessary that tower is to keep people safe. Just because you're landlocked doesn't mean your existence isn't that of a Keeper."

Logan fought to keep the air from audibly rushing from his lungs, but his chest felt tight. He'd felt the importance of his job every day that he was a SEAL. But now, there were days he struggled to get out of bed and face another group of tourists. His bottom lip pulled in, and he bit down as his mind sifted through everything Mace suggested. "Why me, though?"

"You've already got some kind of setup here. Or is my information wrong?" Mace asked.

Logan paused, his thoughts carefully pondering his next actions. Then he took to his feet. "Follow me." Without any explanation, he walked toward the kitchen and stopped at a closet. He didn't turn but could hear Jack and Mace following. He opened the door, revealing a set of stairs, and offered one word as an explanation for now. "Basement."

He led the way downstairs, flipping the light switch as he went. At the bottom, he entered a code into a security panel and walked through the door that opened. Inside, several computers lined two walls of the small room. A white screen filled the third wall, ready for maps, computer images, and intel to be projected. Turning around, he faced the two whose eyes were not showing surprise.

Logan's revelations unfurled. "I work missions… predominantly rescues. At least overtly. But at times, I get called in for my expertise in strategic planning or oversight in critical situations. Other than using my computer skills for planning and my pilot skills for rescues, I only take a few active cases… sometimes for a termination that never goes on the books… usually for Homeland Security. But I haven't led a team since I got out. So I'm not sure what you think I can do for you."

Standing before him, Mace seemed undeterred, his conviction unwavering. "You're just the person. You can't tell me that you're not twitching at night with the restless tug to want to lead a team again. You wake up wishing there was more to your retirement than flying tourists around and rescuing dumbass hikers who have no business climbing mountains they didn't prepare for."

He sucked in a deep breath and looked around his room. Mace's words struck a chord deep inside. He had sometimes sat in here alone, planning a mission for someone else to go on while he forced down and nearly choked on the desire to get back out. But what Mace proposed was life-changing, forcing Logan to a crossroads he was not prepared to navigate. Logan had already lived through a change in career trajectory he hadn't planned on. He scrubbed his hand over his face.

With his hands on his hip and his eyes on his boots, he thought over how his life would change. Finally, lifting his head, he looked Mace in the eyes. "I need to think it over."

Mace nodded, acknowledging Logan's hesitation. "I can give you that. I know it might take longer than a night, but I'll have to start looking for someone else if you're not interested. We're staying at the Glacier Hotel tonight. We'll meet you at the bar in town for lunch to see what you think before we head out. You can let me know by the end of the month." With nods, Jack and Mace turned and headed up the stairs.

Logan followed, then stood stoically on the porch as their departure stirred up clouds of dust, leaving a trail down his long lane. He wandered over and sat in one of the chairs, its familiar creak underneath his weight somehow comforting. His gaze scanned the expansive vista. He owned all the land he could see, including the hills at the base of the mountains. He'd lived in this old house for several years, fixing only what broke and not worrying about making it a true home. He now wondered about that inert decision and felt strangely unsettled. *Did I think something else was on the horizon?* A snort erupted, and he shook his head at the fanciful notion.

Continuing to cast his gaze around, he thought about how Jack and Mace had made it to his house without him knowing. When he'd moved in, he had security on his hangar but had never bothered with his house or property even though he had a great deal of expensive equipment in his basement. Rubbing his chin, he thought of the kind of security he should have around his perimeter. *That would be necessary if I started a company.*

Like the incessant sound of a mosquito buzzing about his head, he couldn't shake the thoughts of their visit. It was unexpected, but he found Mace's unusual proposal both flattering and humbling. Of all the men Mace knew who had the ability to be a partner, he chose Logan.

Yet the weight of the proposition settled upon him, the magnitude now filling his mind. He would relinquish the solitary existence he'd grown accustomed to. Lazier days would give way to the structure of being in control. It would take a new house… a new security building… a new hangar… maybe even a new helicopter or airplane. It represented a tidal wave threatening to upend the life he'd constructed.

I'm too set in my ways. It would take money, time, and changing my life.

But the call to action was strong. He looked at the scrub brush around the yard leading to the towering pine trees. Lifting his gaze, he settled his eyes on the majestic, snow-capped mountains in the distance. He drew in a deep breath of the crisp night air, filling his lungs. At that moment, he pondered the possibility of embracing the change, wondering if the upheaval might hold unexpected rewards.

3

"Jesus, Preacher, you crazy son of a bitch!" Sisco screamed.

The blades of the bird whirled as they lifted off the ground, and I rolled over from where I was lying on the floor just enough to see if Devil was alive. Not seeing my squad member's chest move, I rolled back, my heart pounding with adrenaline.

Devil had taken a bullet to the chest, dropping him like a stone, as we had moved through the mountainous terrain. I was the closest, turning as I heard the cry. With the helicopter almost to us, I yelled ahead before turning back. Dropping down beside Devil, whose face was a mask of pain and anger, I leaned over my comrade's body, trying to shield him from more gunfire.

"Goddamn fuckers got me," Devil growled, his hands clutching his bloody chest. Bending low, I picked my fellow SEAL up, slinging him over my shoulder. Blood was pouring, but there was no time to waste. Jogging toward the helicopter now on the ground, I ducked as bullets zinged through the air

near my head. Just as we were fifteen feet from our destination, an explosion rocked the earth, and I tumbled forward. Sisco grabbed Devil at the last second, keeping him from hitting the ground, but my knee gave out under the weight and angle of my fall.

Arms reached out and dragged me into the bird. Lying on the floor, I writhed in pain. Sisco leaned over, his face right in mine. "Hang in there, man. Hold on."

The pain in my knee was excruciating, but as soon as the needle in Sisco's hand hit me, the pain went away. Looking down, I knew. Fuckin' knew. It was over. My career. Lifting a hand over my face, wanting to keep my squad's eyes from seeing the despair, I sucked in a ragged breath.

Suddenly, a flurry of activity caused me to jerk my eyes open, and I watched as some of the others worked on Devil. "He's alive!" the shout came from someone, barely heard above the helicopter's noise.

As the bird flew back to our base, I slowed my breathing, relaxing slightly against the hard, metal floor. Devil was alive. I'd saved him when I ran back to get him after he fell to enemy fire.

Turning my head to face the open door, I watched as the land below rushed by, the knowledge this was my last SEAL mission filling my mind. But Devil was alive...and I knew, if I had to, I'd do it all over again.

Waking up in the early morning hours, Logan sat up in bed, ensnared by the remnants of his turbulent dreams, the memories of his last mission haunting his restless slumber. Recognizing the futility of pursuing further sleep, he swung his legs over the side of the bed and scrubbed his hand over his face. He dressed for the chill of the Montana morning before moving into the kitchen. Activating the coffee maker with a flick of his wrist, he leaned his hip against the worn counter, the aroma soon filling the air.

Taking the mug of black brew onto his porch, he sat again in one of the old wooden chairs, leaning back so he could place his feet on the rail and watch the sun rise.

The dream reminded him of his call sign, Preacher. A play on his name of Bishop, it came to mean more. But those days were long behind him. Now it was time to think of the future. A future he hadn't thought he would have.

He had spent a long time the previous night weighing the pros and cons of Mace's proposal. His life in Montana was stable…if not exciting. He looked out over the land that was his… all two hundred acres. He lived so simply that no one in town thought much about him. But his grandfather had owned a massive ranch in Kansas that had been farmed by the family. Thankfully, his dad understood that ranching wasn't in Logan's future, and when his sister married a local man, the ranch went to them. A significant trust was given to Logan, and it had been invested for years. He'd hardly made a dent in it when he bought the acreage in Montana.

Now, he scanned the area leading up to the base of the mountains and imagined how the property could be used for a setup like what Mace proposed. *But… can I make this decision and commitment?*

He didn't believe in signs but couldn't deny that

sometimes a beacon guided decisions in life. His gaze lifted to the mountain peaks where an old light tower still stood, a stalwart reminder of the lights guiding aircraft to safety. It was still used as a beacon for lost hikers to have a point of reference. And now, that tower was clearly visible in the light of day.

Then he thought of Sisco and Devil. For the first time since he'd left the service, he allowed himself to think of them in terms of what they were doing, whether they were fulfilled in their lives now and whether they would be interested in joining forces again. And the small spark from last night flamed a little brighter.

Walking into Cutter's Bar hours later, he allowed his eyes to adjust to the dim light of the old building. Built on the outskirts of the small town, the watering hole was a gathering place for locals. A few tourists came in but rarely stayed long. It was a bar, not a nightclub. No jukebox. A simple menu of burgers, fries, and nachos. No fancy drinks. Just a bar. Wooden plank floors, scuffed from years of boots walking on them, met plank walls adorned with a few vintage metal beer signs. Booths were in the back, and the bar was on the left, as plain as the rest of the building except for the liquor bottles lining the shelf.

Nodding to a few regulars seated at the long bar, he spied Mace and Jack sitting in a booth. With a head jerk toward Sam, the bartender, he stalked to the booth and slid onto the wooden bench next to Jack, facing Mace. Sam brought him a beer and headed back to the bar.

Mace's gaze followed Sam but cut back quickly as Logan said, "Told you, no one here gets in your business."

The three men drank in silence for a moment, the sounds of the bar being the only noise filling the air. Yet Logan noticed that there was no tension. Jack was just along for the trip and to provide the introduction. Mace appeared calm, and Logan knew it was because Mace was secure in his new life, whether or not Logan decided to join him.

He knew he could shake their hands, pay for their beer, and say goodbye. He could go back to his tours and local rescues, continue the single mission planning that occasionally came his way, and live and die in his little house on two hundred acres—alone.

Or he could reach out and grab a crazy-ass proposal, work at it, make it his own, partner with someone he would respect, yet get to be his own boss. He could be a leader again. He could live again. A snort slipped out, and Mace's eyes moved to Logan's face. The iconic man lifted a brow but remained silent.

"It'll take a couple of years to get it off the ground, won't it?"

Mace simply nodded.

"Lot of money invested. Lot of work. Lot of pressure," Logan pressed on.

Mace continued to nod.

Sucking in his bottom lip, he hissed as he inhaled. Shaking his head slightly, he chuckled and reached his hand across the table. "I'm in."

A wide, white-toothed smile crossed Mace's face as his hand clasped his. It was impossible for Logan not to reply in kind. The smile stretched facial muscles unused to curving his lips upward while deep inside, the spark continued to flame.

4

ONE YEAR AGO

Logan stepped out onto the porch, a steaming mug of coffee cradled in his hand, the warmth seeping into his chilled fingers through the ceramic. His gaze swept over the transformed vista before him, a testament to the changes in the past two years. His new, much larger home perched closer to the edge of the rolling hills at the base of the mountains. The house was more than he would ever need by himself, but he'd listened when Mace told him it would be better to start large and have the space when needed. Logan could have sworn he saw a twinkle in the eyes of the otherwise stoic man. Even though he disagreed, he bowed to the expertise and experience of his partner.

The expansive front porch offered a panoramic view of his sprawling land. Behind him was a two-story, four-bedroom, two-and-a-half-bath house with a full basement and attic space. A sigh left his lips at how he'd overdone the house. But both Mace and Carson had convinced him that it would not only provide a place for him to work since the basement extended into the hills behind the house but also just in case he started a family.

They'd sprung that little tidbit on him, and he'd nearly choked on his drink at the time. Now, he waited for the deep chuckle to end before taking a sip of coffee. He was glad his sister and her husband had children because he was afraid that particular life event would pass him by. Even though he was starting a new career where he would be leading again, his personal life was still very much alone, and he was fine with that.

This life was not for the faint of heart. He knew most of Mace's and now Carson's employees were married and wondered how the hell they managed, but then the coastlines of Maine and California were a lot different from northern Montana. *Yeah... 'fraid that's not for me, and probably not for the people I'm hiring.* So far, the former special ops he had now employed were rougher, tougher, and a lot more stoic than many. They'd have to be to make it out here.

As his gaze roved over the landscape, it landed on his hangars. They were expanded to house the newer helicopters there. He no longer flew tourists but still completed rescues when needed. But his main job, for which he was well paid, was to get LSI Montana up and running. Mace had projected that it might take a full three years, but Logan was ahead of schedule.

Casting his gaze toward the old house he used to live in, he was in awe at how it had been expanded. It was now a bunkhouse, complete with six bedrooms, a common area, a kitchen, and three large bathrooms, ready for Keepers needing lodging.

As two men emerged from the bunkhouse, he grinned. Two of the best men he'd known as a SEAL walked toward him. When he'd thought about his former teammates, the only two who immediately struck him as potential Keepers were Sisco and Devil. Sisco had served as their medic, and Mace had advised having someone with medical experience. Sisco had been excited to hear from him—so much so, that Logan felt guilty that the past years had passed by, and he'd let everyone from his former Navy life just fade away.

Sisco was out of the Navy, now living in Texas, working as a paramedic for the city of El Paso. He reported he liked his job, but now that his parents had passed, he no longer felt any ties to the area, considering his brothers and sisters were dispersed all over the country.

When Logan informed him of his new change in career paths, Sisco encouraged him. "There's no one better to take this on than you, man!" he had enthused.

And when Logan asked him if he would consider coming on board, which included moving to Montana, Sisco informed him he was already looking into flights. Logan thought he was joking, but Sisco showed up at the ranch a few days later. They'd talked long into the night while sharing whiskeys, and by sunrise, Sisco had agreed without hesitation that he was all in on becoming a Keeper. And for Logan, it was the affirmation he hadn't even realized he was searching for.

Devil was a different matter. Hard to track down

and elusive to get hold of when Logan finally had an address. Logan was dumbstruck to discover Devil was living in Montana on the Flatfeet Reservation. It is one of the Indigenous American reservations that allow non-tribal members to live there. When Logan finally got Devil to answer his phone, his old teammate cried out, "Preacher? What the fuck, man? Where the hell have you been?"

Logan had laughed, having thought the same thing about his teammate. When he told Devil he was in Montana, too, more exclamations followed. He'd invited him to visit, and much like his time with Sisco, he and Devil let the years of separation float away as they reminisced and caught up. It turned out that Devil was still making deals, only now to aid the residents on the reservation. On their team, Devil had been able to get just about anything they needed... extra or better food, a specialized weapon, a vehicle repair, fixing a broken transmitter, or acquiring a state-of-the-art radio. Someone once said that all it took was to make a deal with the devil and Devlin could get it. Thus... he became known as Devil.

He'd discharged from the Navy about a year after Logan did and spent time moving around the States, living and working as he traveled. He finally ended up in Montana. He spent time on the Flathead and the Blackfoot Reservations, finding their need called to his sense of helping.

After Logan and Devil had enjoyed a sunset evening of sipping beer on the front porch, Logan felt the same connection with Devil that he'd continued with Sisco.

He told him of his new endeavor and asked if he was interested in joining. He'd barely gotten the words out of his mouth before Devil shouted, "Hell yeah, man! I'm all in!"

"You know it'll never be for the glory—"

Devil's eyes had narrowed. "When the fuck did I ever go all out for the glory?"

Logan chuckled. "Never." They sat in silence for a few minutes, then Logan reached over to shake his old teammate's hand. "Welcome aboard, Devil. You and Sisco make my first employees."

"You once saved my life. I've spent years trying to figure out if there was any kind of meaning in that. I've done some good, and I'm still close enough to the reservations to keep helping. I'm not joining you out of a sense of duty, but you'll get my promise that you won't regret this offer, boss."

Logan had nodded, but he didn't need the reassurance from Devil… he already knew he was getting the best.

Now, as the two men approached, Logan's attention snapped to the arrival of a large black SUV. It's arrival was followed by a cloud of swirling dust. He was no longer surprised when someone arrived. Between the construction workers and Mace's visits, there were often people around… sometimes too damn many. He hadn't included a gate yet, but his new security system at the lane entrance let him know exactly when someone arrived.

The SUV appeared first, and he wasn't surprised when Mace and Carson exited the vehicle, but the three-row SUV emptied three more men. Standing straighter, Logan remained on the front porch as the five men approached, with the two from the bunkhouse not far behind. He recognized the three new men from their résumé photographs. *Looks like I'll need more coffee.*

He greeted Mace and Carson, having met Carson a year ago when he made a trip with Mace. Logan had the chance to assist with a mission Carson was involved in and had as much respect for the LSI West Coast leader as he had for Mace.

After greeting his partners, he turned to the others and shook their hands, needing no introduction. He'd video-conferenced with these men but had never met them in person. Cole Iverson. Frazier Dolby. Todd Blake.

Leading them inside, he waved them toward the large, informal living room and then turned, saying, "I'll get coffee."

The soft sound of wheels met his ears, and he looked down at the woman in the wheelchair with a tray fitted to the arms filled with coffee mugs. At a glance, he noted she had the exact number of mugs needed, including for the two men coming from the bunkhouse. He could never figure out how she managed to be a step ahead of him at all times. Lifting his gaze, he caught the frustrated expression aimed at the back of her head, coming from the man walking behind her with another tray of coffee fixings.

Focusing his attention on the woman, Logan said, "Mary, you don't have to serve—"

"I'm here. Coffee's here. Not much of a hardship to bring it in."

He clamped his mouth shut, having learned that Mary did things her way, and they were usually right. He stepped to the side and watched Bert set his tray down and then turned to take the tray from Mary's wheelchair.

He turned and watched as Mace and company all came to their feet when Mary entered. Logan said, "I'd like to introduce you to Mary Smithwick. She's local. She served in the Army and worked logistics for a colonel I know and trust his recommendation. She's agreed to work support for LSI here, was available, and is already taking charge of most things around here... including me."

Mary shot him a glare, then turned to the other men, shaking their hands with introductions.

"And this is Bert Tomlinson. He's former Navy who worked support for my team's SEAL missions, and he has agreed to work support for LSI here. He's in charge of the physical compound, equipment, and weapons."

The front door opened, and the two men from the bunkhouse entered the room. They glanced at Logan, who nodded and then turned to the gathering. "Sisco and Devil are two comrades from my former SEAL team who have also agreed to become Keepers... Sisco Aguilar and Jim Devlin."

Mary and Bert left the room, and as they all sat down, Mace continued the more in-depth introductions.

"Carson and I flew in with some of the men who

have made it to the interview portion of the recruiting process you have in place. These three also have our recommendation. Of course, you have the final say. It's your team, and the fit has to be right. I know you already have your hiring system in place. Take time with each of them to discover what works for you."

For the next several hours, while Sisco and Devil showed Mace and Carson around, he interviewed the three men, one at a time. The experience was a bit unnerving... in the Navy, he had no say over his team members.

As a new LSI partner, he'd easily reached out to Sisco and Devlin, and once they'd heard what he had to offer, both were in. Mary and Bert had also been easy employees to choose, and their acceptance was filled with his gratitude. He'd talked with quite a few who hadn't made the final cut. Some were more interested in seeking adventure, and a few gave off an angry, aggressive vibe that would have spilled over to the other Keepers or even their missions.

Now, he sat opposite exceptional men with impeccable backgrounds and experience. He'd already studied their résumés and had a video chat with each of them, but face-to-face was different.

He should have known that Mace and Carson would not have recommended prospects if they didn't already know they were a fit.

Cole Iverson was a current Keeper with Mace in Maine. He was also a pilot, serving with the Air Force Special Operations. When Logan talked with him, he discovered that Cole loved the work he did for Mace and the camaraderie of the other Keepers, but he'd been raised in North Dakota, so Maine never felt like home. Logan realized Cole's experience would be invaluable as they got LSIMT off the ground.

Logan bonded quickly with former SEAL Frazier Dolby but was surprised to hear that Frazier's youngest brother worked for Carson in California. "You didn't mention this before."

"No, sir. I wanted to be considered on my own merit, not the fact that my brother works for Carson."

"And you don't want to work in California with your brother?"

Frazier smiled and shook his head. "Jonathan is already established out there and loves the California life. Me? I'm interested in making my own mark after the Navy and don't mind being landlocked while I do it." He then lifted a brow and added, "You might as well know that there's another brother. Dalton is the middle one and currently a Marine. He just might show up on your doorstep sometime."

Logan chuckled. There was a time when anyone showing up on his doorstep would have made him twitchy, but in the past two years, he'd learned that he never knew who might appear. "It'd be fine if he did."

Next was Todd Blake. Career Marine. RECON. The man didn't smile much, but then Logan had spent his career with few smiles, so he understood Todd's demeanor. He also had no problem realizing the qualities that Todd would bring to the missions, but his connection to LSI won the day. His brother had been Army Delta and now worked for Mace. His sister had been in the Army and then recruited by the CIA. She now worked for Carson, and ws married to another of LSI West Coast Keepers.

By the end of the interviews, Logan had no problem agreeing to hire Cole, Frazier, and Todd. They acknowledged that they'd be ready to assist with the continued building of the company as soon as Logan could use them. With a firm handshake, he said, "I can use you now, so welcome to LSI Montana."

5

EIGHT MONTHS AGO

"Boss?"

Logan, still not used to the term, looked up as Todd approached him. He had been buried in paperwork, which he loathed, until Mary pushed him to the side and insisted it was for her to deal with. He'd almost argued, but then Bert just walked past and said, "Leave it to her. It'll be done faster and, no offense, but probably more accurately."

Logan wasn't offended and had to agree. Now, he watched Todd approach.

"There's a woman here to see you. Sadie Hargrove. Says she's expected."

Logan winced at his oversight, then nodded. "Yeah. Damn, I lost track of time. Show her to the outer office. I'll be right there." Todd dipped his chin and walked back out. In the past six months, the core group Logan had hired had been invaluable, saving him from deciding that he'd made a major error in agreeing to start an LSI.

Now, he was slowly interviewing others who had passed the initial paperwork, security check, referral check, and video interview. He only invited the ones who had passed all the other employment roadblocks he'd put in place to the compound. The last thing he wanted was for anyone to see what he was building if they weren't going to be a part of his Keepers.

He'd met and interviewed several possibilities, but few made the cut. For one thing, relocating to northern Montana, where the weather was unforgivable and the nightlife nonexistent, wasn't a location for everyone.

So far, though, he'd added several more to his contingent of Keepers—Dalton Dolby, Frazier's brother, and Timothy Clemons, a former Army Ranger whose sister was with one of the West Coast Keepers.

He had turned a small outbuilding into an office where he met with potential employees, not wanting them in his house unless they were hired. Arriving, he walked through the door and observed a woman standing erect, her gaze never wavering from him as she thrust out her hand.

"Sadie Hargrove, sir. It's an honor to meet you."

His brows lifted. "Honor? That's an interesting word, Ms. Hargrove. I'm not sure what I've done to elicit that greeting."

She held his gaze. "I've served with some of the best, Mr. Bishop. Some I've respected more than others. But what you're doing here is accomplishing something to be proud of. I've heard of Lighthouse Security Investigations. I had once hoped to be considered by either Mr. Hanover or Mr. Dyer."

"What stopped you?"

"When I first left the military a year ago, my mother needed my assistance. Now, I'm looking for a position with LSI, and Mr. Dyer let me know that you might offer me a chance to interview."

"Sit down, Ms. Hargrove."

She did as he asked, and he settled behind the utilitarian desk. She appeared calm, collected, and ready for action, but he could sense her alertness. He looked down at the tablet in front of him, which he had already studied. She wouldn't have made it this far if he wasn't willing to see if she would fit. Lifting his gaze, he said, "I'm sorry about your mother. My grandfather died of cancer. It's a bitch and takes something from those left behind as well as the victim."

A flash of pain moved through her eyes as she nodded her agreement. When he'd interviewed her on video, she came across as hard and almost too closed off. But with the pain that had quickly filled her face before her professional mask fell back into place, she seemed much more human. Her competence with computer software engineering and cyber security was well documented. After he asked more questions about her work, he only had one concern left. "Can you hack living and working here? Montana can be unforgiving."

Her gaze shifted out the window for the first time during the interview. She swallowed for a moment, then brought her eyes back to him. "Mr. Bishop, I spent my mother's dying months in Florida, where it was hot as hell. And crowded. No matter where I went… to the grocery, to the doctor's offices, then finally at the hospital, I was surrounded by people. Some were rude, some wonderful, some indifferent, and some did all they could to make life better. But I never had a chance to be alone and just breathe. As soon as I stepped out of the plane and started the drive here, this place called to me." Her lips pressed together tightly. "I realize that may sound stupid, but if I'm going to work for you, then I need to be honest. I can do the work required to take on whatever LSI Montana needs. I can be part of the camaraderie of your business. But I also want to be somewhere that allows me just to breathe."

Logan nodded, realizing that she had just verbalized what he so understood. Reaching across the desk, he offered his hand. Her gaze snapped down, and she eagerly clasped his, letting out a long breath.

"Welcome aboard, Ms. Hargrove."

"Sadie, sir."

"And you can call me Logan." He smiled as he stood and walked her outside where Todd was standing. "Todd, this is Sadie. Would you give her a tour? Introduce her to the others, and then get her with Mary for all the employment necessities." He watched as the two walked away, and he headed back into the office.

His feet came to a halt at the sight of a man standing in the shadows by the chair that Sadie had occupied. Narrowing his eyes, Logan growled, "Who the fuck are you?"

The man stepped into the light. "Aldo Caspani, sir."

Logan inhaled sharply, his gaze assessing. "Code name Casper for the ghost, I presume."

"Yes, sir."

"I wasn't expecting you until tomorrow."

"Yes, sir. I arrived early and hoped I'd be able to see you today. If not, I'll return."

Logan waited, carefully weighing his decision. He'd heard about Casper from one of Carson's Keepers—his second-in-command who had served with Aldo Caspani. He moved so quietly, and his skills were deadly. Logan recognized the potential of having someone like him on his team. He also knew he'd get few answers from the man beyond what he'd already ascertained from the interview.

"Mr. Caspani, I know what you can do for this organization. I've only got two questions for you." He watched as Casper's eyes flared with a hint of curiosity. "Why a Keeper? And why here?"

Casper's gaze never wavered, and Logan felt sure the man in front of him missed very little around him.

"Why not a Keeper?" After asking the rhetorical question, Casper shrugged. "It's where I can find... redemption."

Logan scoffed, his chin jerking back. "Redemption?"

"Perhaps a new start would be a better way to describe what I seek. Redemption may follow."

Logan nodded slowly, understanding more than he let on. Most special forces understood the fine line between serving their country and serving the needs of those in charge and how the line could often be blurred. Perhaps Casper had simply stated it correctly the first time. "And here?"

"A man can get lost out here, sir." Breathing deeply,

Casper added, "And from what I see, a man can find himself, too."

The two men remained standing for a long moment before Logan lifted his hand. "Welcome to LSI Montana, Casper."

Almost no emotion had shown on Casper's face during their entire exchange, but now a breath released from his lungs, and Logan had the feeling he'd just witnessed something profound.

6

SIX MONTHS AGO

Logan's radio sounded, and Dalton said, "There's a man on a motorcycle at the gate. Cory Brighton. Said he'd like to talk to you."

Logan didn't recognize the name and hadn't set up any more interviews recently, but he wasn't so aloof that he wouldn't talk to someone. "Send him on through with an escort. I'll meet him at the office."

"Roger that."

Logan reached the office just as a motorcycle roared up the lane behind Timothy's SUV. As soon as the motorcycle came to a stop, Logan watched as a tall man kicked down the stand and pulled off his helmet, hanging it on the handlebars. The dark-haired man waved toward Timothy and then walked toward Logan with his hand extended. "Mr. Bishop? I'm Cory Brighton. It's an honor to meet you."

The handshake was firm, and Logan escorted him into the office, inclining his head toward a chair before sitting behind his desk. It still felt odd to be behind a desk when talking to others, but he knew it was expected for the business aspect of LSI. "Mr. Brighton , what can I do for you?"

"We have a mutual friend... Donald Markham."

At that, Logan had to force his expression to stay the same. Donald Markham belonged to a branch of the Department of Homeland Security that few knew about. Donald would occasionally task Logan with a special assignment—always for Logan to act alone and usually for a target that needed to be eliminated. Remaining silent, he waited.

"I fully expect you to check my claim. But, for now, let's just say that I served two tours with the Rangers, then was recruited for CIA special ops. I separated from them after an assignment went fubar, and I didn't receive the support I needed. Mr. Markham first contacted me then, and I agreed to work on occasional assignments at his behest. I take it that you're familiar with those assignments."

Logan neither confirmed nor denied, and Cory simply nodded his understanding. "I wanted something different. I'd heard of LSI, but it wasn't until Mr. Markham suggested I interview for your group that I felt ready."

"I don't usually take drop-in interviews, Cory. A vetting process has to occur with referrals, recommendations, and experience. And then I have a video interview to see if you understand what is required, expected, and demanded. Only then do I grant a face-to-face interview."

Cory nodded, but his lips quirked upward slightly. "Then I guess we're just doing things backward, sir."

Logan held the man's gaze for a long moment, but Cory's confidence never wavered. He couldn't define it as cocky, but something in Cory's demeanor made Logan feel that what he was looking at was exactly what Cory was. Logan pulled his secure phone from his pocket and dialed Donald Markham's direct line.

"Preacher, what the fuck are you calling me for? I thought you were busy setting up your own shop."

"Got a man in front of me. Says he knows you." Logan held the phone up and snapped Cory's picture, then hit send.

"Hells bells, he took my advice," Donald said. "That's Cory Brighton. Former Ranger. Former CIA. And it looks like if he's in your office, he'll be a former employee of mine. But if you hire him, then I know I have two of the best to call upon when I need something from LSI."

"Is that your recommendation?" Logan never took his eyes off Cory while talking privately to Donald. And it didn't pass his notice that Cory's cool demeanor never changed. He didn't look bored, but he sure as hell didn't look worried.

Donald softened his voice. "Cory reminds me a lot of you, Preacher. Always reliable. Always professional. After military service, he worked alone, but I know he'd work well for you. Personally, I think he misses the team atmosphere more than he admits."

"Strengths?"

"Sniper. You need someone with aim, accuracy, and

experience, you can't get a better marksman than Cory. He'll be your weapons expert."

"Final thoughts?"

Donald sighed. "Preacher, you're pulling together a whole new crew, which I know hasn't been in your experience. But from what I gather, you'll have a helluva team. And Cory Brighton will only make it stronger." Before Logan had a chance to say anything, Donald added, "You like things planned out... no surprises. But my guess is that one day, you'll be surprised as hell to find out that there's more to life than just having every day planned."

Logan snorted his response. "Yeah, like what?"

"Figure you'd find someone special to share that lonely life with. Now? I just hope you find someone special to knock you on your ass."

"I don't see that happening. Anyway, thanks for the info." After goodbyes, Logan disconnected the call, still never taking his eyes off Cory. Pulling in his bottom lip, he pondered the man in front of him and the words of recommendation given by a man he trusted. Finally, nodding slowly, he said, "We still need to go through some of the hiring steps I mentioned above, but you've just made it past the first hurdles toward becoming a Keeper."

At that, Cory grinned while nodding. Leaning forward to shake hands again, he said, "Looking forward to serving with you, sir."

LOGAN

Two months ago

Logan's lips quirked upward as he walked out onto his porch. "It's good to see you again, Landon."

He eschewed the handshake and offered a back-slapping man-hug to Landon Sommers, an FBI agent he'd met and worked with when he'd flown assistance for one of Carson's missions. At the time, Landon had talked to Logan, expressing his interest in leaving the FBI and desiring to pursue a career without the constraints of the bureau.

Landon had made a trip out to Montana the previous year. The two of them spent time sipping whiskey while talking about the plans Logan was bringing to life. He'd told Landon then that he'd gotten used to being a loner, but the idea of leading a team again finally took hold, and making LSIMT functional was now his goal.

Landon confessed that as much as he enjoyed the camaraderie he experienced with Carson's California Keepers, he felt he needed to start over somewhere new. He also talked of his pre-FBI career. Landon had been in the Air Force and then recruited for CIA special ops. After a couple of years of that, he'd come back home to a steadier job while helping elderly parents. Now, with them gone, he was looking to move into something else that gave him more freedom.

When Logan first met Landon, he didn't think the button-up, suit-wearing FBI agent would settle easily in the wilds of Montana. But the more trips Landon made out, the more rugged he became until the straitlaced man was now in the background. A close bond formed as soon as Logan had seen how easily Landon also slid into a friendship with Sisco and Devil.

Logan offered Landon a job, and for the past few months, Landon had spent time with Carson's best security system designer-installer team, Fred and Tricia Poole, learning everything he could about security systems designs. Logan didn't fence in his entire acreage, but he'd fenced around the house, bunker, compound, and hangars. He used contractors that Mace and Carson vetted, but his Keepers, not willing to sit around, jumped in and provided much of the labor.

Poole and Tricia came to Montana to assist with the security installations on the perimeter of the fenced-in area, set up security around the entire acreage, and teach the other new Keepers about security systems.

Logan was reminded daily that when Mace and Carson wanted to partner with him, he truly benefited from the partnership.

"I'm fuckin' glad to be here." He jerked his head toward the bunkhouse. "It looks like more trucks and SUVs are here. Is everyone settling in?"

Logan had involved Landon in the decisions for hiring, valuing the other man's insight. "Everyone is here full-time. Some are in the bunkhouse, and some are renting in town."

"What do the locals think?"

"It's no secret that I've started a security company and been building on my land. They don't care as long as money comes their way. The town will welcome the newcomers, especially since only one bar gets our business." Clapping Landon on the back, he said, "How about we head down where the others are?"

Logan led the way through the house to a hall along the side.

"The house looks good. Fuckin' huge."

"I have no idea why I agreed to build it so large. It was Mace and Carson's idea, and I was eager for their input at the time."

Landon laughed. "You know, now that they have wives and most of their employees are married, that's where their minds go. They think everyone will find someone and need a fuckin' huge house for kids."

Logan shook his head. "'Fraid that's not what'll happen here. If some of my Keepers get married, that's fine, but it's not for me. I've been alone too long. I can't even imagine sharing my space with someone."

"I wouldn't mind it," Landon confessed, "but that's not been in the plans for me."

Logan stopped at a door where he flipped open a panel, entered a key code, then placed his hand on the fingerprint scanner. The door swung open, and as the two entered another hall, the door closed behind them. This hall led to stairs but had an elevator there as well.

Descending the stairs, they stopped outside another keypad and retina scanner.

"The outside entrance is secured?"

"Yes, and also one at the back that leads into a passage through the hills. We don't anticipate needing it, but the entrances give us access to outlets in case we do."

Through the next door, they entered the cavernous basement that extended beyond the foundation of the house and into the hill beyond.

"Fuck, Logan. Down here, I could easily imagine that I'm back at LSIWC."

"I took all the assistance from Mace and Carson that I could get. We incorporated everything that worked for them here. And the things they learned they'd wished were different, I made sure to add them at the beginning. Our munitions and equipment rooms are here, but the gym is in a separate building just off to the south."

They walked into the most significant room that housed all the computer equipment, large screens, and tables where the Keepers sat with their laptops in front of them.

The others had met Landon in person at one time or another, and they all stood to greet him before taking their seats again and looked at Logan. His gaze swept the group. Landon, Frazier, Dalton, Cole, Casper, Cory, Todd, Timothy, Sadie, Sisco, and Devil. Once seated, Logan was filled with a mixture of pride, awe, and a few emotions he'd rather not admit to—a trickle of fear of failure raced down his spine.

He was also struck with the realization that the success of this endeavor rested on all of them. So far, they'd worked well together, but they were untried. They had several small contracts and security assignments, and he could tell they were anxious to get started.

Glancing over at Bert, he grinned. "Everything ready?"

"You got it, boss."

"Good." Looking around, he said, "I had you bring PT clothes today. Everyone meet outside in ten minutes. We've got some team building planned and a bit of a workout."

Once everyone was gathered, he pointed at a trail leading into the hills at the mountain base and said, "Three groups of four. Divide up and give the group in front a five-minute lead. Go until you come to the place marked by Bert. Starting now."

He and Landon held back, and he watched with interest how the ten others quickly formed teams with no sense of egos or deliberation. He liked that they had naturally formed bonds with each of the other members. Sadie was the only female so far, but he intended to add more as soon as he could. She fell into step with the first group, and none of the other three seemed to mind. Casper and Cory held back, joining him and Landon.

The run lasted almost forty minutes, and he had to admit he was sucking air when his group arrived. Bert had energy bars and water at the area where the trail came to a wide space before the climb into the mountains became steeper. They all sat and caught their breaths, with good-natured joking going back and forth between each Keeper.

From that spot, the tall tower at the top of one of the mountain peaks was clearly visible. Logan moved to stand in front of the group, gaining everyone's attention. Jerking his head upward toward the light tower, he began. "Historically, beacon fires were lit on hills, both for signaling over land and for sea navigation. The term pyres came from ancient Greeks. The Chinese used a sophisticated system of beacon towers on the Great Wall. By the tenth century, hill forts were used throughout Europe as part of beacon networks. In the nineteen hundreds, aerial lighthouses were established to guide aircraft with lighted beacons. Some are made of metal, and others are concrete."

He noted that all Keepers' eyes were on the tower above them, then turned to him as he paused. "Today, most of the beacons in the United States have been decommissioned or removed since aircraft have navigational systems. Except for in Montana. This was the last state to maintain aerial towers as lighthouse beacons to assist aircraft in navigation over the mountainous terrain. But as of a few years ago, only six are now part of the National Register of Historic Places."

He chuckled. "You're probably wondering why the fuck I had you run all the way up here just to give you a historical lesson on mountain light towers. It's because of who you now are. You don't just have employment with Lighthouse Security Investigations Montana. You are part of an elite group known as the Keepers. That name came from Mace Hanover. He once told me of how his grandfather talked of the lighthouse keepers of old who guided others to safety and often faced peril when they rescued those in need. It was a mantra... a calling to him. And it is still true today. The lighthouse tattoo each of you now has on your arm isn't just a testament to who you work for. It's a testament to who you are and what we can accomplish."

Everyone took to their feet, eyes sharp and fierce expressions of determination on their faces.

"So if you're ready, head back down to the compound. And let's get to work."

7

PRESENT DAY

Logan leaned back, rubbing his chin as he maintained eye contact with Donald Markham on the large screen. Donald could only see Logan, not the rest of the group or the background.

In the past two months, LSIMT accepted numerous assignments, all important, but none of them were dangerous or difficult to plan. There were security systems to design, security escorts to provide, and search and rescue for hikers who disregarded the weather warnings. It had been both Mace and Carson's recommendation that Logan start slow, let his group continue to get used to working as a team, and pick the assignments that felt right at the time.

But now, seeing Donald Markham on the screen, Logan wondered how LSIMT could help the DHS in a way that used to be one of Logan's lone assignments. Utilizing his group for whatever Donald proposed would be a new challenge for him.

"So what need does the DHS have, Donald?"

"The president is worried about active terrorist cells. Until recently, Alaska was the only state in the country that didn't have them. But now, they do. ISIS is still a factor, and now our intelligence says they're working on biological weapons…the kind that can wipe out cities very quickly. Not bombs. Not guns. But the type of weapons that, when added to food, drinking water, or whatever the hell they think of, can cause death or illness to whole populations. Once perfected, they have plans to use them across Europe, and you know, we'd be susceptible to the same threats."

This produced lifted brows from Logan and most of the Keepers around the table. "Why Alaska?"

"I asked the same question. Seems the remoteness, smaller populations, and definite smaller government policing agencies make it a perfect draw."

"What specifics do you have?"

Donald sighed. "We have identified a house that a cell has taken over in a small Alaskan town. The leader is a suspected terrorist, and it appears he's recruiting from the local university. We need someone to move in next door and investigate what contaminant is being produced. Find out…and neutralize."

"That's it? Move in and investigate. That's the mission? Surely, someone else can do that job. You don't need LSI for that."

Donald continued to push his plan. "I don't need someone who will burst onto the scene to take down terrorists or jump out of planes. I need someone who can move in next door and look just like any neighbor. I need someone who can find out what's going on covertly. Someone who won't get in their face. Someone who can set up cameras and monitor their chatter on phones and computers." Snorting, he said, "If the fuckin' FBI sent someone, they'd send Mr. All-American who'd try to get the terrorist neighbors to come over for a backyard barbecue. You? Hell, they won't suspect a grumpy guy who acts like he couldn't care less about his neighbors. Someone who's not afraid, at the end of the day, to eliminate the… threat."

"Eliminate?"

"In the past, I probably would have called an individual such as what you used to do. But, right now, officially DHS has unofficially shifted this case to my office. I've been tasked with finding out for sure, then eliminating the threat after you find out their plan. You're the person I'm choosing." He threw his hand up before Logan could retort. "I know, I know. You lead a team now. But you… and LSI is still who I choose. Your team will provide the backup needed."

Quiet settled over Logan as he pondered Donald's request. It was the first major request for services that LSIMT had received. It would be a boost to prove that his people could handle a job of this nature. But the word *eliminate* held him back. Eliminating the threat was interpreted as terminating. It was what he would do in the past, but now? Being part of the LSI partnership changed everything.

"Donald, you need to understand that LSI is not a hired assassin group. We can investigate and assist DHS, but then we'd turn over what we have to you or whoever you indicate."

"I understand," Donald agreed, a little too readily for Logan's peace of mind. "Then we need the threat eliminated. Whatever they have created in their labs, we need it destroyed."

"We'd be doing our own planning? Because it's no secret that no one on my team specializes in biological chemical warfare."

Clearing his throat, Donald uncharacteristically hesitated. "The DHS has biologists trained in ferreting out chemicals and biologics that could be used for terrorism in drinking water and food processing. They also have a few people who specialize in the types of biological warfare that could wipe out entire cities."

Logan sat, his face impassive, as he listened.

"I know you ran a rescue several months ago for one of the Saints Protection team members and a scientist who was stuck in a snowstorm in Canada. I even know that scientist, Kendall Rhodes, worked for a lab identifying some of the threats."

"What's that got to do with this?" he asked, his curiosity piqued.

"You have the skills to identify terrorists and eliminate the threat if it is proven that there is one. But you don't have the scientific background to analyze the biologics. You can't just blow up a lab without knowing if any organisms present would be deadly if airborne. For that, you need someone's assistance."

"We won't be working alone? We'll have a civilian to contend with?"

Donald's lips pinched together in frustration. "The DHS employee I've chosen has a background in biology, but they're not an agent. Just a biologist. They will simply be there to assist with the detection of a true threat. Once that's done, they're out of there. It will be up to you to destroy the threat."

A frown knit his brow as Logan's mind raced through the proposed mission. "Doesn't the necessity of the other person negate the absolute secrecy?"

"Not at all. They work for DHS, and I fully vetted them. They hold a security clearance. They don't have your skills…at all," Donald added for emphasis. "But they would be able to detect what the terrorists are cooking up. Then, like I said, they're out of there, and the elimination is up to you."

Logan's mind continued to filter through the possible mission. As a SEAL, he had no say in what missions the team was sent on. But now? He had final control of any assignments his company undertook.

The addition of a partner was troubling, but he understood the necessity. None of his Keepers had the scientific background to know what biologics he would find. Eliminating the threat would rely on what biological terrorism might be let loose in the process. "So there's little working together with the biologist? We track the terrorists to see what they are creating, and he analyzes the threat to see how to get it destroyed and then leaves so I can finish the job?"

"Yes, basically, you're on your own." Donald's expression held steady.

"And when would this assignment commence?"

Donald pressed his lips together for a moment, then

said, "In two days. You'd need to be in Alaska the day after tomorrow—"

Logan hid his surprise and irritation. "How the hell do you expect us to be able to plan for a mission of this scope in less than forty-eight hours? Need I remind you that we're still obtaining equipment and training?"

"You can do this. I know you can," Donald retorted. "It comes down to whether you think you can handle this type of assignment."

Silence reigned for a moment, with neither Donald nor Logan giving an inch in the stare down worthy of an old western standoff. Finally, Logan shifted his gaze around the room to see the other Keepers watching him. His skin felt uncomfortably tight, as he knew they waited to see what his decision would be.

"Give me an hour to talk to my team, and I'll let you know." Disconnecting, he turned to the others at the table, but they remained quietly waiting. Not one to blurt every thought that came to him, Logan drummed his fingers on the table.

The chance to work a dangerous but necessary mission. The chance to investigate. The chance to do something more than deal with security escorts, lost hikers, and security systems. It was exactly the type of assignment that called to him. Sucking in a deep breath, he nodded before lifting his gaze back to the Keepers.

All eyes were on him, and he continued. "I've explained that I accepted a few missions like this before I started LSI. I worked alone, and when asked to eliminate a threat, it usually meant to *terminate with extreme prejudice.* Each one of you knows what that means. I wasn't a hired gun, but when the mission called for it, I had no problem completing what was required."

Heaving a sigh, he kept his gaze moving around the table. "When you were hired with LSIMT, one of the things talked about was your willingness to do whatever was required, within reason, of a mission. This assignment involves a dangerous biological agent that creates a threat to whoever is sent to destroy it. This isn't what LSI typically takes on, and we can turn it down. And, as you just heard, I've reiterated what we will contract to do and not do. But, as with any mission, situations may arise that cause us to act with force... even deadly force. Any problems? Say them now, 'cause there's no judgment here."

Frazier shook his head. "What we do is keep people safe, no matter how that may come about. No problem from me."

"Or me," Dalton said, shaking his head.

"Nothing we haven't done in the service," Casper said, his voice as soft as ever. "No problem."

Sisco scoffed as he shook his head. "Me and Devil are all in, no matter what."

"Done it plenty of times in the past," Cory said, his face impassive.

Cole added, "My missions with the original LSI didn't include elimination, but that's exactly what happened with a few cases." He shrugged his large shoulders. "It comes with the territory."

Todd, Timothy, and Sadie shook their heads. "No problems," they said, almost in unison.

Landon looked at Logan. "The question is, who will you assign to take on the mission?"

Logan speared them all with an intense gaze. "Me." Seeing several about to speak, he said, "First of all, Donald was asking me to take this on even though he presented it as something to LSI. But this is something that I feel is necessary." At that statement, he could feel the heavy stares of those around the table. He reached behind and squeezed the back of his neck. "I know every person in this room is capable of taking on this mission. I trust each of you. But I can't be a leader and send someone out on our first major mission if I haven't proven myself."

"Boss, you don't need to prove yourself. None of us would be here if we didn't trust you to have our back," Dalton said, and the others nodded.

"I appreciate that. But we're not up to our full capacity as a security company worthy of LSI. We still need some equipment, and I know we're working through some issues with a few of our vendors. Sadie, I need you here on logistics. Cole, I want your pilot skills here in case I need to call on you. I just gave out three security assignments yesterday, so Timothy, Frazier, and Sisco, you already have jobs to do. The rest will assist with whatever I might need. This assignment might last a week or a month. Landon, I'm leaving you in charge while I'm gone." He chuckled as he shook his head. "And Bert can take care of the animals."

An hour later, he made the call to Donald. "Okay. LSIMT is in. I'll be the one taking lead."

A slight smile crossed Donald's face, but Logan had no idea why.

8

Sanders.

Where the hell is he? Logan stepped out of his H10 at the small airstrip closest to Ester, Alaska, a tiny suburb of Fairbanks. Originally, it was the site of a goldmine strike in the early 1900s. Now known more as an artists' community, he had read that most Ester residents were employed in Fairbanks or at the University of Alaska Fairbanks, an interesting fact since terrorists were recruiting from the university.

It was only two days after Logan had agreed for LSIMT to work the DHS mission, giving the Keepers little time for preparation. Donald had made the preliminary arrangements, including the compensation for the owner of the small airfield to *hire* Logan as a part-time mechanic. It seemed the man was more than happy to do so, getting paid while having a licensed mechanic help him out. Donald had already taken care of the house arrangements with the landlord and had sent the information to Logan, including a street view.

Mary acquired the key, and Sadie scoped the area, reviewing the aerial photos and maps.

Now, in Ester, he only spied the airfield owner, but no scientist to greet him. He introduced himself to Oscar, a tall, lean man with a wide grin. Logan wondered if he was always happy or just very satisfied with his compensation from Donald. Glancing around the small facility, Logan had a feeling Oscar could use the money and the mechanical assistance.

Once the introductions were made, he discovered Oscar to be unconcerned what hours Logan worked, when he'd show up, or why he was even in Ester. Hiding a grin, Logan felt sure Donald had impressed upon Oscar the need for discretion.

"You haven't seen a Mr. Sanders around, have you?"

The wrinkles in Oscar's forehead deepened, and he rubbed his chin. "I can't say that I know anyone by that name."

"Well, he was supposed to meet me here today."

"It's only been me around today that I've seen," Oscar said.

Thanking him, they shook hands again, and Logan moved back to his helicopter for his bags. Grabbing them, he walked over to the vehicle the Keepers had arranged for him. Eyeing the old, beat-up, dark blue Ford F-150 with approval, he climbed inside and started the engine. He'd told Casper to make sure that his vehicle would serve his needs while blending into the local environment and not stand out.

Setting his GPS, he looked at his watch. Donald had assured him the scientist would meet him at his arrival to coordinate when they would begin working together. Normally, he would have already communicated with anyone involved in the mission, but Donald had been adamant that they wouldn't meet until their arrival in Alaska for security reasons.

It was now already thirty minutes past the time Logan said he would arrive, and he wasn't willing to wait longer. *Sanders can find me... I'm not waiting around for him.*

Reporting in, he called the compound. "Sanders isn't here. I don't know what hotel Donald put him in, but I'm heading to the house."

"Logan, why wouldn't he give you his contact info? This is bullshit," Mary argued.

"Sanders is on a need-to-know basis, but I agree. Keeping us in the dark until we finally meet face-to-face seems like overkill, even for Donald. Well, fuck it for now. I don't need him until I discover what's being concocted, and then I'll only need him to find out how to neutralize it. I'll let you know as soon as I get to the house."

"There's one more thing," Mary said, her voice sharp. "The inside security cameras you ordered to be delivered have been delayed. I'm so pissed and gave the company my assurance we wouldn't be using them anymore."

"Fuck," he grumbled. "Can we get more, or do I need to look here?"

"It's already taken care of. Bert found a new vendor, using someone Carson's group has contracted with. I've assured them that if they get the items to us tomorrow, then we'll continue to use them. Cole will fly them to you once we have them."

"Okay, but I'll coordinate with Cole once I get the lay of the land."

"Yes, sir."

"Oh, and Mary? Good work, and pass that on to Bert, as well."

"No thanks needed, boss. Only doing what we were hired to do."

He disconnected, pissed as hell about the delay but certain that Mary and Bert would take care of the vendor issue. He sighed and scrubbed his hand over his face. Starting any new business certainly meant there would be multiple issues, especially finding vendors that would fulfill the orders for the special equipment required in many of their various missions.

A few miles down the forest-lined road, he pulled into a shopping center, eyeing a grocery store Sadie had already discovered for him in her planning. An efficient trip inside allowed him to grab the necessities. Grumbling at the uncertainty of whether the house had a microwave, he skipped the nuke-ready meals in the freezer case, opting for sandwich fixings. Placing the bags into his truck, he continued on his way.

Seven miles later, he turned onto a gravel road, observing the occasional house dotting the lane surrounded by thick trees. The area was heavily wooded, maintaining privacy for the residents but also keeping the satellite images Sadie wanted to search from being visible—the encroaching forests hid the houses. Reaching the end of the street, he came to a round cul-de-sac with only two houses.

A quick look assured him this was the right place. The twin houses, single-storied ramblers, were adorned with weather-beaten wooden planks that gave evidence of their age. Todd had checked the floor plans of the original houses, and Logan knew they were mirror images of each other, a fact that would undoubtedly streamline his efforts to gather intelligence.

A sedan was parked in the neighbor's driveway, and another small, energy-efficient black car was parked on the cul-de-sac. *Looks like the terrorists already have visitors.* Donald had reported that surveillance determined the terrorists spent several days a week at the university and traveled to the mosque in Fairbanks on Fridays.

Pulling into the driveway of the house he would be occupying, he parked with deliberate nonchalance, opting against concealing his presence. *Might as well have them get used to seeing who's here.* Stalking to the side door with several grocery bags in his hands, he used the key Mary had received from the landlord and stepped inside.

Halting immediately in the small kitchen, he narrowed his eyes, momentarily uncertain he was in the right house. A used coffee cup sat on the counter next to a coffee maker that was turned off but still contained the dark liquid. A few dishes were in the sink, rinsed but not put away. He cursed under his breath, pissed that no one had cleaned after the previous occupants.

Grimacing, he stepped farther into the kitchen, looking around at the scrub-worn countertops, wooden cabinets, and, glancing at his feet, the faded and yellowed linoleum floors. The appliances appeared to be clean but older models. Placing the bags onto the floor, he rounded the counter dividing the kitchen from the dining area, where a scarred wooden table with four mismatched chairs sat. His scrutiny moved sharply to the living room, pleased to see a clean, albeit worn sofa and two wooden chairs with thin, but also clean, cushions tied to the seats.

A faint floral scent lingered in the air, offering a feeble attempt at air freshener by the landlord who hadn't bothered to clean the kitchen.

A wood-burning stove sat in the corner on a brick platform, surrounded by wooden plank flooring. An entertainment center held a not new but not ancient TV. To his right was a hall leading to what he knew were two bedrooms and one bathroom.

The front door was to his left, straight from the living room to the worn front porch. Sighing, he turned to go back to the truck to get the rest of his supplies when the hairs on the back of his neck stood up.

Cocking his head to the side, he listened carefully, hearing the faint noise of someone in one of the back rooms—not footsteps, but the sound of someone opening a drawer. Withdrawing his weapon from his holster, he moved stealthily down the hall. Quickly determining the sound came from the bedroom on the left, he glanced through the partially opened door. The person was behind the door, out of sight, but he heard a drawer being closed. Sliding slightly to the side, he peered through the crack in the door on the side of the hinges, seeing the intruder bent away from him, looking down at what appeared to be the chest of drawers.

With practiced ease, he flung open the door, causing them to stumble backward and lose their balance. With one arm, he flipped them onto their stomach across the bed and planted his hand on their back, growling, "Don't move, asshole."

The intruder was not only short but slight in stature, easily held in place by his hand. The fleeting idea of a teenager ran through his mind. He stared dumbly at the long, silky black hair tumbling across the bedspread, and the floral scent filled the room. The body underneath his hand grunted as they tried to breathe.

Jerking his head, with his hand still pressing down in the center of their back, he raked his gaze down his prisoner, seeing a dark green T-shirt that had ridden up over white panties with long, naked legs hanging over the bed. *Fuckin' hell...a woman!*

Grabbing her right shoulder, he flipped her again so she was facing up. Her dark, wide eyes stared back at him, flicking to the side where the gun rested easily in his grip. Her chest rose and fell with each shaky gasp. She opened her mouth slightly, as though to speak, but closed it quickly as she glanced at the gun once more.

"Who the hell are you?" he growled, his rough voice filling the small bedroom.

"I...I'm Vivian." Swallowing audibly, she cast a nervous glance toward the weapon again. "Vivian Sanders."

9

Logan stared in silence, not bothering to hide his surprise at the realization that the woman on the bed was his biologist contact. From the rumpled bed linens, it appeared she had slept in the rental house.

Vivian's eyes stayed on him, and she didn't seem to breathe until his stance relaxed slightly. She swallowed deeply, and her voice shook as she said, "You now know who I am. I'd like the same consideration, please."

With another glance, Logan stepped back from her legs, watching as her hand moved to the bottom of her T-shirt, pulling it down to cover her underwear. Glancing up, he saw the fear in her eyes. An uncomfortable guilt slid over him, an emotion he was unaccustomed to and immediately decided he hated. He stepped back quickly, keeping his gaze on her face. "Sorry, I wasn't expecting anyone to be here. I'm Bishop. Logan Bishop."

Her large eyes popped open even wider as she exclaimed, "You're the man I'm supposed to be working with?" Pushing up on her elbows, she stared at him unabashedly before narrowing her eyes on the weapon. "Do you mind putting that thing away before you accidentally blow my head off?"

Irritation now moved into the already crowded emotions sweeping through him as he re-holstered the gun. "I assure you, when my gun goes off, it's not by accident."

Scooting to the edge of the bed and standing, Vivian skirted by him, returning to the chest of drawers to pull out a pair of jeans. She looked at him expectantly for a moment, but he wasn't willing to turn his back until he verified her identity. Stepping just outside the room, he heard material shuffling around before a zipper sounded out.

Another drawer opened, and he hastily stepped back into the room to see what she was searching for, only to find she had simply retrieved a pair of thick green woolen socks. She sat on the edge of the bed and slipped them on each foot, wiggling her toes when finished. Fully dressed, she turned to him, but with the height difference, her eyes were at the level of his chest. She tilted her head back and held his gaze, offering no explanation as to why she was in his house.

She was a natural beauty, and in another time and place, he might have been tempted to flirt with her... if his flirting skills weren't rusted over from unuse. Blinking at the random path his thoughts had taken just from being in her presence, he shoved them down, reminding himself this was a job and nothing more. Frustrated, he demanded, "Where were you?"

His voice sounded harsh, even to him, but her brow simply crinkled as she tilted her head to the side. "What do you mean, where was I?"

"You were supposed to meet me at the airport today so we could discuss arranging our work schedules."

"Tomorrow. I was given your arrival date as tomorrow."

"Today."

She rolled her eyes. "I was told tomorrow. Sorry if your people can't get things right."

At that, he bristled. "My people? Listen, missy, you've—"

"Missy? Oh, no, Mr. Bishop. You can call me Vivian or Ms. Sanders. Your choice. But if you *Missy* me again, we're going to have problems."

"Gonna have problems? Clue in, *Ms.* Sanders, we've already got problems. Where's your vehicle?"

Pinching her lips together, she jerked her head toward the window. "I parked on the cul-de-sac. It's the Fusion. It was the only energy-efficient car I could rent. Everything else was a gas-guzzling truck or—"

"Okay, fine."

Her fists landed on her hips as her eyes flashed. "What the hell is your problem? I was told to come to this house, get settled, and meet my partner tomorrow. Which, I might add, made no sense to me because you obviously have a vehicle. You didn't need me to pick you up."

"Settled? Get settled?" he growled, his eyes narrowing even further as he took in more of the room. He noted that her suitcase had exploded toiletries on top of the chest of drawers. "Why the hell would you need to get settled in my house?"

Blinking, she snapped her brows together and stepped back, her hands dropping to her sides. "How else are we supposed to work together? I was told we would live here, pretend to be a married couple, and investiga—"

"Pretend to be a married couple?" Logan's voice rose with each word as the blood rushing through his veins caused a buzzing in his ears greater than one of his helicopter rides. "Hell, no." Turning on his booted heel, he stalked from the room, pulling out his secure phone. He was pissed, but at the moment wasn't sure who would bear the brunt of his frustration. Donald, for orchestrating the situation, or the woman he'd left back in *his* bedroom.

He walked into the front room, his phone pressed to his ear. "Mary, what did you know about the biologist I was meeting with, who appears to be planning on staying in the house with me?"

"Nothing, Logan. Mr. Markham was very closed-off about the security surrounding this mission."

"Who's available there?"

He heard lowered voices in the room, and Cole came on the line.

"What's going on, Logan? No one here knew any more than you about the mission. Do you need backup? I can fly—"

"No." He sighed. "I'm fine. But get whatever you can on Vivian Sanders. She's the biologist. I'll talk to

Donald, then I'll be in touch. Tell Casper the truck is just what I needed."

"You got it," Cole agreed.

Disconnecting, he dialed Donald. "You know this is not how I work."

A few seconds of silence passed before Donald said, "Look, Logan. I knew you wouldn't have a problem working with a woman, but I also knew you'd balk at the idea of the subterfuge."

"Subterfuge? Hell, I've worked missions with more subterfuge than you can ever imagine. But I never had to pretend to be married to someone—"

"Then consider it a new experience."

"You're fucking kidding me, right? This is not how I work—"

Donald's voice hardened. "You took the mission; now see it through. Vivian Sanders is there to work with you and provide cover. Otherwise, you'd be too suspicious on your own."

He pinched the bridge of his nose and breathed deeply. Donald was right. This was just an assignment. One that he wished he'd been fully briefed on before agreeing—a mistake he wouldn't make in the future for any of his Keepers. "Fine. Consider it done."

"Good. I knew I could count on you."

Logan could swear he heard Donald chuckle before he disconnected. Turning, he watched Vivian make her way down the hall to the front room. Lifting his phone, he snapped her picture. Sending it to both Donald and Mary, he texted for them to verify that she was Vivian Sanders.

He and Vivian stood silently, staring at each other. When his phone indicated messages received, he looked down. Donald confirmed. Mary also confirmed, then, in an uncharacteristic manner, she sent a wide-eyed emoji. Another message came from Mary. **Do I need to make alternate housing arrangements for Ms. Sanders?**

For a moment, Logan almost confirmed, then he sighed and typed, **Negative.** Shoving his phone back into his pocket, he continued to stare as tension filled the air as well as in his stance.

Vivian finally moved first. Sucking in a fortifying breath, she skirted around him, moving to his unpacked grocery bags on the floor. "I also bought some groceries, but more is always better." Her voice was natural, almost sounding friendly.

But Logan was anything but comfortable. She began putting the groceries away, haphazardly tossing the cans into the cabinets next to her purchases and the cold items into the refrigerator.

"I see you bought two percent milk. I have one percent, but I suppose it doesn't matter. I've never really tasted a difference, but I figure I don't need the extra fat." She smiled as she turned away from the refrigerator. He still glowered, so she quickly turned back to her task.

He moved forward, but the tiny kitchen had little room for both of them. "I've got this."

She stepped to the side and nodded, her lips pressed together, but he didn't speak, not sure what he'd say. He arranged the canned goods in the cabinet, labels facing out in a neat stack. After he finished placing the cold items in the refrigerator and freezer, also arranging them neatly on the shelves, he stowed the plastic bags and turned to face her.

She walked straight to him with her eyes flashing. "Mr. Bishop, please... stop the silent pouting."

Irritation morphed into anger at Donald's duplicity in a mission, but seeing her take a step backward, he reached out to stop her retreat. Seeing the flash of fear in her eyes, Logan grimaced, immediately mumbling, "Sorry." Filling his lungs with air before letting it out slowly, he knew the situation needed to be salvaged.

Vivian stared up at him, resignation in her voice. "Look, why don't we sit down and talk this out? Obviously, neither of us was completely informed about the situation, but we have to work together."

Nodding, Logan knew she was right and was galled to admit she was coping better than he was. SEALs adapted. SEALs reassessed at a moment's notice. And now, he hoped that as the leader of the Keepers, he would do the same.

He walked into the living room, which was only a few steps from the kitchen, once more forcing him to realize how closely the two of them would be working together. *Living together.* Not hearing her follow as he sat down, he turned his head to see her returning to the kitchen and retrieving two beers from the refrigerator before making her way to him. Setting them both on the old coffee table, she sat in one of the chairs, now facing him.

He dipped his chin in appreciation and held out his bottle in a silent toast. She smiled and clicked her bottleneck to his. Taking a long drink, he began, "I suppose we should start over. I'm Logan Bishop."

Her lips curved up ever so slightly as she responded, "Nice to meet you, Logan. I'm Vivian Sanders." Taking a sip of her beer, she continued, "We might as well be forthcoming so we each understand exactly what we've been told."

At his slight nod, she said, "I'm a biologist employed by the Department of Homeland Security. I was hired to study and test the different chemicals and biologics that terrorists—"

"I'm aware of the interest in biological warfare." He interrupted. "I had the opportunity to meet Dr. Kendall Rhodes a few years ago." Now that he thought about it, it was more like five years ago. And once more, he felt the passage of time rushing by.

Her eyes widened as her smile brightened. "Kendall? You know Kendall? I visited her lab in Louisiana when I was training. She's brilliant. Her research for the International Olympic Committee is valuable for all of us in this field... and... uh..."

He stared at her blankly. Her shoulders slumped, and her smile became less bright. His gaze moved over her face, noting her striking features. High cheekbones and silky, straight black hair. Her dark eyes were clear and shining, no longer filled with fear but doubt. His gaze dropped over her body, observing her slight stature paired with feminine curves. Jerking his eyes back to her face, he was relieved to see her tearing off the beer bottle label. That meant she missed his perusal of her body.

Clearing his throat, he gained her attention once more. "What were you told about your work here?"

"I was approached by a supervisor and told that I was to attend a meeting with another person in the department, someone high up… Donald Markham." She shrugged. "I hadn't heard of him before, but that's not unusual since I'm just a lab rat. I went to the meeting to discover it was only him and me. He told me terrorist groups in Alaska were feared to be working on biological contaminants that could easily be used to incapacitate thousands of people from all over the world. Either killing them outright or causing severe illness. After COVID, you can imagine how we all have a heightened awareness of this."

He nodded, and she continued. "So they needed someone to do the testing to determine what was being created."

"Why you?"

Snorting, she said, "I'd like to say that it was because I was the best person they could send…but more likely, it was because of my heritage."

"Heritage?"

"You're not much of a conversationalist, are you?" she joked, but her mirth died as she observed his unchanging expression. She blushed as her lips pressed together and nervously tucked another strand of hair behind her ear. "I'm from California, but my parents were born in Alaska. My mother is full-blooded Tanana Athabaskan. I think because of my appearance, it was thought that I would easily be disguised here. You know…integrating into the area and not really being noticed."

"And the so-called *marriage*?"

Vivian visibly bristled, then shrugged again. "I was told that I would be in charge of determining what was being produced in the suspect's house, and since I would be sharing a house with a security investigator, we would have the cover of being married so as not to draw unwanted attention to ourselves."

"Security investigator," he muttered to himself. *Donald wants me to investigate… and then he wants me to exterminate.*

Her eyes narrowed. "Are you just going to keep asking questions? What about you? What do I need to know about you?"

"I'm the investigator," he said, leaning forward to snag his bottle off the table. He took another long swig. "And what else were you told?"

She must have been lost in thought when she didn't speak, and a chuckle erupted at the lunacy of the plan.

Snapping out of her trance, she blushed. "I'm sorry. What did you say?"

Now he was lost in thought at the slight rose spreading across her cheeks. Pulling himself back to the subject, he repeated, "What were the rest of your instructions?"

"I was told that the security investigator would be in charge, letting me know what I needed to do, and would let me know when there were samples for me to test. I was also told that we would be sharing a house next to the suspects and that our cover would be to appear as a newly married couple." Seeing his eyebrows lift, she hastened to say, "I assure you, I was equally surprised, but it makes sense. Why else would two people be moving to this remote location and live in the same house? A newly married couple who can't afford anything nicer right away is perfect." Her shoulders lifted again in a shrug. "Anyway, we certainly don't look like relatives."

Logan had to admit the logic was sound—he just wished Donald had informed him of the complete cover. *But then, would I have agreed to take the mission? And which other Keeper would I have sent?* A strange flash rushed through him at the thought that he wouldn't want any of his Keepers to be in this room with Vivian except him. As soon as that crossed his mind, he shut it down. *Mission only. Get it done... go home. Just like every other mission.*

10

Vivian's attempts to steady her breathing proved futile as she sat in the cramped confines of the small living room. Her companion's large and unhappy presence loomed over her, and since meeting him, her thoughts had flown from one thing to another.

At first, she felt heart-stopping fear at being accosted in the bedroom by a man holding a weapon while she was changing clothes. She'd never been around guns, much less had one pointed at her.

When she discovered he wasn't a threat and her breathing had returned to normal, she noticed just how imposing he was. Well over six feet tall, he dwarfed her as he had peered down. He had broad shoulders and a chest that tapered to a trim waist. He was handsome in a rough-around-the-edges way, with a chiseled jaw covered in stubble. His penetrating eyes held a hard glint that paired with his deep, gravelly voice.

His jeans fit perfectly over his ass. She'd have to be

dead not to notice that particular asset, and she was definitely not dead. Yet. The way he glowered and growled, she wasn't sure how long that would last. Despite the ruggedness of his appearance, there was an undeniable magnetism about his raw masculinity that both captivated and unnerved her.

By now, her beer was drained and so were her emotions. She'd successfully shredded the label in a fit of nervousness but no longer had anything to do while he continued to ponder their situation silently. Taking the opportunity, she observed her partner in more detail. His square-jawed face, with its day-old scruff and short, dark hair, gave him a dangerous, *don't-fuck-with-me* appearance. But it was his eyes that pulled her in. Greenish-gray. Or greenish-blue. Or bluish-gray. They seemed to change as quicksilver with his mood. Blinking, she stared...mesmerized. *He'd be perfect for the cover of a romance novel.* She pressed her lips together to keep from letting a nervous giggle slip out at the thought.

He shifted on the sofa, leaning forward to place his empty bottle on the coffee table.

Uncomfortable with the silence, she said, "I can see this doesn't make you happy, but that's what I was told. I don't see any other way for us to make this work." Vivian sighed as she also leaned forward, her gaze landing squarely on Logan.

He nodded and confessed, "I was basically given the same information, although I was just given the name of Sanders and had no idea we were sharing a house. I made the assumption you were male, and that was a stupid, sexist error on my part." Blowing out a breath, he added, "And I wasn't given any need for a cover. Certainly not pretending to be married."

Standing, she collected the bottles and headed into the kitchen, chucking them into the trash. Her mind swirled with the new information. He wasn't prepared for this, and she had no idea what he was going to do. There was no wedding ring on his hand, and she wondered if it was the state of matrimony or pretending to be married to her that he found so distasteful.

If he refused the mission the way it was, she would have to report back to work with nothing, and she hated not knowing what the neighbors were possibly cooking up in their house. Hearing a noise behind her, she startled, whirling around to find him standing right behind her.

"Jesus, you scared me," she said, her hand to her throat. "You move so quietly for such a large man in boots."

"Sorry," he muttered. "I've lived and worked on my own for a number of years before having others around me recently. Guess I've lost my manners."

Leaning her hips against the counter, she peered up at his face, holding his gaze. "Have you decided what you're going to do?"

"I admit to being surprised, but I agreed to the mission, so I'll do what is needed in order to adapt."

Letting out a huff of air, she opened her mouth, but he got there first.

"But," he added, "I have no idea about the marriage thing. Never been married. Never figured I would."

She burst into laughter, thinking that a man who had no problem facing terrorists and could handle a weapon as easily as he probably handled a toothbrush seemed daunted by the idea of the simple pretense. "Logan, you don't have to know about marriage. After all, we're just pretending. We'll just act like a normal couple for a week or so. It's not like they'll be peeking to see that we sleep in different rooms. It's no big deal."

Logan remained quiet, and she now wondered if she had said something to offend him. Sighing, she stepped closer and placed her hand on his arm. "Come on, let's get the rest of your stuff inside, and then we can put our heads together."

Still smiling, she walked to the kitchen door leading outside, and he followed in her wake. "Good God, you've got one of those old gas-guzzling trucks as well," she huffed. Shaking her head, she missed the eye roll behind her.

"I'll get my things. No need for you to assist."

She sighed and nodded. "Sure. I'll just go nuke something for linner."

His expression remained the same, but his question came in the form of a slightly tilted head. She mimicked his head tilt and said, "You know... when you eat a meal between lunch and dinner. *Linner*." When he gave no response, she shooed him away with her hands. "Well, that's what my mom used to say. Just go. I'll nuke some food."

Vivian dug into the food that she'd bought. She

looked over, glad to see him eating but wondering what he was thinking since he'd said very few words after coming back into the house. "I should apologize for the food. It was just simple for now, but I really can cook."

"No need," Logan commented, keeping his eyes on his plate as he shoveled another forkful into his mouth. "I didn't buy anything like this because I wasn't sure there would be a microwave. You don't need to cook for me."

"Well, I'm certainly not going to cook for just myself." Popping the last bite into her mouth, she took a hearty gulp of tea before standing to take her plate to the sink. Washing it, she reached her hand out for his dish as he moved toward the sink.

"I'll get it," he said, sliding in next to her at the sink.

"How about you wash, and I'll dry?" she offered, smiling up at him.

Logan nodded, lifting the dour frown on his face. Once finished with the plates, cups, and utensils, he wiped his hands as she finished drying. She stood on her toes to set the cups on the top shelf, and he reached around her, his front at her back as he took them from her to place them there. Their proximity hit her, and her breathing hitched. She tried not to think about the heat emanating from his body. Tamping down those thoughts, she forced her professionalism to take over. "Thanks," she said, twisting her head around to smile up at him. "See? We'll get along just fine."

"Insufferable man!" Vivian grumbled under her breath.

Their pseudo-relationship devolved quickly after they'd eaten with an argument over her phone and their rooms. She had wanted to discuss their plan, but he appeared to be as closed-mouth about it as he was about everything else. Her earlier attempts to draw him out had been met with silence, and now he was invading her space and making demands. He'd asked for her phone, and as soon as she handed it over, he powered it off before shoving it into his pocket.

"As of now, this phone is off-limits for you—"

"What?" The screech she emitted was a sound she almost never used, but it seemed as though he managed to pull it from the depths of her lungs.

Handing her a burner phone, he said, "Use this. Only when you have to."

She held out her hand, palm up, and demanded, "Give me my phone."

"No. I can't trust that you won't forget and use it. While we're here, you can't have your personal phone in your possession. It's just a precaution. And you need to get your things out of this room and into the bedroom across the hall."

At that, she blinked, her mouth hanging open. "Why? My things are already in the closet and drawers."

"I need the room on this side."

Standing in the hall, she watched as he set his bags onto the bed she'd slept in last night. "The rooms are the same size," she argued, following him into the bedroom and grabbing the handles of his duffel bag, attempting to lift it. Barely able to budge the heavy bag, she grimaced as he swiftly moved in, putting his hand on the top.

"Don't," he ordered. "Don't touch my things."

Whirling around with her hands now on her hips, she huffed. "Seriously? I normally wouldn't consider touching someone else's property, but you've entered *my* room, putting your bag on *my* bed, not to mention you stole *my* phone!"

"I'm taking this room," Logan declared once more, his tone firm. "I need to be in this one."

Stepping closer, with her hands clasped together in front of her, Vivian attempted to calm by taking a deep breath before letting it out slowly. "I will not leave this room without you giving me a reason. A good reason. You may be in charge of this assignment, but you owe me the courtesy of talking to me. You need to—"

"I need to be on this side because it faces the neighbor's house."

Her mouth snapped closed as her eyes darted to the window, knowing the neighbor's house was in view or would be if the blinds were open. "Oh," she muttered. Turning, she found him staring at her. Swallowing audibly, she complained, "If you had just said so to begin with, I would have understood."

He scrubbed his hand over his face, sucking in a deep breath. "I'm sorry, but I'm not used to having to explain myself." Moving to his bag, he unzipped the duffel, pulling out some sweats and running shoes. Moving silently around her, he stepped into the bathroom, shutting the door firmly behind him, leaving her standing in the middle of the bedroom.

A moment later, he walked out of the bathroom, bypassed her, and headed down the hall. She hurried after him, calling out, "Where are you going?"

"Running."

"But why now? We need to talk about what we're doing! I'm not sure when I need to—"

Turning on his heel, he faced her, and she skidded to a stop.

"Vivian." He said her name as though it pained him to do so. "We will talk, but not now. I'm going for a run, and you're going to get your things set up in the other bedroom. It'll be late when I get back. Don't wait up."

Her jaw dropped. He placed his forefinger on her chin and lifted, shutting her mouth.

"And Viv? Get used to this, 'cause as of right now, I *am* your boss." With that, he turned and walked out the front door, closing it behind him.

Fifteen minutes later, Vivian found herself going between the two bedrooms, transferring her clothes from one to the other. She hadn't been told how long this assignment would last but had been told to prepare for a few weeks. As she put the last of her things in the chest, she slammed the drawer in frustration. It became stuck, and she shoved all her weight against it with her hip, crying out in both anger and pain. Stepping back, she sat on the bed, blinking back tears.

Glancing out the window, she saw the sky as the sun set, much earlier than she experienced in California. The beautiful, ever-changing colors over the deep green of the fir trees held her spellbound. Realizing this bedroom was gifted with the glorious sunsets and didn't suffer from the glaring morning sun made it the better room even though they were the same size. *He couldn't have known that...he wasn't being nice...just demanding. And now I look like an idiot for standing up for myself when I wouldn't have had to if he'd just come out and explained things to begin with.*

Hours later, Logan had still not returned. Walking back into his bedroom to make sure she had all her possessions, she looked at the bed, his large bag still sitting on the quilt. Heaving a sigh, she thought of the sheets that needed to be changed since she'd slept on them last night. Standing next to the bed, she grabbed the handles of his bag once more, struggling just to lift it. Indecision moved through her, but she decided to take some of his clothes out so she could move the duffel. *He didn't mind taking my phone!*

Burying the feeling of guilt, she unzipped the top and reached inside to lift out a pile of clothes. Her fingers hit cold metal, and she snatched them back as though burned. Sucking in her lips, she hesitated before her curiosity got the better of her. Leaning over, she peered inside, seeing two guns in holsters, and another one partially visible underneath some clothes. Her breath left her lungs in a whoosh, and she plopped down heavily on the bed as her thoughts tumbled.

Lightheaded, she began to breathe deeply, acknowledging that nothing was going the way she thought it would. *I thought I'd share a house with some nice man who would just sneak in next door, do his thing, get some samples for me to test, and then we'd be out of here. Guns? Weapons? And who knows what else is in that bag?*

Jumping up, she bent over the bag again and fixed the handles the way they were before she began her ill-fated sheet changing. She stepped back and looked at the bed before letting out another sigh. Glancing around, she hurried out of *his* room.

11

Logan walked back into the house, locking the door securely behind him and turning off the porch light that Vivian must have left on for him. Staring at the lock, he knew he needed to add extra security since she'd be on her own a lot.

While running, he'd taken the time to report to LSIMT, receiving some good-natured teasing about how he must have known about Vivian, which was why he was so keen on being the one to take the lead in the mission. He'd allowed his Keepers their laughter, but he still couldn't stop the gut clench that occurred when he thought of how this mission was already off the rails.

Now, he didn't want to leave her vulnerable. Pulling out his phone, he called the night Keeper on duty.

"Hey, boss, it's Dalton. What can I do for you?"

"I need security locks for this house. Didn't think about it when it was just going to be me, but I want to make sure Ms. Sanders is safe when I'm not here."

"You got it. Bert can stick them in the shipment he's preparing with your new cameras. Anything else?"

"Yes, I'm going to get a list from Ms. Sanders as to what she'll need for the makeshift lab. I'll send it to Bert to include."

"No problem. When it's ready, Cole will fly it up."

"Thanks. Appreciate it."

After ending the call, he noticed the warm glow of a lamp illuminating the living room and the adjacent hallway. It was a thoughtful touch he silently appreciated.

Meticulously checking the back door in the kitchen, he turned off the lamp before heading to the bedroom. A quick glance inside his room satisfied him that she had completed the task of moving her things from that room. However, a handwritten note perched on the bed captured his attention. Curiosity had him immediately pick it up, and his gaze skimmed the words.

I didn't want to touch your belongings, so I couldn't change the sheets on your bed. They were clean when I slept on them last night, and I assure you I took a shower before I went to bed. See you in the morning, Vivian

He sighed heavily at the mix of emotions that her note sparked within him. He'd gone out to accomplish reconnaissance, as well as to actually run to drain the frustration from his body. Frustration he wasn't used to feeling when on a mission. Vivian was a distraction he didn't need. Or at least he didn't want to need.

Glancing back at the note, he realized he'd been gone for a long time and hadn't told her what he was doing or where he was going. When he worked alone, he didn't have to worry about a partner or telling anyone his whereabouts. In a significant shift, he acknowledged that if he was going to be an example for the other Keepers, he needed to work and communicate with Vivian.

After chastising himself, he looked across the hall to where her door was closed. He moved to it, his hand on the doorknob before hesitating. The desire to open the door to see that she was safe was unnervingly strong. *I can't just open her bedroom door. I can't just peek in. What if —fuck it, I need to see that she's safe.*

He opened the door slowly, and his eyes quickly adjusted to the dark room. The soft moonlight peeked in through the slit in the closed curtains, revealing an unmoving lump in the bed. He stepped closer, allowing light from the hall to shine on the bed. Her dark hair flowed out behind her on the pillow as she lay on her side facing him. Her eyelashes made thick crescents on her cheeks, and her mouth, for once not talking, was slightly open, her breaths deep and even.

Nothing about the day had been what he'd expected. From her defiance to her melodious voice, he was caught off guard. When she'd laughed at his reticence over pretending to be a couple, he refused to admit he hadn't been part of a couple in a long time and that his only experience with it was just a college romance that lasted a few months. When wanting company, it was easy enough to find a willing woman, usually a tourist passing through Cut Bank or the SEAL bunnies years earlier. Lately, it had been his hand he'd been wedded to.

Now, unwanted, unexpected, and unneeded ideas of what he'd like to do with Vivian slid through his mind. From the moment she announced who she was, he'd felt this assignment was a mistake. Comments about his gas-guzzling truck and then defiance in following orders had him recognize fully that this wouldn't go easily. Used to those under him obeying without argument, her defiance had rubbed him the wrong way. But her willingness to work with him and eagerness to do what she could to make the situation better caused guilt over his earlier harshly spoken words.

The floorboards creaked underneath his weight, and he inwardly cursed, but Vivian never moved. Satisfied she was safe, he backed out of the room, closing the door behind him. A slight grin slid over his face as he thought about how deeply she slept. He was trained to sleep light, to be awake and aware in an instant. But her? She looked as though she could sleep through fireworks.

His cock stirred at the thought of her tucked into bed, but he tamped down any thoughts of sex with the pretty Viv. His frown now back firmly in place, he headed to wash up in the tiny-ass, shared bathroom. It didn't miss his notice that it was neat, with no evidence of her personal items at all.

Glad for the hot water, he showered quickly. Back in his bedroom, dressed in cutoff sweatpants and a T-shirt, he set his bag off the bed after checking his weapons. The rooms were small, only fitting a twin-sized bed with a scuffed wooden headboard, a chest of drawers, and a wooden door that opened to a small closet. Vivian had closed the curtains, but he moved to the window, barely pulling them to the side once his light was out, and looked next door. Their lights were out as well now. His run in the dark included reconnaissance on the neighbor's property.

And that was what led him to his next call. Glad to hear Donald answer sleepily, he hoped he woke up the fucker. "What the hell were you thinking?"

A heavy sigh met his ears. "Look, Logan. You were the best person for me to send. I know that your LSI team is involved, but I also knew you'd be the one to take this assignment. Ms. Sanders was chosen because she had the scientific knowledge you need and the appearance to fit in easily. I know I can trust you to take care of her, work with her, and figure out a way to make the mission successful."

"And the end of the mission? If termination is necessary?"

"Then I also trust you to keep her out of it."

Silence fell between the two, and Donald finally broke it. "Look, Logan. You're making this more difficult than it has to be. If you're going to lead a team for LSI, then you need to figure out how to work with people in all kinds of situations again. Not just the ones who call you boss, but ones who will challenge you."

"And you think little Ms. Sanders is the one to challenge me?"

A deep chuckle came across the line. "Logan, my man… I think she already has."

Donald disconnected, leaving Logan to stare at his phone for a few minutes. Finally, giving up the pretense of wondering how the hell everything would work out with the aggravating woman, he tossed his phone to the nightstand.

Satisfied there was nothing else to be done tonight, he pulled back the covers and slid into bed. As his head hit the pillow, the soft floral scent of Vivian encircled him, filling his nostrils. For an instant, he thought that perhaps he should have changed the sheets. But as he relaxed into sleep, he liked that her scent surrounded him.

12

Vivian's eyelids fluttered opened, and the world gradually seeped into her consciousness. It took her a moment to remember where she was. Always a deep sleeper, she lay for several minutes, enveloped in disorientation until the sunlight coming through the slit between the curtains and the sound of boots moving down the hall pierced through the mental fog.

Swinging her legs over the side of the bed, she pulled on her woolen socks as a desperate, primal urge for coffee overrode all other needs. She staggered out of her bedroom in a mindless quest for caffeine, barely noting Logan's bedroom door was open. Shuffling into the kitchen, she rounded the corner and viewed the back of him.

Tall and sinewy. His tight, long-sleeved T-shirt pulled across his back and fit along his trim waist. His jeans hung just right on his ass, but she could tell he didn't care about his clothes or how they looked on him. He exuded confidence just in his bearing.

She was still gawking when he looked over his shoulder, catching her standing there. His lips quirked slightly, sending a jolt of awareness coursing through her veins. Holy hell. It wasn't much of a smile, but she wasn't sure she'd be able to handle the force of his gorgeousness if he offered a full smile. Especially not without caffeine first.

"You've got a pillow crease on your cheek."

"Huh?" She kept her gaze down, now focused on the mug of coffee he had in his hand.

"Viv? You awake?"

Her eyes jumped to his, and she shook her head. "Nuh-uh. Coffee."

He filled another mug and set it down before placing the creamer and the sweetener packets on the counter.

She fixed her coffee and then glanced at the very black brew in his mug. "How'd you know how I liked my coffee?"

"Creamer was in the refrigerator, and the sweetener was on the counter."

Wondering if she'd ever get used to his short way of speaking, she circled her hands around the warm mug, holding it close. Her eyes closed as she inhaled deeply. After taking a few sips while he stood at the stove fixing bacon and eggs, she finally asked, "When did you get in last night?"

"Late. You were already asleep."

No response seemed necessary, so she continued slurping. He plated the bacon and eggs, then moved past her to set them on the table. She remained standing in the same position, her hip leaning against the counter as though it were holding her up.

"You gonna eat?" he asked, taking a seat.

"Uh-huh," she mumbled as she shuffled to the table and sat down. Sniffing appreciatively, she nodded her thanks as she shoveled a forkful of scrambled eggs into her mouth. "This is good."

He eyed her carefully. "Are you always this much of a zombie in the morning?"

Blinking, she halted the fork on its path to her mouth. "I'm not a zombie."

"Viv, you sleep like the dead. I checked on you last night, and you didn't even stir. I checked on you this morning, and you were lying in the same position as though you hadn't moved all night. Now, you can barely speak a sentence and look like you're going to face-plant right into the middle of your eggs. I'd call that a zombie."

Vivian opened and closed her mouth several times, but no response came. How did he do that? Reduce her to silence. *And he calls me Viv. No one calls me Viv.* Her parents sometimes called her Vivie, but that sounded too much like her teenage years. *But Viv?* Her lips curved up slowly as she turned her attention back to her plate. "I just need caffeine in the morning."

As he finished his breakfast, he pushed his chair back, stretching his long legs in front of him. "Thanks for taking care of changing bedrooms last night. I need to be on that side to keep track of the house next door at night for any unusual noises or visitors."

Realizing he was ready to talk business, she finished

quickly and took their plates to the sink. Rinsing them, she left them for later and poured two more cups of coffee. She doctored hers and left his black before setting it in front of him. "Here's your unsullied cup of coffee." Taking her creamed and sweetened cup to the opposite side of the table, she sat down.

"Unsullied?" He chuckled.

Not having heard him chuckle before, she stared for a second. The rumble came from deep in his chest, wrapped around her like a hug, and her breath caught in her lungs. She looked down, trying to hide her grin. "Yeah…it's unsullied with anything to make it remotely drinkable. But that's the way you like it, right?" she asked, looking up to see him smile. And her breath caught once again.

After taking a sip of his brew, he nodded. "Okay, we need to talk about our plans." He leaned a long arm over to the counter, snagging a folder and laying it out in front of them.

She slid her chair next to him so they could view it together.

"Were you given any details about the suspects?" he asked.

Shaking her head, she answered, "No." Biting the corner of her lip, she altered her reply. "Other than they were suspected terrorists. But, honestly, that means little to me."

His sharp gaze met hers, and she quickly added, "It's not that I'm ignorant, but there are many terrorist sects, and the particulars weren't shared with me. I'm just interested in the possible chemical and biological combinations and mixtures that can be made. Unlike explosives, the results can be easy to hide. They don't have to be completely volatile."

Turning to the first page of the notebook, she observed the pictures in front of her: one man and one woman. Tapping the two pictures, he said, "This is Akram Zaman. The house is rented in his name. The lease includes his wife, Farrah. Whether or not they are actually married, we can't say for sure. We do know they didn't come straight to Alaska. They immigrated to Chicago, and it appears they spent time in Denver as well. He's been on the radar because of the past company he's kept—members of other known ISIS cells. They moved to Fairbanks almost two years ago, where they leased an apartment near the university. Akram was active in the local mosque and began spending time at the university, hosting gatherings for other Muslims." Snorting, he added, "That sounds good, except he was recruiting for his organization, not socializing with peace-loving students."

She listened attentively, studying the photographs carefully so she could identify them when she saw them.

"They took out a lease on this house about two months ago." Flipping to the next page of photographs, he continued, "And these people seem to be the most frequent visitors. Malik Jones, Rashad Smith, and Nafisa Fariq. All university students majoring in biology or chemistry. There have been other visitors since they've been under suspicion, but these are the most frequent."

"How on earth do you already know all that?"

Logan looked up, his brows lowering. "I may have just been handed this mission a couple of days ago, but DHS has been gathering intel for a while."

Eyes widening, she asked, "But if they know all that, then why are we needed?"

"Not all intel can be gathered by computers or satellites or—"

"Satellites?" She leaned back in her chair, shaking her head. "But...but...that sounds like something out of a movie."

"Movies are shit. I work in the real world."

Vivian sucked in her lips, her mind swirling with questions.

He held her gaze. "What are you thinking?"

Her gaze jumped to his. "How did you know I was pondering something?"

"Viv, you'd better not play poker. Your face hides nothing. In fact..." His mouth pinched as he rubbed his jaw. Leaning back in his seat, he pinned her with a hard stare and sighed. "This whole thing may be a big mistake."

She bristled. "Are you saying I'm a mistake?"

His gaze was piercing as he nodded slowly, but his voice was softer. "That's exactly what I'm saying."

"I'll have you know—"

Throwing his hand up, he said, "Don't get riled up. This isn't personal. But why the hell did the DHS security think it was a good idea to put a woman with no investigative, security, or military experience out here? Viv, your face is an open book, easy for anyone to read."

"I was sent to analyze the materials and compounds

they're using and creating. I can test what you find and let you know what it is."

"And our cover? Jesus, it's more than just us living in the same house. We'll see them out in the yard... maybe at the store. Sure, you can act the part of my wife from a distance, but how will you ever shutter your face so they can't see your suspicion when we're close?"

Shoving her chair back, she stood quickly and entered the living room. Embarrassment and frustration moved through her. He might be a man of few words, but he sure knew how to make her feel inadequate with those words.

Logan sighed heavily, then she heard the sound of his chair scraping along the wooden floor. As she stood motionless in the middle of the room, his boot steps came closer until he placed his hands on her shoulders and gently turned her around.

"Viv, I'm sorry," he said. "I swear, I'm not trying to be a hard-ass. I'm just used to working either alone or with a trained team."

Vivian's eyes stayed on his chest, not trusting herself to look higher although his muscles right in front of her face were distracting. Nodding jerkily, she continued to stare straight ahead. She blinked while refusing to let him see the moisture in her eyes.

He lifted her chin with his finger, and for a long moment, the silence hung between them. Finally, he said, "Let's get back to planning, okay?"

Shrugging, she lifted her gaze. "What's the point? As far as you're concerned, I'm not right for this job."

Logan simply tugged on her arm, leading her to the sofa. Once seated, he twisted to face her. "I was a SEAL."

A SEAL? At that pronouncement, Vivian's gaze jumped to his as her mouth opened in stunned silence.

"Guess you know something about SEALs."

Not wanting to admit she read SEAL romances, she snorted. "Not officially, but yeah, I know a little. Mostly from TV, movies, and…uh…books." She thought about what she knew—they were some of the best of the best, could take on any mission, and were highly trained. Understanding dawned, and defeat filled her voice. "I'm so not what you're used to. You're right… this is a mistake."

They sat quietly for a few minutes, and she tried to think how her superiors would react if she went home in disgrace. While she'd never had aspirations of espionage, she still hated to fail at anything.

Finally, Logan said, "Look, maybe we're both thinking of this all wrong." Her brows lifted in surprise, and he continued, "In a SEAL team, we each had our own strengths, our own particular jobs that we were to accomplish, but we worked as one—seamless. We spent so much time together that we could read each other's faces and body language."

A faraway expression filled his eyes for a few seconds, then he seemed to snap back to the present. "We knew the mission, planned it out, but could change on a dime and reassess what needed to be done. And this only came with intense, twenty-four-seven training over a long period. When I started taking on assignments by myself, I had no one else to consider in my decisions."

She nodded, dejection still on her face. "What you're saying only proves why we can't make this work."

"No, no," he said, shaking his head. "It just means that I need to change what I'm used to. And so do you. I'm not on a SEAL team anymore, and you're not stuck in a lab."

"But how do we do this now…with no time for training together?"

He stared into her eyes and seemed lost.

"Logan?"

Blinking rapidly, he looked away, clearing his throat before turning his attention back to her. "We need to be clear on what our different roles are. We need to carefully review the information we have, but I'm not going to force you to learn anything outside your need to know. After all, if we were just newlyweds moving to the neighborhood, you wouldn't know their names ahead of time. You'd stumble over their names. Hell, you might even get the names mixed up if you saw a different person over there."

Nodding, she agreed. "Okay, so I need to review the information as to what you know and what you'll be doing, but I need to keep to my role of just a neighbor until you bring over samples for me to analyze?"

"Yeah, that sounds about right." Looking up suddenly, he ordered, "But I don't want you over there by yourself. At all. Do you understand me?"

Crinkling her brow, she shook her head. "But why?

What if we get invited over for…for…I don't know. Maybe coffee?"

Incredulity hit him. "Jesus, Viv. You think a terrorist is going to invite you over for coffee?"

"No, I'm sure they won't," she floundered, feeling the blush heat her cheeks.

"You do not go inside that house by yourself. Ever. I won't yield on this, Viv, so you've got to promise."

"Okay," she agreed hurriedly, hoping to reassure him.

"What do you need to do for your analysis?"

"I brought equipment with me, but honestly, I haven't figured out where to set up—"

"How big a space do you need?"

"A room about as big as one of our bedrooms, but not in this house. It could be potentially deadly materials—"

"I found a shed."

His constant interruptions would typically drive her crazy, but she quickly realized this was the way Logan worked. It appeared his mind was so efficient he was already ready with an answer halfway through a question.

Sighing, he said, "I'm sorry."

"What for?"

"Just…just for…hell, being me, I guess."

A smile slipped out, and she accepted his apology, knowing this situation was as difficult for him as it was for her. "No problem. And, yes, a shed would be good, but where can we find one that'd work?"

"On my run last night, I was doing a reconnaissance of the area—"

"That's why you were gone so long?" she asked, now the one interrupting.

"I had limited time to gain knowledge of this area before coming, so I wanted to check it out myself. Going on a run was the perfect way to explore the neighborhood and surrounding woods. My people looked into the area and discovered a shed at the back of the property, and I found it about fifty yards to the west in the woods. It's abandoned. It hasn't been used in years."

"To the west…that's away from their house, isn't it?"

He nodded. "Makes it perfect for you to get to the shed without being seen."

"So can we make this work?" She couldn't hide the hesitation in her voice as her eyes searched his.

Rubbing his hand over the back of his neck, he said, "Truthfully? I have no idea. But I've never failed in a mission before, and I sure as hell don't plan on failing this one either."

Her smile widened as she took his words to heart. Slapping her hands on her legs, she said, "Okay then. Tell me what's next."

13

An hour later, Vivian stretched her arms over her head, working out the kinks in her neck and back. Her shirt rode up slightly, and Logan averted his eyes, trying not to look at the sliver of skin now exposed. They had reviewed the pictures of the major occupants of the suspect's house and formulated a basic plan of action.

Viv would monitor the neighbors and catalog their movements, including cars, license plates, and descriptions. He'd explained that while his people could monitor some intel from satellite images, there was still value to boots-on-the-ground reconnaissance.

Logan explained his part-time job at the small airfield as a mechanic, just enough hours to provide cover until the covert part of his mission kicked in, which was something he did not divulge, assuring her that it was best for her not to know. He would be *running* often at night and had intel to gather. "I brought some cameras for the outside but will put them up tonight when it's dark. Once they're up, you can watch the cameras and won't be stuck right at the window to keep up with their comings and goings."

He also let her know that as soon as he could get inside, he would smuggle samples for her to test. But before that, she needed to look at the shed to let him know if she deemed anything else essential to complete her work.

With a plan in place, she glanced down and groaned. "I'm still in my flannel pajamas." Grinning, she added, "Dibs on the shower!"

Watching her jog down the hall, he was unable to keep the smile from tugging at his lips. Once the bathroom door was closed, he sat and leaned back in his chair, his mind in motion as he reviewed their plans. Closing his eyes for a moment, he wondered if this mission had any chance of succeeding. When he heard the water in the shower turn on, his mind slid down another path—one where he imagined her body, wet and naked.

Jerking his eyes open, he stood quickly, forcing those thoughts away. *Fuckin' hell...she's a scientist... coworker... fake wife... not some girl for me to pant over.* Grimacing, he thought of her innocence in this situation and wondered why Donald set her up on this mission based on her heritage and not her experience. The mere thought that she could be in danger caused him to pace the room before heading into the kitchen, where he gripped the counter, his knuckles turning white. *Not on my watch*, he vowed, knowing part of his mission was keeping her safe.

While the water still ran, he called back to the

compound. "Sadie, what have you got for me?" Last night during his run, he'd called to ask the night duty Keeper what they found out about Vivian Sanders. When they had nothing to report, he asked them to check again.

"Boss, there isn't much. She's twenty-nine years old. She has no record, not even a speeding ticket. Everything she told you is true. I talked to her supervisor, and Donald chose her because he felt like she had what she needed to work with you on this assignment."

Landon was also on the line. "Is there a problem? It's not too late to change the plans."

"I can fly up," Sadie offered. "We can have Ms. Sanders stay in a hotel until you get the samples, and I can work the case with you in the house next to the terrorist group."

Logan considered the offer for a few seconds, then sighed as he dismissed it. Since she parked in the cul-de-sac, he felt sure the neighbors had already seen Vivian going in and out of the house. "No, that's fine. I don't want to take a chance that the neighbors see too many people come and go. But it'll be nice to know I'm not alone in this and have you all as backup."

"Whatever you need, let us know," Landon said.

He disconnected and bent down to grab the tools he'd found under the sink, planning to replace the locks on the doors. As he performed the mundane task, he thought of what he'd said to Vivian earlier about working with his SEAL team. Then after a few years of being alone, he had to develop the skills of a leader again and utilize his new team. He'd been so quick to throw in the towel with this mission at the first sign of a problem, and that wasn't like him.

But the *problem* had deep brown eyes, so dark it was hard to distinguish the pupil from the iris. Dark chocolate. His mom used to make a rich, dark chocolate cake for his birthday because that was his favorite when he was a kid. He slowly shook his head... *I haven't thought of that memory in years.* But all it took was Vivian's eyes to remind him of something he'd loved—decadent dark chocolate.

Finishing the locks, he placed the tools back where he'd found them and stood at the counter once again. Scrubbing his hand over his face, he sighed heavily. The last thing he needed to do was think of Viv's eyes. *This mission may not be fucked, but I sure am.*

While inside the bathroom, Vivian lathered her body and quickly washed her hair, unsure how long the hot water would last. Closing her eyes as the water sluiced over her, the image of her fake husband filtered through her mind. Tall, dark, and handsome. A strangled snort erupted as she realized how conventional her description sounded. *How about towering, somber, and athletic? Soaring, shadowy, and muscular?* Another snort slipped out. *He's more like glowering, angry, and irritable.*

Shaking her head, she knew there were infinite ways to describe him, each one accurate. Rinsing her hair, she turned the water off, knowing she also had to turn off her physical attraction to Logan. It was time to do her job and do it well. Determined to accomplish that feat, she dressed for the day, hoping the new alliance she and Logan had begun would make their working relationship easier.

That afternoon, Logan drove to the small airfield to work for a few hours and check on his helicopter while Vivian sat by the window waiting to see the neighbors. Reading on her e-reader, she lifted her head to see a woman coming out of the house next door. Hurrying to her car, she intended to take out a bag she had left in her trunk for the express purpose of having an excuse to go outside. From a distance, it was hard to see if the woman was Farrah, but she was desperate to make contact as soon as possible.

"Hello!" she shouted over at the woman.

The woman looked over quickly, her gaze jumping from Vivian to her house, then back to Vivian again. Finally, a shy smile crossed her face, and she nodded slightly.

Vivian began walking toward her, smiling widely in return. Recognizing Farrah, Vivian noted the black skirt, white blouse, and the hijab worn by the young woman. A beautiful leather belt cinched Farrah's waist, but the stylish leather boots on her feet were most surprising.

Feeling frumpy in her jeans and heavy sweatshirt, Vivian thrust out her hand. "I guess we're neighbors. I'm Vivian. My husband and I just moved in."

"And I am Farrah," the woman said, shaking her hand delicately. "I also live here with my husband."

"The houses seem nice here although kind of old."

She shrugged while still smiling. "But we just got married, and the rent fits our budget."

Nodding, Farrah agreed. "We have not been here long, but I have tried to make it our home."

"We should get together sometime," Vivian blurted, her heart pounding as she wondered what Logan would think of that plan. They hadn't worked out all the details of what she was supposed to do when she met the neighbors, and she realized, belatedly, that she had no clue what she was doing.

Farrah's eyes widened at the suggestion. Thinking she was going to deny her outright, Vivian pressed, "We've got a grill out back that I'd like to try sometime. Um…you and your husband could join us."

"That is very kind of you to offer," Farrah said, her smile not reaching her eyes. "But I will have to speak to my husband. He…does not often have time to socialize. His work with university students takes up a great deal of time."

"Well, he has to eat sometime, doesn't he?" she asked, returning her smile. "But if not, then we can get together for coffee or tea or something. You could tell me the best places to shop."

Farrah's smile faltered. "Of course. It would be an honor to have tea with you sometime. I… well, my husband has me go to the grocery on Thursday afternoons, and there really is only the one store close by."

A slight movement in her peripheral vision caught Vivian's eye. A man looked out of the window, his hand pulling the curtain partially back. Too far away to determine whether he was one of the men in the pictures, she continued smiling at Farrah.

Hearing Logan's truck rumbling down the road, she quickly stepped back. "Oops, I need to get dinner started. I'll talk to you soon, and we'll figure something out. Nice to meet you, Farrah."

"You too, Vivian."

Hurrying back to her car, she reached inside the trunk to take out the bag she had placed there earlier. Seeing Logan's narrowed eyes on her, she smiled as she parked next to the house. Rushing over to him as he stepped out of the truck, she threw her arms around his neck while giving a little hop, causing him to catch her as she wrapped her legs around his waist.

Logan's arms encircled her waist as she plastered her front to his. She had no doubt his fast action was due to surprise and instinct, but she was also shocked at how her body reacted to being held by his. It was as though she fit perfectly against him. Her romance novels would have described it as two halves creating a whole. Or maybe the steamier ones would have said his hold awakened the parts of her that had slumbered too long. And she knew just what parts they would have referred to.

"Viv," his deep voice rumbled in her ear, jerking her back to the present.

"Hey, sweetie!" she called out, tamping down her desire and plastering a joyful smile on her face.

14

Stunned, Logan held on to Vivian as she clung to him. He'd seen jungle monkeys not hold on to trees as tightly. Concern sent his heart racing. "Viv, what's wrong?"

Placing her mouth close to his, she whispered, "Is she looking?"

Blinking slowly, he crinkled his brow as he glanced over her shoulder, then returned to her face. "She was, but she's headed back inside." He held her easily, finding her weight in his arms comforting. And as she wiggled slightly, his comfort quickly became discomfort as his cock reacted to the beautiful woman plastered to him. Her breasts were pressed against his chest, the soft feel against his hard body making his growing erection hard to ignore. He was still uncertain of why she clung to him so tightly, but the smile on her face gave evidence she wasn't in danger.

"Just in case she or the man inside who was peeking out the window earlier are at the window watching now, we should stay like this for a moment," she whispered. "I told her we were newlyweds, and she'd expect me to greet you this way."

Dawning slid over him as he continued to hold her in his arms, enjoying the feel of her body pressed to him more than he wanted to admit. "Oh, she would, would she?" he said, keeping his mouth close to her cheek.

"I tried to invite her over for tea, thinking that would be a way to get to know her without her getting suspicious."

Holding her close, Logan felt her warm breath wash over his cheek, and he fought the urge to wish her lips were closer. "I think it's safe now." His gruff voice effectively sliced through the distraction that was Viv in his arms. Irritated that she had made contact with the neighbors without a plan or him around, he forced his arms to loosen, afraid they might go from holding her waist to throttling her neck.

Startled, she settled back on her heels with a jolt. "Uh…yeah. Right." Turning quickly, she walked toward the front door with him following. Once inside, she faced him again, only this time from a respectable distance. "I went over to introduce myself to her."

Cocking his head to the side, he placed his hands on his hips and said, "You should have waited for me."

"Oh, no. I didn't go to their door. I just waited until I saw her come out, and then I went out like I was going to my car to get something. I stowed a bag there just in case the opportunity arose. And it did! It was easy to introduce myself to her."

"And what name did you give her?" he asked, his voice unyielding.

"Uh…Vivian?" she said, a question in her tone. "You and I didn't talk about names, did we?" Her smile fell as she muttered, "Damn."

"You should have waited, Viv. I'm the one with experience planning. I'm the one who has to anticipate what they might think or do." He worked to keep his voice steady, but his words held an undercurrent of anger.

"But it seemed like such a good idea. Really spontaneous."

"Did you give your last name? Did you say Sanders?"

"No. No," she hurried to say. "I just told her my name was Vivian. And she just said she was Farrah."

A relieved breath rushed out of Logan as he dropped his chin to his chest, closing his eyes on the way down. A soft touch reached his arms, and his eyes jerked open again. Vivian stood right in front of him, her face peering up into his, her dark eyes searching.

"I'm sorry, Logan. I just saw her and wanted so much to make contact. I figured they might get suspicious of us if they never saw us out together. Now they know we're a newly married couple who just moved in. I thought you being gone would be a good thing, not knowing if she would approach if you were here."

Nodding slowly, he reached up. His fingers itched to cup her cheek but rested on her shoulders instead. "Right. It's done, and it appears nothing untoward occurred. But"—he pinned her with a stormy stare—"from now on, you don't make a move unless I know about it. I don't want them inside this house any more than I want you over there. Agreed?"

Vivian pursed her lips, appearing to try to hide her irritation but failing at the effort.

"Does that include the labs as well?" she asked, unable to keep the snarkiness from her voice. "I might not be a covert operator, but I'm sure as hell not stupid." As soon as the words left her mouth, she slumped her shoulders. Sighing loudly, she said, "What a mess this is."

Logan stepped backward, his thoughts tumbling once more. He was used to precise planning and execution, so this mission drove him batty...*and it's only been one day.* "Okay, let's plan more after we eat. I stopped at the bar in town and grabbed some burgers."

Seeing her eyes light up, he turned and headed back to the truck to retrieve the bag he had abandoned when she threw herself at him. It reminded him it had been a long time since a woman had jumped into his arms.

In the Navy and then SEAL training, the bars near the bases were full of women just waiting to bed a SEAL for bragging rights or wanting to snag one as a husband. Leaning into the truck to grab the bags, he knew how different it was for Vivian to be in his arms. Sure, it had been for their cover, but it still felt...*real.* He could have sworn she was glad to see him return and not just for their cover.

Shaking the thoughts from his head, he stalked back inside, his earlier grumpiness returning.

Vivian quietly grabbed water bottles for them as his dark mood filled the room. She sat at the table, reaching for her food and thanking him softly. He sat down, hating that his bad mood permeated their meal, and tried to think of a way to apologize.

She bit into the burger, and her eyes closed as she groaned as though in ecstasy. Logan leaned back in frustration, hearing the sounds emitted as her mouth closed over her hamburger. He knew all too well he would love to listen to those sounds in a different context.

With her woolen sock-covered feet on the coffee table and toes pointed toward the wood-burning stove, Vivian crunched on an apple as she watched Logan work on his plan. His dark brown hair was the color of milk chocolate, and while it was thick, it appeared silky, not coarse. He had reading glasses perched on his nose, giving him the look of a sexy professor. Thinking back to the lab she had worked in, no men had his virility. Sighing, she shifted her gaze out the window, watching the sun as it dropped behind the tree line.

"It gets dark so early this time of year," she commented.

"Uh-huh," he agreed, not looking up from the laptop perched on his lap.

"It's been a long time since I've spent any time here…not since college. The last years in California have me spoiled to more daylight and warmer autumns."

"Uh-huh," he muttered again.

Stifling a laugh, she said, "Do you want me to run around the house clucking like a chicken or crowing like a rooster?"

"Uh-huh."

"Logan!"

"What?" he asked, his brows drawn down as he looked at her over the top of the computer. "What's wrong?"

"You haven't been listening to a word I've said!" She pulled her feet off the coffee table and plopped them on the floor, leaning forward. "I know you're busy, but you still haven't told me what I'm supposed to talk about with Farrah."

Turning toward her, he set his laptop down and offered a slight grin. "I'm working on our backstory. I only created one for myself before I came, and frankly, the whole thing about supposing to be married has completely thrown me."

She forced a blank expression on her face, refusing to admit his words stung. *Is it that hard to imagine me in a romantic light?* "What have you come up with?"

"Okay, you've given your name as Vivian, which is fine. I can still be Logan, but our last name is Preacher."

"Preacher?"

"Old name from my SEAL days...never mind. Just go with it."

"Vivian Preacher. Vivian and Logan Preacher." She tried the names out, and a smile spread across her face. "I like it."

"I'm thrilled," he muttered. "My cover job is working as a mechanic at the airport. Before I came, it was arranged for me to have a part-time job at a little airfield a few miles from here. Usually, I'll leave each morning but return in midafternoon."

Bobbing her head in agreement, she listened more eagerly. "And me? What's my cover?"

"You're working on a college degree but taking online classes for now until you start at the University of Alaska next semester. That gives you a reason for being at home during the day. And they can't check to see if you are a student since you won't be enrolled until later."

"My major?"

"I think we'll stick to the truth. Biology."

Her eyes widened. "But—"

"When creating a cover, it's often best to stick to certain truths so as not to get tripped up. Giving you another major could possibly cause problems if they ask you questions you don't know the answers to."

"Gotcha," she agreed, seeing the wisdom in his explanation.

"Tonight, I'll install the outside cameras on our house to give us surveillance on their property. My people will also be able to monitor what is happening. They won't be watching them as much when you're here during the day since they'll have other work to do. I have more equipment arriving today, but I will have to know their schedule—"

"They grocery shop every Thursday afternoon," she blurted.

"How do you know that?"

"Farrah told me."

He was surprised but then wondered if there would be a day when she didn't surprise him. "As I was saying, we didn't have time to do surveillance before I came, so this was more rushed than I would have liked."

"What kind of things would you have done?" She leaned forward, interested in what his job entailed. "This is so different from what I do or can even imagine!"

He held her gaze for a moment, then said, "If an area can be monitored by satellite, we could have gotten a visual on the area, houses, their cars, and even who came to visit. But we didn't have time to do much, and this area is so wooded that our resources were needed elsewhere."

She nodded, then leaned back again. "So what will I be doing during the days when you're at work?"

"You will need to monitor the comings and goings next door. Even with the equipment that will come in—"

"You never told me what equipment was coming."

Heaving a sigh, he said, "Equipment necessary for what I'll be doing. Until then, I need you to keep a log of who comes and goes. Descriptions, car makes and models, and if you can positively identify the people, all the better. You also need to get your lab ready."

Interest sparked throughout her. "Finally!"

Logan shook his head and met her grin with a slight quirk of his lips. "In fact, we can start that today."

Clapping her hands, she jumped up from the sofa and announced, "Just let me get my boots!"

15

The dense woods enveloped them in a cloak of shadows as the vestiges of dusk barely filtered through the trees. They were far from the house, but with walls of thick trees on either side, the narrow path wound its way deeper into the forest.

Vivian trailed Logan, and when he finally stopped, she stumbled into his back. She reached out, her fingers gripping his coat. "Sorry," she mumbled. A small shed was in front of them, and the wooden planks of the walls and roof appeared sturdy. There were no windows, but as Logan swung the door open, they could discern a skylight in the roof. He stepped in, setting the lantern on the wooden table against one wall.

"I wiped it down yesterday," he explained. "But I know it will never be as clean as it should be."

She looked around, her gaze surveying the interior of the shed. He had no doubt her mind was working overtime on how to make the shed functional. "I'll cover the interior in plastic, so I'll need a staple gun to make it quicker."

"Good. That's smart."

She shrugged while still looking around. "I was told that I might have to prepare a temporary lab room. This should be okay. The table is small, but we can easily bring in a folding table as well." Looking up toward the ceiling, she added, "The skylight will give light, but I can bring in lanterns, too."

"We need to cover the skylight. We can't have any light escaping to give evidence that you're in here working."

"Oh, yeah... right." A sigh left her lips. "I think in terms of the lab and testing. I forget about the need for no one to be able to see anything."

"I'll buy some battery-operated lanterns. With halogen bulbs, they'll give you a lot of light to work with."

Turning to him, she crinkled her brow, asking, "Do you think this place will be safe? I know it's actually close to our house and well hidden with the trees, but..." Her uncertainty crept out for the first time since he'd met her. Until now, she'd appeared fearless.

Facing her, he put his hands on her shoulders. "This is why we need to be smart. We need to be cautious. There's no reason for them to suspect we are on to them. Just be a friendly neighbor, but do not attempt to question them. This shed is easily accessed through our kitchen door, which they can't see. Your car is parked on that side and can hide you as you enter the woods. You should be able to come and go very easily, but..."

He stopped for emphasis, bending slightly to peer into her eyes. "I want to be out here when you are. So when I'm gone, you watch their house. When I'm home, we can come out here together."

Together... somehow that had his thoughts scattering in directions that had nothing to do with the mission.

She nodded, her lips curving slightly as his blue-green eyes locked onto hers. "Right," she agreed, her voice coming out breathier than before.

Squeezing her shoulders, he forced his thoughts back to the task at hand. "Okay, do you know what you need my people to get?"

Looking around again, she blew out a breath. "Yes. I'll put a list together for you when we return to the house."

He nodded and sent a message to Bert, letting him know they would need Cole to fly up with supplies as soon as they could get them. "Let's get back to the house. I have work I need to do once it gets dark enough."

As they stepped outside, a rustling to the left caused her to stiffen, her hand reaching out to grab Logan. His gaze jerked over, focusing on the leaves to the side of the path.

"Meow."

He looked down to see a small, thin, tabby cat looking up at them. Vivian gasped and bent forward, but Logan was faster and held his hand out to the scared cat. She immediately moved to him, allowing him to scratch her head, and the rumbling of a purr released from her throat.

"Oh, Logan, can we take her back? Please. I promise I'll take—"

He scooped up the cat. "Of course, we'll take her with us. Looks like she could use a good meal." As his gaze moved to Vivian's, he could have sworn she was staring at him as though he held a treasure and not just a scraggly cat. Shaking his head slightly, he said, "Come on. We'll get you two inside, then I have some work to do."

Two hours later, he lay flat against the roof, hidden from view, and spied headlights coming down the lane. Akram and Farrah alighted from their car and walked silently into their house. Lights shone through the cracks in their curtains as they moved through the house, first in the front and then toward the back.

Rolling onto his back, he stared at the clear, night sky dotted with stars. They twinkled brightly with no pollution or atmospheric interference and appeared close enough to touch. Bundled up against the cold, he remembered the warmth of Viv in his arms. What started as a continuation of their cover quickly became a need on both their parts. *Is it just lust based on proximity? Or something more? Something based on real emotions?*

A gust of cold wind hit him, bringing him back to the present. Frustrated that the situation took his mind off the mission, he rolled over. Continuing to work, he set up the transmitter and hid it behind the TV's satellite dish. Finally, completing his tasks, he moved toward the back, where a ladder was hidden. Entering through the kitchen, he stopped at the counter and looked into the living room, where Vivian sat on the sofa with the cat curled up on her lap.

"I see she's made herself at home."

Viv's eyes lit as she held his gaze. "Is it okay if I named her? I thought Sakari would be nice. It means *sweet* in Inuit."

"It's perfect." He meant the cat's name, but as he took in the domestic scene before him, he had to admit the vision was also perfect.

She carefully set the sleeping cat on the sofa and walked over to the other side of the counter.

"Did you get it all set up?"

Letting go of the vision of domestic bliss, he nodded. "Yeah. Let me work on my laptop for a few minutes, and then I can show you what we need to focus on next."

"Sure, that'll be great." Her lips curved, but the beaming light he had grown accustomed to from her wasn't present.

Not knowing what else to say, he headed to the kitchen table and opened his laptop. Half an hour later, he called her over. She hurried to the table, clearly anxious to see what he had completed. Sitting in the chair next to him, she leaned close as she stared at the laptop screen. His nostrils filled with the floral scent of her shampoo, and he leaned slightly closer.

He showed her the various screens she could now monitor from the computers—a straight shot down the street to see someone coming, the cul-de-sac where someone would park, and the front and side of the house next door. "These images will be available to my people, but remember, they won't be watching them twenty-four seven. Much of the day, you'll log the comings and goings and the times so we can document their patterns."

"Okay," she agreed, eagerly nodding her head. "I can do that."

"Perfect, so now, give me the list you've come up with for your makeshift lab, and I'll have my people order it. They can bring it up along with my things."

It was late, and they had a lot to do tomorrow.

"Go on to bed. I'll take a shower and get some shut-eye, too."

She agreed, smiling sleepily, then offered a yawning good night as she turned and walked down the hall. He stared for a moment until she disappeared into her room. Then he shook his head, wondering when his thoughts about her had changed. No answer came in the dark room, so he stood and headed into the bathroom.

Logan stood in the old bathtub as the warm water from the showerhead poured over his body. He wanted to make sure there would be enough to last for Viv's shower. He tried to shake the image of Viv in the shower out of his mind but was unsuccessful.

He had come to Alaska expecting a male scientist, never anticipating a beautiful woman to work with him. And once he'd met her, the reality that they would pretend to be married shocked the hell out of him. His cock stirred at the thought of her soft body tightly held to his earlier when he arrived home. The way her breath warmed his cheek as she spoke. The way her small waist felt in his arms as her hips and breasts pressed against him.

As the water rained down, his hand found his cock, and with thoughts of Viv filling his mind, he quickly worked his way to release, the force making his knees weak. Choking back a groan, he hoped his low growl hadn't been heard. By now, the water was cooling, and with guilt hitting him that she'd have to wait for more water to warm, he washed away the proof of his desire before turning off the spray.

Regretfully, he realized that this was all he would be able to have of her... just thoughts of her beauty as he jerked off while pretending to be her husband... *What a fucking mess.*

Wrapped in a cocoon of bedcovers, Vivian lay awake. Despite having slept soundly the night before, sleep now eluded her. Rolling over, she punched her pillow.

She had attempted to compartmentalize her feelings toward Logan, relegating him to the role of colleague only—someone necessary for the shared mission, like one of her lab partners. But she'd never counted on his rugged handsomeness or the way his stone-like features melted when he smiled—not that he smiled often. But then, that might be why the smiles he did offer were so breathtaking. And his eyes...*my God, his eyes!* Gray-green-blue... ever-changing. Granted, mostly they appeared stormy but mesmerizing, nonetheless.

Her hand slipped inside her panties, finding her folds slick with need. She shoved the thoughts of Logan as her boss into the box of not-to-be-touched and slammed the lid. Instead, he filled her mind as she imagined it was his fingers tempting, taunting, and teasing her body until she pressed her mouth against the pillow to stifle her groans.

The coil tightened inside, and when her release finally came, it was all she could do not to cry out his name. Riding her fingers until the tremors subsided, she inhaled a shaky breath, uncertain her lungs could take in enough oxygen. Certainly not enough to clear her mind of forbidden thoughts of him.

Letting out a frustrated sigh, she attempted to recall the last time she had felt a genuine attraction toward someone. Her recent dating escapades had all ended in disappointment. Blind dates, dating sites, someone from work... *yep, all disasters.* Cursing her luck, she knew the one man who had held her interest for more than a day was off-limits, even while supposedly being her husband. And when the job was over with, he would go back to wherever he came from, and she would head back to California. *What a ridiculous mess.*

16

NEXT DOOR

"Come away from the window," Akram ordered, his dark eyes on Farrah.

She dropped the curtain and turned toward him, saying nothing. He stepped forward, his eyes sweeping the tiny bedroom.

"You seem taken with the new neighbors," he said.

She wondered if she heard an accusation in his voice. "Just curious," she replied. "The house has been empty as long as we've been here, so I find it strange to see people over there."

Nodding, he said, "I should have rented that place when I had the chance. That would have given us more privacy."

Akram turned and walked toward her, noting with pleasure how her gaze dropped as he approached. Without speaking, he moved toward the bed, shedding his clothes, knowing she would follow. And she did.

Later, as Akram snored in his sleep, Farrah lay awake, her body still aching from his rough treatment.

When recruited by ISIS at the university, she had been promised a future where she would hold a valued place of honor. But so far, Akram had been demanding and coarse.

Rolling to her side, she faced the window and wondered about the couple next door. The woman appeared happy, and as she greeted her husband with enthusiasm, he seemed to be just as pleased to see his wife. Sighing, she closed her eyes, willing sleep to come. It certainly could not hurt the cause to speak with the simple woman who was now her neighbor.

17

The following day, Logan headed to work as Vivian watched him from the front door and waved goodbye. Her eyes jumped to the neighbor's house, only to see all was quiet. One car was in the driveway, and she wondered if Farrah drove. Shutting the door, she fixed a second cup of coffee before settling on the sofa to read. She'd placed his laptop on the sofa next to her so that she would read while watching next door without having to awkwardly turn to face the window.

Turning to Sakari, she said, "Ready to keep me company?"

The cat replied by jumping onto the sofa and turning around in circles until she found just the right place to curl up. Vivian smiled, her heart warm at the remembrance of Logan scooping up the little stray cat with such gentleness.

Growing bored didn't take long, but remaining vigilant was necessary. After another half hour, she heard a vehicle's tires crunching over the gravel road. Moving out of sight, she trained her binoculars on the sedan as it pulled to a stop outside the neighbor's house. Jotting the license plate number onto a small pad of paper she had handy, she observed two men alighting from the car. Using the telephoto lens on the roof camera, she zoomed in, wishing they would turn her way. The driver answered her wish as he looked toward the passenger, a smile on his face as he reacted to something said. Unfortunately, the passenger continued toward the house, only giving her his back.

She pulled up her laptop and quickly made a spreadsheet with the time, car make and model, and attached a few of the photos.

Sitting back on the sofa, she waited another hour, but no more activity was seen. Pondering the idea of using the ancient grill outside the rental house, she sent a message to Logan. **Going to grocery.**

He responded with a thumbs-up, so she grabbed her keys and headed to her car.

Three miles down the road, she pulled into the parking lot of the small grocery store. Entering, she smiled at the same cashier who had greeted her the day she had arrived in town.

"Back so soon?" the woman called out.

"I wanted to have a cookout but realized I need charcoal and steaks. Oh, and cat food!"

Nodding, the clerk jerked her head toward the back. "Charcoal is against the far wall, and the steaks are in the back. Got beef, elk, and some venison. Cat food is in aisle four."

"Thanks!" Vivian pushed her cart toward the back. A few minutes later, she stood at the register and placed her few items on the counter.

"I see you got some wine this time," the woman commented, lifting an eyebrow as she held up the bottle.

Laughing, Vivian said, "I'm definitely not a wine connoisseur. I love the lighter wines with everything."

"Hey, no judgment here!" the cashier replied, joining in laughter. "By the way, I'm Betty, part owner and full-time worker here at the best grocery store in Ester. Of course, we're the only grocery store in Ester."

"Nice to meet you. I'm Vivian Sa…uh…Preacher." Seeing the questioning look in Betty's eyes, she blushed. "I'm a newlywed and still forget to use my married name."

"Well, congratulations," Betty said, her smile wide. "I think I saw your husband in here the other day. Big guy…dark hair…handsome as they come?"

"That's him," she agreed, taking out the cash that Logan had given her for incidentals. He had warned her about using her credit card and given her a wad of cash to use in town.

"You're renting that place over on Ester Creek Lane, aren't you?" Seeing her eyes widen, Betty laughed again, saying, "Honey, Ester's not that big."

"I guess not."

"You only got one set of neighbors out there. That family where the wife covers her head? I mean no disrespect to their culture, but I've never gotten her name. She doesn't come in here by herself, and the times her husband comes with her, they're not too talkative." Shrugging, she continued, "But they don't cause any trouble and seem to be nice people."

"I met her yesterday," Vivian said. "I'm a bit lonely up there, so I'll keep trying to get to know her."

"It's not a bad idea, especially before winter sets in. Sometimes you need your neighbors around here when the weather is harsh."

It was on the tip of her tongue to tell Betty that she wouldn't be here in the winter, but she wisely kept her mouth shut. Saying goodbye, she took her purchases out to the car, her mind already planning on spending some time outside. And she loved the idea of grilling for Logan.

Once home, Vivian hurried inside to show Sakari the bounty. "I didn't know what you'd like, so I got dry food, canned food, and treats. I also got a litter box and litter. Plus a scoop." Digging into the bag, she laughed. "Oh, and a mouse toy."

Once Sakari was well-fed and had found another spot in the sun to sleep in, Vivian went outside. She dragged the old grill over the gravel drive until it was a safe distance from the house, not trusting her fire-building skills. She poured charcoal into the grill's drum, but her attempts to light it were in vain. Match after match extinguished before the charcoal ever managed to light. Frustrated, she turned when she heard a vehicle on the gravel, seeing Farrah and a man drive up in a car.

Plastering a big grin on her face, she jogged over,

waving as she went. "Hey, Farrah!" Seeing the expression of fear on Farrah's face as her eyes cut over to the man, she hoped she was not making a mistake.

Stopping a few feet from them, she looked at him and smiled. "I'm Vivian. Vivian Preacher. Can I ask for a favor?"

The air immediately electrified as his face registered blatant irritation, but she rushed ahead. "My husband is at work and will be home in a bit. I wanted to grill some steaks but have no idea how to get the charcoal lit. My matches keep burning out before it lights."

The man opened his mouth, but before he could speak, another car drove into the driveway, parking behind them. Two other men and a woman alighted from the second vehicle. The woman, dressed like Farrah, with modern clothes and a beautiful hijab covering her hair, cast a narrow-eyed gaze toward her. The two men, one much darker in skin color than the other, smiled widely at her.

"Hello," the taller, darker man greeted, his white teeth gleaming against his skin. Walking closer, he asked, "And who do we have here?"

"I'm Vivian…from next door."

"I'm Malik," the smaller man said, his eyes not leaving her face.

Suddenly feeling like one of her specimens under a microscope, she forced her smile not to waver. "I was hoping to get some help starting a fire with the charcoal in my grill. My husband will be home soon, and I wanted to grill steaks for him."

The taller man stepped up, introducing himself. "Rashad." He glanced behind her to the grill and said, "I'll help you."

"Oh, thank you. That would be so nice." Emboldened, she moved toward Farrah and thrust her hand out to the man she stood beside. "Are you Farrah's husband? It's nice to meet you."

"Yes," he responded, ignoring her outstretched hand.

She caught Farrah's blush as she started to turn away, but she twisted back as though just having a thought. "You know, I have tons of food. We'd love to have you join us for a cookout…out here."

She caught Farrah's eyes flare in interest while the other woman's eyes went cold and hard. Rashad and Malik grinned in response, though Akram did not change his expression.

Pushing forward, she said, "I have steaks and potatoes." Farrah said nothing, so she added, "It'd be so nice to meet some people around here."

"I have no time," barked the unnamed woman as she moved toward the house.

"Well, we have to eat," Malik said, not looking back at the others.

"Right," Rashad agreed, his smile firmly in place.

"We will be happy to join you," Akram finally spoke, his eyes unreadable. "My wife and Nafisa will prepare some food as well."

At this, Nafisa whirled around, her glare now focused on Akram. "I have things to do—"

"Silence!" His voice sliced through her objections.

Nafisa's mouth snapped shut, but her chest heaved. Facing Vivian, he repeated, "We will join you and your husband. Rashad can go now to assist with the fire."

Smiling with accomplishment, she turned to walk back to her yard, praying Logan would not be pissed.

18

Logan offered a chin lift to the man behind the bar in the only establishment in town that offered a drink as well as something to eat. The rough building, like most in the area, looked worse for the wear. Harsh winters had obviously pounded the weather-beaten wooden exteriors. He cast his gaze around the clean interior, and it appeared just as worn as the outside. It reminded him of the bar in Cut Bank.

A large man, his tan skin, eyes, and cheekbones giving evidence of his native Alaskan heritage, smiled widely as Logan settled onto a barstool. "Whatcha havin'?"

"Draft."

"You've been here two days in a row, newcomer." This came from behind him, and as he turned, his gaze landed on the server he met yesterday when ordering the burgers. Even with her sleek black hair and dark, twinkling eyes, he knew she was fishing.

"Yep," he replied, lips twitching upward.

Huffing, she slapped her dish towel on the bar and said, "So you gonna talk or what?"

"Woman, leave the customer alone," the bartender growled and winked simultaneously.

"Iggie, if we want fresh blood in this joint, we need to be friendly with the customers," she groused back.

"And I'm tellin' you, Sally, we gotta give the man a chance to have a drink before you pepper him with questions."

At their lively banter, Logan let a grin slip out despite his efforts to rein it in. "Either you two have been working together for a while or you're married."

"Both," Iggie and Sally said at the same time.

The man held his hand out, grasping Logan's in a firm handshake. "Guess you figured out I'm Iggie. Igaluk's my name, but Sally nicknamed me Iggie about twenty years ago when we met as teens. It kind of stuck. Welcome to the Goldmine Saloon."

"Logan Preacher."

"Nice to meet you, Logan," Sally said, her smile genuine. "You living around here or just passing through?"

Eyeing her carefully, he said, "Why do I get the feeling you already know?" Seeing her grin, he confirmed, "My wife and I just moved here. We live off Ester Creek Road, right at the end."

Sally and Iggie shared a glance, which wasn't lost on him. He continued to drink his beer as he added to the story. "Got a part-time job as a mechanic. Wife's taking online classes for now."

"Met your neighbors yet?" Sally asked.

He acknowledged her attempt to keep her voice neutral but heard the inflections nonetheless. "Nope. My wife met the woman who lives there."

Her eyes flared with interest. "They don't come in here, but then I heard from Betty, over at the grocery, that when they come in there, they don't talk much." Hearing Iggie making a grunting noise, she hurried to say, "It just seems weird to me when someone moves to a small town yet don't make any attempt to meet the people they come in contact with. That's just not neighborly."

"He's got those college kids around," Iggie said, "so they probably spend a lot of their time in Fairbanks."

"Whatever," she grumbled, then smiled again as she looked over at him. "So, Preacher, when are you going to bring your wife in?"

He startled at the sound of his SEAL name being used so easily by someone else. He had to admit he had chosen it as a way to connect with his former missions —well, *the ones taken with a bunch of badass SEALs and not an impetuous scientist.* Clearing his throat, he said, "I'll get her in here soon. She's a real sociable girl and would love to meet you."

Sally's eyes sparkled. "Well, that's good because I doubt she'll have any luck making friends with your neighbors!"

As Logan's truck rumbled up the lane, his thoughts alternated between strategizing the infiltration of the

Zaman house to gather vital intelligence and the image of Viv. Thoughts of her won out, fueling his eagerness to get home. Knowing she might be bored and lonely, he rounded the curve, anxious to see her again. And not remembering the last time he'd ever been so anxious to see anyone.

His gaze landed on a gathering of people in front of his house, and his heart raced as he blinked to take in the scene before him. Wisps of smoke curled upward from an old grill that had seen better days and probably better decades. A few weather-beaten lawn chairs were scattered across the grass, while a card table was set up in the center, complete with bowls and platters.

And there, in the middle of the group, was Vivian, standing at the grill, surrounded by two men. Her smile was bright, and her hands waved while she chattered. Two women with traditional hijabs wrapped around their heads were nearby, one sitting in a chair and the other standing by the table. As he pulled closer, he noticed Akram standing to the side, his face set with distaste.

Fuck me. I'm gone part of a day, and Viv's managed to get the whole gang together. Thoughts of throttling her were becoming more of a reality. He'd never had anyone get his emotions in such a tangle.

Stepping out of his truck, Logan felt the weight of everyone's gaze upon him, but the beauty running toward him captured his attention entirely, taking his eyes off the terrorists. He anticipated and readied his stance this time when she jumped into his arms. One hand supported her ass, and the other arm banded around her back. He held her close as she pressed her lips to his, catching him off guard yet igniting a fierce longing.

He angled his head for maximum contact. Deep, wet, and long, but no tongue. That last part nearly undid him, but while he wanted to take advantage of the kiss, he didn't want to take advantage of her. He tried to tell himself he was just determined to play the part of devoted newlyweds, but he knew it was more about the desire to taste Vivian.

She leaned back slightly, eyes wide and glazed. "Wow," she breathed against his lips.

"Yeah," he whispered back, her face filling his sight.

Blinking, she said, "I know it's crazy. Don't be mad… it just all happened."

"Viv, with you," he growled softly in her ear, "I already know nothing *just* happens."

Settling her feet down to the gravel drive, he peered down at her, assessing. She hid her nervousness, but she smiled up at him brightly. "Hey, sweetie, I've met our neighbors and asked them to eat with us. It's such a lovely afternoon. I thought we could grill out."

Meeting her smile with one of his own, he inwardly rolled his eyes at her subterfuge but quickly decided to make the most of their intelligence-gathering opportunity.

"Sounds good, babe." They walked over, and she began the introductions.

Rashad and Malik greeted him with practiced smiles, but he noticed their gazes were not nearly as warm as when they were aimed at Viv. Jealousy, mixed with protectiveness, shot through him, but he tamped it down. Moving to shake hands with Akram, he observed the man's dark, penetrating gaze as he took his hand in a friendly shake, giving his name.

Looking at the women, he noticed none of the men introduced them, but Vivian stepped forward.

"This is Akram's wife, Farrah, and one of the university students, Nafisa."

He greeted Farrah, not allowing his eyes to linger on her, especially with Akram eagle-eyeing him, but noted her nervously glancing toward her husband. Nafisa barely acknowledged him, giving a slight nod before turning away.

Grinning as he walked over to Vivian, he glanced at the table loaded with several Middle Eastern dishes. His arm encircled her waist, and his fingers gripped slightly as he said, "Looks like it's going to be an interesting dinner, babe."

19

The food was delicious, and having skipped lunch, Logan ate heartily. Chicken on skewers, falafel, and hummus with naan bread, combined with Vivian's steaks and corn on the cob. Interested in the participants, he easily slid into the cover of just a mechanic looking for work. As they sat in lawn chairs with the late afternoon sun still shining warmly over the treetops, he sipped his drink, disguising his study of the various players. Casting his gaze back toward Vivian, he gave a nearly imperceptible nod, relieved when she seemed to pick up on his nonverbal command.

"What are you studying?" Vivian asked, smiling at Rashad and Malik.

Rashad's mouth was full, but Malik answered for both of them. "Science. I'm a grad student in chemistry, and Rashad is working on a master's in biology."

Eyes wide, she exclaimed, "Oh my goodness, me too! Well, not my master's degree... I'm just working on my undergraduate. I have most of my credits but am taking some online classes in education because I'd like to teach biology someday."

Rashad smiled as he swallowed. "Great—"

"Really?" Nafisa asked, her eyes narrowed. "You? Biology?"

Maintaining her smile, Vivian nodded. "Well, actually, my major is microbiology."

Nafisa leaned forward, a sly smile firmly in place, and asked, "And what particular type of microbiology are you interested in?"

"Nafisa!" Rashad growled.

"What?" she argued, shrugging her delicate shoulder. "I'm just seeing what she's majoring in." Turning back to Vivian, she provoked, "If you can tell us."

"I'm particularly interested in microorganisms used for drug delivery. Of course, they can be suitable for high-value medical applications such as tissue engineering. I studied the biotechnological production of biopolymers with tailored properties and a variety of other biopolymers, such as polysaccharides, polyesters, and polyamides. Obviously, these are produced by microorganisms." Smiling widely, her eyes twinkling, she focused on Nafisa. "Is that what you were looking for?"

Nafisa scowled and leaned back in her seat, and Logan hid his smile at the way Vivian had proven she knew what she was talking about, helping to solidify their cover. Rashad and Malik burst into laughter.

"What do you plan to do with your degrees?" she asked the two men. "What are your specialties?"

Malik's smile drooped slightly as his gaze shifted to

Akram. "For now, I just want to continue to learn as much as I can. I sometimes think that perhaps I'm best as a student but not so much as an employee."

She nodded, sympathy in her eyes. "It's so hard to have an unending love of learning, don't you think?"

Rashad wiped his mouth, his eyes on her as he said, "I had thought about pre-med. I don't know…maybe."

"That's so noble. To be able to save lives is such a gift," she commented pointedly. "I hope to work in the pharmaceutical industry."

Silence fell over the group as they continued to eat, Farrah standing occasionally to serve the men, always starting with Akram. As she approached Logan, he smiled genuinely, saying, "No more, but thank you. It was delicious."

"Mr. Preacher, what do you do?"

Logan shifted his gaze to Akram and gave a self-deprecating shrug. "I work on aircraft. Been a mechanic for several years."

"And where did you learn such a trade? The military, perhaps?"

A heavy silence hung in the air. With an aw-shucks attitude, he grinned. "Nah. My parents were farmers and had their own crop-dusting plane. I learned how to fly it, and my dad taught me how to fix it when needed. After high school, went to technical school to learn more."

Akram seemed to relax slightly in his chair, his eyes less wary than before. "And Alaska? Why here?"

"My grandfather," Vivian said quickly, interjecting before Logan had a chance to reply. He kept his expression neutral, but inside, he quaked. *What the fuck is she doing? We haven't talked about that yet—*

"My mother is full-blooded Tanana Athabaskan. My parents are in California, but my grandfather is still here. He's not well, but I wanted to be closer to him." She beamed at Logan. "My husband was sweet enough to tell me he could get a job anywhere, so...we're here."

His pulse eased as he noted the others appeared to relax with Viv's biology response and the story of her grandfather. Surprised at her ability to think quickly on her feet, he smiled at her in return, his face a mask of an indulgent husband completely in love with his wife.

Turning his focus toward Akram, he leaned back, patting his stomach. "And what do you do?"

Akram's dark eyes penetrated his for a moment. Just when Logan thought Akram wasn't going to speak, he answered, "I work at the university. I counsel a variety of students, particularly those from other countries."

"Been in Alaska long?" Logan continued.

"For a while." That was his noncommittal reply.

"Where are you from originally?" Vivian asked, turning her wide eyes to the gathering. "I find that Alaska's cold can be hard to get used to after the California sun."

Farrah nodded enthusiastically. "I much prefer the warmer weather of—"

Clearing his voice loudly, Akram interrupted her, causing Farrah to clamp her lips shut, her eyes darting anxiously toward Akram.

"I was in Northern California," Vivian jumped into

the breach. "So we certainly had snow, but it was nothing like here."

"Well, this was *lovely*," Nafisa said, sarcasm dripping from her words as she stood. "But I gave up an evening of studying and need to get back to work." She gathered two almost empty dishes from the table and looked down at Farrah. "Helping?"

"Of course," Farrah said, jumping up from her chair. "Vivian, it was truly very nice of you to invite us to share a meal with you."

Vivian stood also as Nafisa handed the two platters to Farrah. "It was our pleasure. Your food was wonderful, and the spices you gave me for our steaks made my poor attempts at grilling more successful than if I'd been on my own."

The men stood and, with goodbyes, followed the women back to Akram's house. Logan folded the card table and carried it inside their house as Vivian brought in the last plates. Once inside, she set her dishes on the counter before immediately turning to him.

"Look, Logan. I know you're probably mad as hell at me. It was just all so unplanned, really. Well, not completely. I had mentioned a cookout to Farrah yesterday and went to the grocery store just in case. I had no idea if I could meet them or get them to come. It worked out when Rashad and Malik came. I couldn't get the charcoal lit, and my request for assistance appealed to their machismo side, I think. But it worked, didn't it? I mean, we got to meet them all and stayed outside, right?"

Logan leaned his hip against the counter, watching

Viv's arms flying about as she walked and talked, her nervousness palpable. Sakari weaved figure eights between both their legs before Viv reached down to pick her up, snuggling against the sweet cat's fur. He stepped closer, placing his hands on her shoulders and pinning her in place.

"I'm beginning to get used to the idea that you seem unable to follow a plan." Sighing when he watched her face fall, he added, "It's okay. I admit, when I drove up the road, I was caught off guard." Tilting his head back, he stared at the ceiling for a moment before lowering his head so his gaze could hold hers. "Yeah... it was good. We now have confirmation of who's there, but babe, you've got to realize the dangers lurking."

Sucking in her lips, Vivian sighed loudly. Almost in anticipation of knowing a lecture was forthcoming, her body stiffened, and his fingers lightly massaged her shoulders.

Jerking his head toward the direction of the house next door, he continued, "They're not just neighbors. They're not nice people. Any one of them would slit your throat if they had an idea you were looking into them."

At that, she sucked in a quick breath, her forehead crinkling as she pulled the cat closer to her chest.

He noticed the change in her expression and pressed his point further as his fingers lightly trailed over the silk-soft skin of her neck. "Yeah, Viv. You heard me right. Slit. Your. Throat."

She opened her mouth to speak, but with no words forthcoming, she closed her lips, and Logan observed them quiver slightly. He battled the urge to press his mouth against hers to settle the nerves he felt move through her body.

Instead, he blew out a long breath and spoke in gentle tones. "I see I'm starting to get through. That's what I meant when I said I needed you here to watch their comings and goings. Not going over and meeting them. What if I had been late getting home? You would have been here with five known terrorists. And the instant one of them suspected you were anything other than a new wife taking some online classes, they would have killed you without compunction...and I wouldn't have known what had happened."

Tears welled in her eyes, and he hated making her feel as though her sense of accomplishment was decimated. Her shoulders slumped, but instead of Logan pulling away after making his point, he gently pulled Sakari from her arms and set the cat on the floor. He encircled Vivian's shoulders and pulled her forward until her face planted in his chest. His arms slid around her back as he barely rocked side to side, and her arms wrapped around his waist as she held on, accepting the comfort he offered.

"I'm sorry," she said, a silent trail of a lonely tear sliding down her face, soaking into his shirt. "I just wanted to help."

"I know," he said, his voice softer as his hand stroked up and down her back. "But you're here to do the lab work and be my eyes when I'm not. That's all. I can't do my job properly if you're not doing yours."

She unclasped her hands and opened her arms, stepping back. Swallowing deeply, she offered a jerky nod, then smiled wobbly with a quick swipe underneath her eyes. The deep blush on her cheeks gave evidence to her embarrassment, and that was the last thing he wanted her to feel.

"Right...uh...right." Glancing at the dishes in the sink, she said, "I can get these later. I think I'll...uh... take a shower." Slipping around him, she hurried down the hall and closed the bathroom door.

Logan stood in the kitchen, dropping his chin as he stared at his boots for a moment, his heart strangely heavy. Sakari stared up at him, the cat's intense gaze feeling like a judgment. Rubbing his hand over his face, he pinched the bridge of his nose as his eyes squeezed shut.

"Fuck," he whispered. This mission was not like any he had ever attempted, and it appeared to be getting more complicated by the hour.

Walking into the now dark living room, he stared at their neighbor's house for a long moment before pulling out his phone and placing a call.

"What's up, Logan?"

He heard the concern in Landon's voice. "Would you believe I came home today, and she was in the front yard with the whole terrorist group having a barbecue? She said it just happened, but she managed to get them to talk about some things I would never have gotten and did it all under the guise of just being a cute neighbor."

There were three seconds of silence before Landon snorted. "I swear, I can't decide if that's brilliant or fuckin' crazy." Then he started to chuckle. "You know, you've just called her cute. Is there something going on?"

"No."

"Okay, fast but short answer. I'm sorry if that was the wrong thing to assume."

He dropped his head to stare dumbly at the scuffed wooden floors, and his shoulders slumped as a heavy sigh left his lungs. "No, it wasn't. She is beautiful and smart. And swear to God, she's funny. But also maddening. She doesn't seem to get the danger from these people. She's trying to help and manages to do what I ask, but then when I'm not around, she also manages to get herself in situations I can't control."

"Is that the issue? You've met someone you can't control?"

Thoughts of the shared kiss from earlier lingered in his mind. "No," he lied, then offered a kernel of truth. "I'm just not sure how all this works."

"Take some time to get to know her. I know that wasn't necessary for the mission, but it'll make you more comfortable with being around her. You two will seem more natural."

"Yeah, maybe that's what I need. Anyway, I should be able to get the inside cameras up tomorrow since Vivian managed to find out they go shopping on Thursdays, and then we'll make fast work of this. I should have it all wrapped up soon. Thanks."

"Not sure I did much, but what are friends for anyway." Landon laughed.

Disconnecting, he leaned his hands on the countertop, his gaze still aimed downward. *Just think of her like any team member you've worked with.* Not nearly as easy as the other Keepers thought it would be. He'd seen the look in her eyes after they'd kissed and knew she felt something. He wondered if he was brave enough to let her know he felt something, too.

20

Vivian slipped under the covers, her flannel pajamas giving warmth when cold slithered throughout her body. Still feeling foolish from her conversations with Logan after the events of the day, she sucked in a deep breath before letting it out slowly.

Sakari hopped up on her bed and began to paw her way to a comfortable position. Vivian smiled as her fingers trailed along the soft fur, the movement calming her tumultuous thoughts.

Clearing her mind, she began to focus on the next day. *No more Miss Investigator. No more trying to help beyond what I was assigned. I'll take some things to the shed and get them ready. I'll watch out the window and take notes. That's it. That's all.*

Satisfied she had her mind re-centered on what she needed to do, she rolled over, careful of the now slumbering cat before slipping into a restless slumber, thoughts of the earlier shared kiss dancing in her mind.

Shuffling down the hall the following morning, Vivian assumed Logan had already left for work. Her plan was to sit at the laptop and log the activities next door all day, doing nothing but that, no matter her inclinations.

Her gaze landed on Sakari sitting in the middle of the living room, licking her whiskers, giving evidence of having had a meal. She came to a sudden halt at the sight of Logan in the kitchen.

He turned, blasting an unexpected early morning grin her way as his gaze roamed from her head to her toes and back again, landing on her wide-yawning mouth. Without speaking, he pushed a cup of coffee toward her, and she wrapped her hands around it, mumbling her thanks.

After tucking her hair behind her ear and taking a fortifying sip, she peered up at him. "What are you doing here?"

Another grin slipped out as he replied, "I live here, remember?"

She snorted. "Okay, smart-ass. I mean, why haven't you left for work?"

"Staying here today. Got some things I want to do and—"

Frustration spread through her. Setting the mug down on the counter harder than she meant to, she said, "Look, Logan. I get it. I fucked up yesterday. It won't happen again, so you don't have to stay here and babysit me. I'll watch next door and get my lab equipment ready. Nothing else, I promise—"

Logan leaned over the counter, pressing his fingers over her lips, stilling her protest. "Viv. Hush."

The feel of his rough fingers against the softness of her lips sent a tingle throughout her body. She stared into his eyes, drowning in their sea-stormy midsts. His eyes widened almost imperceptibly, and she could have sworn they held lust. He pulled his fingers away, dragging them gently over her lips like the touch of a kiss. She sucked in a ragged breath, still not speaking, but her gaze remained locked on his face.

Swallowing deeply, he cleared his throat. "We're fine, Viv. You and me. I want you safe, and this kind of setup should have never happened. You should be safely ensconced in a lab somewhere, waiting for me to send you samples. Not here, in the middle of Alaska, next door to more danger than you could ever imagine. Not here, in a dumpy little house, sharing it with a grumpy-ass man."

She didn't protest his description, but her lips quirked as she kept her gaze steady.

"But we are here. Together. And I need to make this right. I need to make sure you're safe. And we'll figure out how to work together as a team...not as individuals."

Her head moved in a slow nod, still quiet as she took in his words. "What do you have planned?" Hesitation coated her words.

"I have a delivery to pick up today."

"Okay."

"And I want you to go with me to pick it up. It'll get you out of the house. You've been cooped up here, only going to the grocery. You need a break. We'll pick up my delivery and have lunch somewhere."

"Okay," she repeated.

He leaned back, his weight resting on his hands planted on the counter, a smile still on his face. "You gonna keep being this agreeable?"

Taking another sip of the fortifying coffee, Vivian nodded. "Yes. No more making any decisions without you."

He sighed, and his smile slipped. She watched his eyes change color, getting darker. The idea that the color changed almost every time she looked at him fascinated her. Blinking, she realized he was staring back.

"What?" she asked.

"I just want to keep you safe," he replied, his warm gaze not leaving hers. "And that's what I'm going to do." Standing to his full height, he turned back to the stove and plated eggs and bacon for them both. Grinning over his shoulder, he said, "But first, we gotta eat so I don't have to drag zombie Viv to town."

Energized by breakfast and coffee, Vivian sat in the cab of the old pickup truck and listened to the classic rock music blaring from the radio. Tapping her foot on the floorboard, she watched the scenery roll by as she lip-synched to the song.

Logan glanced her way, and she caught his grin from the corner of her eye. He seemed less grumpy, and her heart felt lighter than it had in days now that the two of them finally seemed to be on the same page. The desire to know more about the enigmatic man she was with filled her.

"How long did it take to become a SEAL?"

His head swung around, surprise filling his eyes as his brows snapped together. "Uh—"

"I know you can't tell me a lot, but I was just wondering how long it took for your team to become a team."

His hands relaxed on the steering wheel. "Well, the easiest answer would be that it can take close to three years."

"Holy moly," she breathed. She sat silent for another moment, thinking of all the training he would have gone through. "No wonder you can't stand working with me."

He reached over and grabbed her hand, then squeezed her fingers. "Viv, that's not true. Yeah, I was thrown for a loop when I first got here, but shit, SEALs are trained to think on their feet and adapt to any contingency. I fucked up. Guess the years I've been out have made me rusty, but considering I'm running a security company now, I need to adapt more quickly to other people. We're in this, and we're in this together."

She remained silent, thinking about the new company he now ran, but didn't want to pry too much.

"You with me, Viv?"

Nodding, she slowly curved her lips up. "Yeah, I'm with you."

"Good. First stop is the airfield, and when we get back, I'll take you to the Goldmine Saloon for food."

For the next few miles, Vivian noted he kept her hand in his, resting on his thigh. Instead of feeling odd or presumptuous, she smiled at the warmth spreading from her fingers to the rest of her body. As they pulled into the airstrip and he came to a stop, his hand let go of hers, and she regretfully felt the cold where his warmth had been.

"Come on," he called out, walking toward a helicopter.

She joined him, admiring the way he walked around the aircraft, taking note of various parts. He climbed inside and, again, began to go through the motions of checking things out. She took the opportunity to look around at the small airfield, barely more than a large barn and runway. A couple of small planes sat near the building, but other than that, the place appeared vacant.

Hearing a noise behind her, Logan said, "I'll be right back."

Nodding, she watched as he jogged toward the barn-like hangar and walked back toward her a few minutes later. For a man so large, she loved the way he moved. He walked like a man in charge—not with an in-your-face attitude but with a confidence that bespoke his character.

He grinned as he neared, and she returned his smile. "All right. We're ready."

Cocking her head to the side, she looked at his empty arms, asking, "Did you get what you came for?"

"Nope. We're on our way to get it now."

"Oh, okay." Turning, she started toward the truck, but he called her back.

"Hey, Viv. This way."

She stared at him wide-eyed as he nodded toward the helicopter. "That? We're going in that?" Her voice rose with each word until squeaking by the end.

"Come on," Logan said, reaching over to take her hand and giving a little pull. She didn't refuse, but her hesitation poured off her. He stepped closer until he was directly in front of her, barely an inch separating their bodies. Peering down, he said, "Are you afraid? I would never let anything hurt you. Believe me?"

Sucking in her lips, she slid her eyes sideways toward the helicopter before returning her gaze to him. She believed him when he said he wouldn't let anything hurt her. With her head leaned back, her former nervousness was replaced with determination, and she nodded slowly. "Okay. Let's do this."

A few minutes later, Vivian was buckled in and watched with interest as he handled the controls. Before she knew it, they were airborne. Her stomach took a few dips but soon settled so that as she looked out the windows, the beautiful Alaskan landscape was the only thing on her mind.

"Where are we going?" she asked, as her courage allowed her to lean forward, taking in more scenery. Thick forests, with slim roads, occasionally cutting through them, stretched as far as the eye could see. She was awed as she leaned over to peer down farther. Crystal-blue lakes, surfaces as flat as a mirror, came into view. Leaning back in her seat, she looked out the front, snow-capped mountains in the distance, standing like sentinels over the water.

"To an airstrip on the east of Fairbanks that has something I ordered. It's in an undisclosed location, so that's why we're not going somewhere more populated."

She smiled and looked down, understanding she had been given all the information needed. About twenty minutes later, they began their descent. Impressed with his piloting abilities, she turned to him, her voice full of admiration. "This was absolutely amazing, Logan. Thank you!" She impulsively repeated the action he had instigated earlier and reached for his hand, squeezing his fingers.

He deftly turned his palm up so that his fingers linked with hers. They sat, entranced, and stared at each other for a moment before a man alighted from a hangar where a small plane sat.

"Hang on, Viv. Just stay here. I'll only be a minute."

With that, he squeezed her fingers before unlinking their hands to climb out, and once again, she immediately missed his touch.

She watched as he approached the man, who greeted him heartily. Dressed in pants and a shirt with sunglasses on, the only thing she could tell from a distance was that he was big—just as big as Logan.

The two men spoke briefly before they walked to the plane, pulled out several boxes, and walked to the back door of the helicopter to set them inside. Glancing behind her, she smiled at the stranger, but he didn't look her way. Sucking in her lips, she turned to face the front again.

They made a few more trips, each time carrying cardboard boxes to the helicopter and stowing them in the back. She wondered what they contained but had learned enough of Logan in the past few days to know that he would tell her if she needed to know. *Few days. Is that all it's been?*

The door closing startled her, and she realized she had been lost in thought over the changes happening in her life so quickly. Twisting around, she watched as Logan shook hands with the mystery man again. Opening her door, he said, "Let me introduce you to one of my Keepers. This is Cole. He flew down some equipment I needed and the supplies for your lab. Cole, this is Vivian."

Cole smiled up at her and offered his hand. "It's very nice to meet you, Ms. Sanders. I hope I brought everything you'll need."

"Thank you for making the trip," she said, thrilled to meet one of Logan's friends, shaking his hand.

Cole stepped away, and Logan shook his hand again before closing her door and rounding the helicopter. He quickly climbed back into the cockpit. He settled the headset over his ears, and in a few minutes, they took flight once more.

Once in the air, he said, "Thanks for coming with me, Viv. How about we take a little detour on the way back, and you can see some more scenery?"

Her wide grin was her answer, and when he smiled in return, her heart beat faster. She was sure it had nothing to do with the dips of the helicopter as they headed back toward Ester. Leaning forward, she stared down at the beauty of the Alaskan wilds. Mountains in the background. Thick forests of evergreen trees. Snow in the distance. What towns they came across were few and far between, containing nothing more than a few streets of buildings.

Looking to the side, she viewed his profile. Strong. Handsome. And just as in charge in his helicopter as he was planning their work. Relaxing in her seat, she felt his hand reach across and take hers, once more linking fingers with her.

21

Logan thought about Vivian asking him how long it took him to become a SEAL. Her face had held such interest, unlike the SEAL bunnies that always asked questions, pretending to want to know about their lives when all they really wanted was either a quick tumble with a SEAL or a ring on their finger, assuming that would grant them a ticket out of whatever shithole they were in.

Now, he found himself wanting to know more about her, and he couldn't remember the last time that curiosity had sparked. "Tell me about your family," Logan encouraged as Viv observed the vista before them, her eyes bright with interest.

Looking over, she tilted her head to the side, her lips curving. "My grandparents were from Tanana descended from the original inhabitants of the Tanana River…Tanana Athabaskans. They grew up together and married as soon as they could. My mom was born there but left for college in Fairbanks, where she met my dad. We'd visit when I was a kid, and I thought it was a great place to spend my vacation. Long walks in the woods, boat rides on the river, fishing in the lakes. And, when I was really little, my grandfather would let me sit with him in the post office, talking to everyone in town who came in." Laughing, she added, "There were only about three hundred residents, and they used the post office as a gathering place, so I got to know everyone."

"You mentioned your grandfather to Farrah—"

"Oh, that." She blushed. "You said it is best to stick to partial truths when making up a cover, so I figured they would believe that. Remember...I was chosen because of my heritage."

He glanced to the side, seeing a tinge of sadness fill her eyes. "I take it your grandparents are..."

Nodding, she said, "Yes. They passed away about five years ago. Within a month of each other." She held his gaze with her eyes bright with unshed tears. "I think it's sweet. To be so in love that you can't live without the other."

Thinking of his own parents and grandparents, he could imagine that kind of love, having seen it as he grew up.

Twisting to look at him, she continued, "Hollywood is making some kind of reality TV show about men in Alaska from that area, and most of it's fake. The show made it sound like there were only a few days worth of food in the local store, but they failed to mention that the store is actually fully stocked, and there's a café with great burgers just down the street."

"Sounds nice." His smile was warm as her happy recollections bubbled forth.

"The funny thing is, though, I really hate the little daylight part of the year. I'm someone who can handle cold and snow, but I need sunshine!"

At her words, a thought flashed through his mind—the idea of Viv at his place in Montana, where cold and snow certainly occurred, but the sun never ceased beaming down on the plains around his home. Blinking rapidly, he forced the thought from his mind. Instead, he said, "Well, how about a trip down memory lane?"

She grinned while crinkling her brow. As realization seemed to dawn, she clapped her hands and exclaimed, "Oh my God, Logan! You'll fly over Tanana?"

"Let's follow the Tanana River and see where it takes us."

It didn't take long for them to circle over the tiny town, the brown dirt roads and old wooden buildings making a small, inhabited square in the middle of the deep green of the trees. Pointing out the post office and café, she grinned as they turned back toward Ester.

"It's a little bigger than I remembered, but I bet the new TV show based out of there has brought in new businesses and visitors."

Once they'd landed back at the airfield near Ester, she reached over and placed her hand on his arm, squeezing lightly. "Thank you so much. This was such a fabulous day."

He leaned forward until his face was a whisper away from hers. "Yeah, it was." He wondered if she would take the chance to kiss him again. Wishing her lips would land on his, he held his breath. Her gaze never wavered, and he could feel the emotional pull between them. But he hesitated, then simply moved his hand toward her chest to unbuckle her harness.

A tiny gasp slipped from her lips when her body, no longer restrained, shifted. Now, their lips were perilously close to each other. Time stood still, hanging in the balance between need and want. But he didn't move any closer, and she jerked back, blushing as she slid the harnesses off her shoulders.

Realizing the moment passed, he opened his door. "I'll come around and help you." Returning to the land of reality and not fantasy, he said, "We can unload the boxes and then head for some lunch at the bar."

It took twice as long to unload the boxes as it did to load them since he insisted on carrying them himself. But, in what he had come to expect, Viv refused to stand idly by. She crawled into the helicopter and pushed the heavy boxes toward the door to make it easier for him to pick them up. Lifting the last box, he winked as he turned to take it to his truck.

He sensed her gaze upon him as sure as a caress. His mind roamed to the kiss from the evening before, the passion igniting a fire within. Turning, he caught sight of her fingers lifted to her lips and wondered if she also thought of the kiss. He could still feel the touch. Though the kiss may have been staged for the benefit of the neighbors, its authenticity resonated deep within him. Blowing out a long breath, he called out, "Are you ready to eat?"

Startled, she looked up, her eyes meeting his, and

beamed a wide grin. Perched in the doorway, she dangled her legs, swinging them back and forth as though carefree instead of worried about the dangers of living next door to terrorists.

Matching his grin with one of her own, she allowed him to assist her down before he secured the helicopter. Walking to his truck, he slung one arm casually over her shoulders. She relaxed as their steps aligned with one another. He could kid himself that the maneuver was for their cover, but it felt natural the way her body fit next to his.

"So…uh…we're going to the bar?"

"Yeah," he said, looking down at her, his eyes bright. "I went yesterday and met the owners. And that's where I got the hamburgers from the day before."

Within a few minutes, they pulled into the gravel parking lot next to the large, wooden plank building. A sign hung over the front, with the name *Goldmine Saloon* painted in reds and yellows. Logan watched Vivian's eyes light up as they walked up the front steps and entered the dark, cool interior.

"Preacher!" Iggie hollered in greeting. His eyes moved to Vivian, and he grinned. "Hey, Sally, come meet Preacher's wife."

He had entered the bar behind Vivian with his hands on her shoulders. At Iggie's yell, she stiffened, and her back hit his front just as Sally came barreling from behind the bar, skidding to a stop directly in front of her.

"Hi! Oh, aren't you a beauty," Sally declared, grabbing Vivian's hand and shaking it profusely. Standing back, she narrowed her eyes and said, "Damn, Preacher, you didn't tell us your wife was Inuit!"

With Vivian's back still plastered to his front, he wrapped his arm around her chest and rested his chin on her head, feeling the tension leave her body.

"This is Vivian. I thought we'd get something to eat. We missed lunch and know it's kind of early for dinner. Can you set us up?"

Vivian's hand went to his arm, her fingers wrapping around his muscular forearm. Trying to remind himself they were only playacting for a cover, he knew the tingle from her touch was, once again, more than just pretend.

"Well, Vivian, I'm Sally, and that old coot back there is my husband, Iggie. We'll get the best burger you've ever eaten out here in just a few minutes."

He gave Vivian a little nudge, and they moved forward toward the bar. He gave her a boost onto the barstool, and they ordered beers from Iggie.

Soon, they were joined when Sally brought out the burgers and fries. Logan grinned as Vivian quickly learned there was no privacy at the Goldmine Saloon. Sally plopped down next to her, and Iggie stayed planted behind the bar just in front of them.

"Tell me about your family," Sally asked.

After swallowing her bite, she explained about her grandparents, including how she had been raised in California.

"Oh, Alaska never leaves your blood," Iggie claimed, a wide smile gleaming against his tanned skin.

"Maybe so," she replied, laughing. "I like my sunshine, and I can't drive in the snow!"

Sally grinned as she waved her hand dismissively. "You'll get the hang of it if you two stay here. That's what you're planning, right, Preacher?"

Viv slid her glance toward Logan, silently handing the question to him. He nodded slowly before replying, "We'll see. Gotta go where the work is. Right now, the airfield here can pay me enough to make it worth our while, but if work comes from somewhere else, then I figure that's where we'll head."

The foursome continued to chat for another hour as they finished eating. "Sally, you're right," Vivian said. "You do make the best burgers."

As the dinner crowd increased, Sally and Iggie moved on to serve other customers. Someone put money in the jukebox, and Viv stood, taking Logan's hand. As she pulled him gently from the barstool, he looked at her in confusion. She led him to the back, where a few tables were cleared away, and another couple swayed to the music.

Halting, he tugged on her hand and glanced around before muttering, "Viv, I don't dance."

She grinned, moving in closer, wrapping her free hand around his waist. Standing on her tiptoes, she whispered, "All you gotta do is hold on to me and rock back and forth."

Not wanting her to let go, Logan pulled her body tightly to his. He placed one hand on her back and pressed their clasped hands over his heart between their bodies. Moving as one with the music swirling about them, their gazes locked on each other, they began to sway to the music. His heart thudded so loudly in his chest that he was sure she could hear the beat over the music.

Her hair hung gracefully down her back, the ends brushing against his arm, making him want to run his fingers through the thick, sleek tresses. As he stared into her eyes, he felt as though he could drown in their depths...and be found again. His fingers flexed on her lower waist as the warmth traveled up his arm. *This makes no sense...I've known her for less than a week.* But his heart warred with his mind. He wanted her. *Maybe that's it...this is just sex I need. Me...a pretty girl...yeah, maybe a fling is what we both need.* But as those thoughts moved through his mind, he knew a fling was not what he wanted.

Bending down, he nuzzled her nose before sliding his lips over hers—just a taste...just a touch. A soft gasp from her lips brushed warm breath across his lips, and he took the kiss deeper.

"Viv..." he groaned into her mouth, no longer caring what his head said as long as he listened to what his heart demanded.

It had been a while since he'd experienced a kiss just for the experience itself. His arms banded tighter around her as her hands slid upward to encircle his neck. His wide chest pressed against her breasts, and each curve seemed made just for him. He took the lead, angling his head as his tongue delved inside. Stealing her breath, he plundered and teased.

As the music ended, their bodies continued to sway.

He lifted his head slightly to see her eyes hooded and felt her breath warm against his face. She stared into his eyes, their gazes locked.

Letting out a long breath, she whispered, "Is that part of our cover?"

Logan hesitated, but the truth won out. "No," he replied softly. His heart pounded, and his body stiffened in preparation for her response.

Her lips curved into a wide smile as she moved in closer so their lips were once more a whisper apart. "Good."

His heart leaped as he pulled away, staring down into her beautiful face. Without a word, he led her toward the bar, his arm around her shoulders, firmly pulling her next to him. Tossing enough bills onto the bar to cover dinner, drinks, and a hefty tip, he waved at a grinning Sally and Iggie. When they stepped outside, the afternoon sun surrounded them as they headed home.

22

The two-mile drive home seemed to stretch into eternity. Logan held tight to Vivian's fingers, placing their entwined hands on his thigh. Casting a nervous glance at her, he breathed a sigh of relief to see her staring back, a smile etched on her face.

"You okay?" he asked.

"Oh, yeah." She nodded, still smiling. "Never better."

He stepped on the accelerator, and the old truck kicked up gravel as they turned onto their road. Approaching the cul-de-sac, he noticed no cars were parked outside the Zamans' house. The reminder of the boxes in the back of his truck was like a cold bucket of water dumped on his head, killing the mood. He parked and turned off the ignition, the sudden quiet of the evening permeating the cab. Hesitating before looking at her, he felt the squeeze of her hand in his.

Her soft voice broke the silence. "The timing's wrong, isn't it? You've got to work with whatever's in the back of the truck."

He turned toward her, her face illuminated by the faint light shining over the kitchen door. Understanding mixed with regret in her eyes caused his breath to stumble. "Viv, I'm so sorry. I didn't mean to lead you on. That's not me—"

"Shh," she said, her smile less wide and holding a little sadness. "We're here on business and have things we need to take care of." She started to pull away, but he held fast to her hand. She looked back over her shoulder in surprise, her brow furrowed in question.

"Viv…what happened back there…that was not business. You need to know that."

She nodded, and he wondered if she had any idea how beautiful she was at all times, but especially when she smiled.

"I know. But it's best we focus on our mission right now." She slid her hand from his and hopped out of the truck, walking toward the kitchen door.

Leaning his head back, he breathed, "Shit." Sighing heavily, he climbed out and moved to the back to unload the boxes. Once unloaded, he hurried into the house to find Vivian at the laptop, with Sakari curled on her lap. "I need to see when they left and—"

"I have it," she said. "They left an hour ago."

"Both of them?"

She nodded, and he reached over to drag his hand over the cat's fur, then cup Vivian's cheek. "Thanks, Viv." He pulled up the tracker he'd placed on the Zamans' car and breathed a sigh of relief. "They're in Fairbanks. That means I have time to get next door to install the equipment that I picked up today. Once that's done, you and I can get to the shed to start the preparations."

Her eyes were bright as they nodded. "What can I do?"

"I'll have my people on my radio since they will be able to monitor the tracker on the car. But just in case there is a change, such as one of the others showing up, I'll need you to watch and call me."

"Damn, this makes me nervous."

All he could do for reassurance was to lean over and kiss the top of her head before he moved to one of the boxes and found the camera equipment he needed. Then moving outside, he slipped around to the side door to their kitchen and let himself in. He worked fast but accurately, making sure each tiny camera was working by having Sadie and Sisco monitor it from the compound.

"It looks good, Logan," Sisco said. "I can see the two bedrooms, the kitchen, and the living room. Angle the one in the living room slightly to the left. Yeah, yeah, that's it."

Once finished, he carefully looked around to ensure there was no trace of evidence of what he'd placed in their home. Hurrying back the way he came, he darted over the yards and into his house. He'd barely set his bag down when Vivian flew into his arms.

"Oh my God! I was a nervous wreck. It didn't matter that I knew they were in Fairbanks. I was terrified the whole time you were over there!" She leaned back and peered into his eyes. "Did it work?"

"Let me show you." He walked over to the laptop and

pulled up the program that utilized the indoor cameras. "Look."

She bent over his shoulder.

"Is that what I think it is?" she asked, her eyes wide as they stared at the inside of the Zamans' house.

"I set up a few cameras in rooms where they're working. The bedroom the Zamans are using appears clear, but the other bedroom, as you can see, has lab equipment set up. I also put visual and audio transmitters in the front room and kitchen, as most conversations occur in those rooms."

"How will they not detect the wires and stuff?"

Logan heard the worry lacing her voice and clasped her hand. "Viv, the equipment I used is not the usual crap most security agencies use. It's not even available to most civilians… although I'm sure some have it. The company I run has access to the best equipment." He snorted. "It just took a little pressure to get it to me." He watched her face as she digested the information, slowly nodding.

"So they won't know we're doing this?"

"It's all transmitted to this laptop, both visuals and audio."

"And you need me to…?"

"We need to know what they're working on. If they're creating something deadly, I can't just go in and steal some random Petri dishes, test tubes, or whatever the shit they're using. I'll need you to let me know what to get. What to take so that you'll be able to transport and test it safely. As boring as this is, I need you to watch them—monitor them. It doesn't have to be all the time, just enough to know what we're up against."

"And no more cookouts, right?" Her nose scrunched as she battled back a smile.

Dropping his chin, he chuckled. "Yeah. We'll ease back on the neighborly thing." As their mirth slowed, he lifted his head and held her gaze. "Look, I know this is fucked. You didn't sign on for any of this. Donald just sent you to do testing. Granted, he at least told you what you'd possibly be facing, but none of this other shit—"

"It's okay." She interrupted, her chocolate eyes piercing his. Offering a small shrug, she added, "I haven't had this much excitement in a long time."

He twisted his head around, finding her temptingly close. Clearing his throat, he said, "We need to get your lab set up in the shed with the other things I picked up today."

On this trip, the dense woods once again enveloped them in shadows as the sun slithered through the leaves. Vivian walked behind Logan along the path to the shed. Her arms were filled with a large box, and Logan carried two boxes. When inside, they set his boxes on one of the tables. He pulled out the two lanterns, and soon, a bright glow filled the space.

Looking at the supplies packed inside the two larger boxes, Vivian slipped on latex gloves and handed a pair to him. Once gloved, she pulled out sheets of plastic and unfolded them.

"I don't need a perfectly sterile environment, but we'll do our best," she said. "A staple gun should be in one of the boxes to attach the plastic sheets to the walls and ceiling."

He nodded, and following her directions, they worked in tandem. The shed was only about ten square feet, so it didn't take long for Logan, with his height, to cover the whole thing. She then had him staple plastic sheets to the ceiling, including covering the skylight. She also draped the table in plastic before pulling out a few items and placing them on the table.

Finally, they draped plastic sheets on the floor, backing out as they went. "I'll take my boots off when I'm in here," she explained. "I have a new pair of sneakers and the plastic booties that go over shoes, along with my hazmat suit. That should be enough."

"Whatever you need, Viv," he promised.

He fitted a lock onto the door as they backed out of the prepped shed. Turning, he found her waiting for him, her smile beaming in his direction. He reached out, and she quickly linked her fingers with his. Holding hands as they returned to the house felt strange and strangely natural. Having someone he cared about while on an assignment had never happened before. But having her hand in his made him want to slay any dragons coming her way. He just hoped he would see the dragons before they got to her.

Once inside the house again, she fed the cat while he sat at the laptop to see what was happening next door. "They're back," he called out when the Zamans' vehicle returned. Vivian walked over and sat beside him, her gaze riveted to the screen. But nothing was happening besides Farrah fixing a meal while Akram sat at his computer.

After looking at the screen, Logan turned and realized they had leaned so that their lips were so close that it only took the barest movement in each other's direction for their mouths to seal together.

Vivian raised her hand to cup his strong jaw, her fingers trailing along the stubble of his beard. He erased the distance. The kiss was slow and sensual, the barest touch of flesh on flesh.

A soft moan escaped from her lips as he pulled back, resting his forehead on hers. Sucking in a ragged breath, she whispered, "What are we doing? I've never been a fling kind of girl... but with you, I'm willing to throw caution to the wind and give in to whatever this is between us."

"I know, Viv. Me too."

His large hands cupped her face, calloused thumbs gently smoothing over her skin. Peaceful silence moved between them, their eyes never wavering.

"I don't want to do anything to hurt you. What started as just pretending now feels like it's something more. But..."

"I know, Logan. I feel it, too. But we come from different places. It's scary to think of when this is over."

Pulling her forward, Logan kissed her again, first on her lips and then on her forehead, resting there for a moment. Swallowing, he dug deeply into all his training and pulled back. "Let's take it slow. Keep working the mission. And this... whatever's between us...let's give it time to see what it is."

She nodded as she let out a long, ragged breath. "You're right. If this is something real, we can take it slow."

"Slow is good," he said, his eyes capturing hers as his chest heaved as though out of breath from a long run.

"Yeah, slow is the right thing to do."

Time stood still. Nothing existed but the two of them in the room, gazes never wavering, hands still cupping each other's faces. The only sound was the old clock on the wall, ticking off the seconds.

"Oh, fuck going slow," Vivian cried as she crashed into him, erasing the space between them. Not just lips, but she shifted her body, crawling onto his lap, her arms moving from his face to around his neck.

Logan's arms encircled her waist as he pulled her tighter to his body, heedless of the chairs they knocked over as he stood with her in his arms. Noses bumped as they twisted, each angling for the closest position. His tongue thrust inside her warmth, tangling with hers as he searched every crevice, determined to memorize the taste and feel of her. With one hand under her ass, he stalked toward the back of the house, his lips still pressed against hers, mumbling, "Thank fuck. No more slow."

23

Logan managed to maneuver them into the bedroom, bumping Vivian's legs twice and only missing her head on the doorframe because he placed his hand on the back of it to protect it. When they finally stumbled into the room and fell sideways together on the twin-sized bed, their mouths separated just long enough for her to say, "Ow," as she grinned against his lips.

"Shut it." He chuckled, grabbing her by the waist and rolling, pulling her on top of him before sealing her lips with his again.

While their lips moved in concert, their hands flew haphazardly between their bodies, trying to pull their clothes off without ending the kiss. Finally, after they fumbled like teenagers, getting nowhere, Vivian sat up, her hand on the wall of his chest as she panted. Sliding her hands to the bottom of her shirt, she pulled it slowly up over her breasts, teasing him as the material caught on the underside first before revealing her lacy black bra. Flipping the shirt over her head, she tossed it to the side.

Suddenly nervous, she held her breath as his eyes moved from her face to her chest. Lifting one hand, he traced the swell of flesh with his forefinger, dipping down into her cleavage before moving over the next swell. Her breasts ached with need, and her nipples hardened.

"God, you're beautiful," he groaned, his voice surprisingly reverent as his eyes lifted back to hers.

Smiling in relief, she reached behind her and unclasped her bra, tossing it into the air. As her naked breasts bounced slightly with the movement, she caught Logan's eyes darkening to a stormy blue. She leaned forward, her nipples now closer, and he lifted his hands, palming their fullness. Rising, he latched his mouth over one, and she gasped as he sucked deeply. He took his time with one breast before moving unhurriedly to the other. She groaned, urging him on.

Rolling, she was now under him as he straddled her body, and his hands moved to her jeans' zipper. He had to slide so that he was standing to keep from rolling off the small bed. Slowly dragging her pants off, he snagged her black panties as he went. Bending, he kissed her stomach, causing her to jerk.

"My skin feels electrified," she whispered as his lips moved down. She'd never been ticklish, but as he stood by the bed, his eyes moving from her head to her toes, her body completely naked for his slow perusal, she felt every tingle. "You make me nervous," she confessed, her voice quivering.

"Don't be." His eyes were once more back to hers. "You're fuckin' perfection."

Licking her lips, still tingling from their kisses, she said, "You're kind of overdressed for what I think is going to happen."

"Oh, what you think is going to happen is going to happen," he assured. Jerking his shirt over his head, he reached for his pants while toeing out of his boots. In a few seconds, he stood tall and proud, his erect cock in his hand as he palmed it. Snagging a condom from his billfold, he crawled back on top of her, halting a whisper away from her lips.

She allowed her gaze to travel slowly over his body. His dark brown hair was clipped close, and his daily scruff gave off a dangerous air. She followed his body with her eyes, from his muscular chest to his defined abs. A smattering of chest hair tapered to his waist. "You're gorgeous," she whispered, marveling at the play of his muscles as he held himself above her.

She watched him hesitate for an instant as though giving her the opportunity to call a halt to what they were doing. Her response was to grab his cheeks again and pull him down to her. Thrusting her tongue into his mouth, she relished the taste of him as their tongues tangled. She heard his groan, feeling it rumble in his chest as it pressed against her breasts.

Her hands clutched at his shoulders, her feet digging into his ass, urging him on. Lining his erection to her entrance, Logan looked down at her expectant face. "Tell me what you want, Viv," he ordered, teasing her sex with the head of his cock. Moving it slowly through her wet folds, he closed his eyes briefly as his movements slowed. He inhaled deeply, then opened his eyes.

"I want you. Now," she answered, her breasts heaving with each pant, her hips bucking upward.

Dipping his mouth, barely touching hers, he whispered, "My pleasure," before plunging his cock into her sex and his tongue into her waiting mouth.

Moving in rhythm, he started slowly, his cock stretching her as it hit every nerve along the way. In and out, creating friction that drove her to distraction. He moved his tongue along her neck, sucking on the tender area at the base where her pulse throbbed.

Vivian's hands wrapped around his back, and her legs entwined around his waist, opening herself up more. She heard him groan as she met him thrust for thrust. Moving her fingertips over the ridges of his arms and back, she felt the power of his muscles as they flexed with each stroke.

"More. Harder," she moaned as the friction built to a crescendo. She squeezed her eyes shut as the world around her fell away, feeling only the rocking of her body as he powered into her.

The bed creaked, and the headboard banged against the wall. He shifted the angle of his hips, grinding them against her taut bundle of nerves. Feeling the world tilting as tremors began in her core, she suddenly felt his cock swell even larger.

"Open your eyes, babe. I want to see you while you come," he begged. Her eyes focused on him, and she smiled. "Christ, you're like a vise. You feel so fuckin' good." He managed to slide his hand between them, pressing on her clit. The tremors exploded outward, and she cried out her release.

As she came down slowly from her personal fireworks, she watched Logan's ordinarily stoic expression change as his orgasm rocked through him. With his head thrown back, the veins stood out on his neck as he powered through.

A moment later, he fell onto his back on the mattress, rolling to the side as he gulped air. She panted along with him, their sweat-slicked bodies cooling slowly as their heartbeats continued to pound.

"Wow," she finally breathed.

Chuckling, Logan leaned up just enough to stare down at her. Pushing her damp hair back from her face, he replied, "Yeah…wow."

He slowly eased from the bed and went into the bathroom. She watched his muscular ass as it walked away and smiled. Then suddenly, the smile dropped away as she wondered if she should get out of his room and return to hers.

A wide yawn nearly split her face, and her eyelids drooped. He came back, and before she had a chance to disappear back to her room, he wrapped his arms around her and shifted to give them more comfort on the tiny twin-sized bed. She draped most of her body on his, her head on his chest, and as he tangled his legs with hers, they just fit if neither moved. But soon, she fell asleep, no longer worried about which bed she was in.

24

Logan woke early to the comforting warmth of a body nestled snugly against him. A smile curved the corners of his mouth as he glanced down at Vivian tucked into the crook of his arm. Her back rested against the wall while the rest of her sprawled over him in peaceful slumber. Her silky hair cascaded over his pillow, the soft tresses across his arm. Her black lashes lay on her cheeks, and her lips parted slightly as soft breaths tickled his chest.

From over her shoulder, he stared into the amber eyes of Sakari, who unblinkingly gave off her annoyance at not having enough room in the bed.

Carefully extracting Viv's arm from beneath her, he suppressed a chuckle at the realization that she was as immovable as a drowsy zombie in her slumbering state. Padding over the wooden floor to the bathroom, he briskly showered, working out the kinks from a night spent in the cramped confines of their tiny bed. Refreshed, he ventured into the kitchen, making sure to place cat food into the dish before flipping on the coffee maker. Soon the aroma of brewing coffee filled the small space. Seated at the table, he ate a bowl of cereal as he watched the comings and goings next door from his laptop. It appeared the Zamans were having a busy morning.

The soft sound of shuffling footsteps drew his attention, and he looked up as Vivian rounded the corner. His initial grin at seeing her blossomed into a full-blown smile. She'd slipped on a pair of form-fitting yoga pants, an oversized sweatshirt, and her feet were snug in the thick socks she was so fond of wearing. Rising to greet her, he poured a cup of coffee, liberally adding cream and sugar. Pushing it along the counter toward her, he watched as she reached out blindly, circling her hands around the steaming mug.

"Good morning, babe," he said through his smile.

Lifting her eyes over the rim as she sipped, her mouth opened as though to speak, then snapped shut. She shook her head slightly before taking another sip. "Wow," she mumbled.

Logan's eyebrows arched as he leaned forward and tilted his head to the side. "Wow?"

She twirled her finger around in a circle, directing it toward him. "T-shirt clinging to your toned chest, showing off your muscles. Finger-combed hair, still damp from a shower. Gray-green eyes that look like the ocean on an overcast day." Her gaze dropped to his forearms resting on the counter. "Even your arms are... they're just... wow. How's a girl supposed to compete with that this early in the morning? I was lucky to find some clothes to throw on just to hide the mess."

His head tilted back as laughter rumbled from his chest, a deep, resonant sound that filled the room. "Viv, you're no mess. You're gorgeous."

A blush moved across her face as she took another sip. "I...uh...I'm sorry about last night."

His brows drew down sharply. "Sorry?"

Bobbing her chin in a jerk, she added, "Uh...about going to sleep. I should have gone back to my room. You could have woken me and...uh...you know...told me to leave."

His face relaxed as he watched her stumble over her words. "Why would I want you to leave?"

Her breath left her lungs in a huff as she scrunched her nose. "Look, I know what last night was. Fun... right?"

"Yeah, it was fun," he agreed. "Was that all it was to you, Viv?"

She blinked, then shook her head. "No."

"You told me you weren't a fling kind of girl. I already knew that. So do you think I'm the kind of man who would enter a fling with someone who wasn't on board?"

Shaking her head slowly, she said, "No. I think you're the best kind of man." She shrugged, then took another sip. "But we had agreed to just work the job. No complications. And then, boom! We were kinda out of control. So I figured..."

"Well, if you figured I was just into having a good time with the most available girl, you figured wrong."

Setting her cup down on the counter, she reached forward, placing her hands over his. He turned his upward and linked fingers with her. "I'm sorry, Logan. I seem to be making a mess of things."

"Why don't you tell me what's really on your mind instead of what you think you should say," he ordered gently.

Clearing her throat, she nodded. "I...I loved last night. I wanted last night. Wanted you. But when I woke this morning and you were gone, I realized I'd fallen asleep in your tiny bed, probably making you uncomfortable. And I guess I was embarrassed. I slept like the dead, and you probably didn't sleep at all." Snorting, she continued, "I've heard friends talk about the walk of shame when a guy kicked them out of bed. Or friends who complained about someone who wouldn't leave when it was over."

His shoulders relaxed, and he gripped her fingers tighter, giving them a little squeeze. "That's better. I've grown used to not having to guess what's on your mind."

She cocked her head to the side, unasked questions in her eyes.

"Yeah, we were stuck with a tiny-ass bed, but I wasn't uncomfortable last night. I got up this morning so I could shower and make coffee so zombie Viv would have the bathroom when she was ready and some caffeine in her." As her mouth quirked, he continued, "I made it clear that I wanted us, but I guess what I fucked up on was not making it clear what I wanted after the sex."

He watched as she sucked in her lips, holding her breath. Leaning forward, he gave her hands a little pull, bringing her closer. "I wanted you. In my bed. In my arms. All night long."

Her eyes widened as he neared, her lips now only a breath away from his.

"And I want that for as long as we both want it." Closing the tiny distance, he latched onto her lips, suckling and tasting, swallowing her moans and his own rumbling from his chest. Pulling back reluctantly, he sighed. "I hate to stop, but—"

"You've got to show up for your job, and I have to start watching our neighbors."

Nodding, he kissed her again before rounding the corner. He stalked straight to her, pulling her into his embrace. His arms wrapped tightly around her much slimmer body while hers rounded his waist. She rested her cheek against his heartbeat, and he couldn't deny it felt right.

"I'm working on a small plane that came in today, but I'm only a phone call away. If you need me, give me a call." When he felt her head nod against his chest, he added, "Viv, babe. Do not do anything on your own. I don't care if they come knocking on the door. You stay inside. Got it?"

"Got it, boss man."

Laughing, he kissed her hard and fast, then headed out for the day.

Pulling her shower-wet hair up into a sloppy bun, Viv focused on the camera angle that gave her the best view of what was in the Zamans' room used for their makeshift lab. Scribbling on the pad of paper by the laptop, she wrote down as many of the chemicals she could now identify. With her laptop opened to the side of Logan's, she could simultaneously search the properties of each. She also made notes of other substances in labeled boxes and bottles.

The work was tedious, but she methodically plodded onward, her interest piqued at what they were creating. Occasionally, she flipped the screen back to the other room, but Akram appeared busy at his laptop, and Farrah stayed in the kitchen, first cleaning up from breakfast and then preparing their next meal. A small TV was on the kitchen counter, and Farrah would watch game shows while cooking.

Vivian stood and rubbed her eyes while moving to the kitchen to fix a sandwich. As she walked back with her meal, she heard the crunch of tires over the gravel. Sliding the curtain back slightly, she saw a car park outside the Zamans' house. Recognizing Rashad and Malik alighting from the vehicle, both with boxes in their arms, she hurried back to the laptop and watched them enter the house.

Akram greeted them with a cursory nod, his voice low and indistinguishable. Malik walked past Farrah in the kitchen without speaking to her, but Rashad nodded his greeting. As Vivian changed the view on the cameras, she saw them enter the lab.

They donned white lab coats along with gloves and

masks. The two men sat at the tables and began taking more test tubes from the boxes they brought in. Zooming closer, she was frustrated when she realized there were no labels. *If only I could get in there.* Knowing that line of thinking would get her nowhere, she continued to monitor their progress as she munched on her sandwich.

Watching them carefully, she leaned back in her chair, sipping her tea as she analyzed what she was seeing. *They are cautious but not extraordinarily so. There is no way they can be working on deadly biologics or chemicals.* Vivian knew bioterrorism did not have to cause immediate deaths or life-threatening diseases to be effective. In fact, with a large gathering, such as the upcoming Olympics in Europe, the only thing that bioterrorism would need to do would be to cause panic, disruption, and chaos. Categorized as "incapacitating agents," they would be effective even if all they did was create a strain on the healthcare system by causing many thousands of sick patients to inundate treatment facilities that contained only limited quantities of drugs and only a few isolation beds.

The concept was much like the COVID-19 virus, which had the same effect of overloading the hospitals. But it didn't have to be as severe as the COVID-19 virus. Just to cause panic when the pharmaceutical companies couldn't keep up with the demand for medication.

Turning to her laptop, she began researching the most common incapacitating agents. Hearing another car approach, she moved to the window and observed as Nafisa arrived. Curious, she watched Nafisa enter the house, barely speaking to Akram, ignoring Farrah, and walking directly to the lab room. Malik looked up, greeting her with a smile, but Rashad never acknowledged Nafisa's entrance. Vivian watched with interest at the relationships playing out before her.

Malik continually glanced in Nafisa's direction. Nafisa ignored him while appearing irritated at Rashad's disinterest. *A love triangle?*

Before she had time to process if that information interested anyone else, her phone rang, pulling her away from her personal soap opera.

"Hey," she said softly, knowing Logan was the only one who knew the number.

"Babe," he said, his voice still sending warm tingles down her spine. "You doing okay?"

"Yeah. I've managed to stay out of trouble and have been working on the security feed all day. Right now, the whole group is over there."

"Good," he replied. "Listen, I'm finished here and will head home soon. Thought I'd stop at the grocery."

"Oooh, I'd love to make pizza tonight. Get whatever you like on it and some pizza dough."

"I can just buy a frozen one—"

"No! I want to dazzle you."

The phone went silent for a moment, and she wondered if the line had gone dead. "Logan—"

"Viv, if you want to dazzle me, all you gotta do is repeat last night."

She smiled as warmth speared throughout her.

"Well, I can certainly do that, but how about I dazzle you in the kitchen first?"

"Kitchen, bedroom, living room...babe, you can dazzle me anywhere you want."

Now laughing, she said, "Just bring the pizza fixings. I'll make dinner, and then...we can see what comes next."

"You got it. See you in a bit."

Disconnecting, she stood and walked into the living room, plopping down on the sofa. Leaning her head back against the cushion, she closed her eyes, a huge sigh escaping her lips. *Girl, what are you doing? You never do flings.* Opening her eyes, she knew he had said what they were doing was not a fling. *So what is it? What happens when he goes back to wherever he came from, and I go back to California?* The silent room gave no answers.

It's okay...I can do this for now...enjoy what we have for now. Standing, she walked back into the kitchen, hoping she was not lying to herself.

25

At the sound of tires crunching on the gravel drive, Vivian hurried to the window, her lips curving into a smile as she watched Logan's old truck come driving up. Moving to the kitchen door to help him with the groceries, she watched as he came in, several bags in his hands.

"Is there more?" she asked, moving to go outside.

He caught her arm, gently halting her progress. "I got it, Viv. Stay in here where it's warm." He kissed the top of her head as he moved past, bent to pet Sakari's head, then headed back to the truck. Re-entering, he brought a six-pack of beer and a bottle of wine. "I got you some Reisling. I know you like sweet white."

Grinning at his memory, she said, "Go take a load off. I've been on my ass all day while working. I'll get the pizza in the oven in just a bit."

He stalked toward the bedroom with a nod, and she busied herself with dinner. Half an hour later, the pizza went into the oven, and she realized he was still in the back of the house. Walking around the counter, she headed down the hall. His door was shut, but hers was open. Peering in, she was startled, seeing two twin bedframes stacked up against the wall. Sakari weaved among the displaced furniture in curiosity.

"Logan! What are you doing? Can I come in?"

The door swung open just as her hand was reaching for the doorknob. His large body filled the doorway, and any thoughts of what he was doing bolted from her mind. He had changed into sweatpants, hanging low on his hips, his bare feet peeking out from the bottom. With a clean white T-shirt straining over his biceps and chest muscles, she stared, speechless.

Reaching above his head, he placed his hands on the top of the doorframe, drawing her focus to his massive arms. Grinning, he asked, "Like what you see?"

She blinked out of her trance and rolled her eyes. "You know I do."

"I like your honesty." He jerked his head toward the inside of his room. "So curious about what I'm doing?"

"Uh…yeah." She laughed. "Why have you put the bedframes in my room?"

"'Cause it's not your room anymore." Stepping back, he stood to the side, allowing her to see into his room.

Vivian's eyes landed on the way he'd arranged the bedding. With the bed frames stored in the room across the hall, he had placed the two twin box springs side by side on the floor, topped with the two mattresses, essentially creating a king-sized bed. With their combined blankets and pillows, she gasped at the perfect bed. She jerked her gaze up to his, and her eyes landed on the hesitancy on his face.

"Hope I wasn't presumptuous," he said, squeezing the back of his neck. "I should have asked first—"

"No. This is perfect."

He stepped closer, his chest a breath away from hers, and cupped her face in his hands. "This takes away all doubt in your mind as to where I want you to sleep, Viv. The room hasn't got a lot of space, so the bed has to be pushed up against the corner, but if you need to go to the bathroom, you can just crawl right over me."

Smiling, she said, "I could sleep on the outside—"

"Nope. It's protection. I sleep closest to the door. No one can get to you unless they go through me... and no one can get through me."

"Oh..."

Leaning down the rest of the way, he moved across her lips, whisper soft. "Babe," he said, his mouth moving over her lips as he spoke, "Have we got time to initiate the new bed arrangement?"

"Pizza'll be ready in fifteen minutes," she mumbled against his onslaught, no longer caring whether they ate pizza.

"That'll do," he said, lowering her to the mattresses.

"So besides whatever they are concocting over there, it appears a love triangle might be happening."

While the pizza was being devoured, Logan listened intently to Vivian as she described what she had learned. "Huh?" Pausing mid-bite, he waited for her explanation.

"It seems Nafisa has eyes for Rashad, who doesn't pay attention to her, but Malik has his attention on Nafisa." Suddenly, her eyes lost their sparkle when she added, "And I don't think Farrah has a very good life. Akram is an asshole to her. She mostly cooks, cleans, and watches some old shows on a tiny TV in the kitchen."

"What is he doing?"

"He's on his laptop almost all the time."

Nodding, he said, "My people have been monitoring him, but so far, it's nothing important to us. He sets up meetings for the campus groups, which is how he first got noticed by the FBI and DHS. Hell, who knows how long the CIA has had him on one of their watch lists? From now on, you can just focus on the lab. You'll need to let me know as soon as I can get in there and tell me what to snatch."

Swallowing the cheesy goodness, Vivian agreed, "I made serious headway today. Hopefully, tomorrow will give me even more. I just wish I could see what they brought in today."

"Any ideas yet?"

"There's no way what they are dealing with is lethal." She watched as he held her eyes, his undivided interest evident. "They only need to wreak havoc...cause chaos. Overwhelm the medical system, including doctors as well as hospitals and pharmaceutical companies. People can even be exposed, not know it, have no symptoms for a while, and then travel to spread the infections. And it can come slowly, giving the instigators time to introduce the bioterrorism agent into food or water and then disappear."

"And that's where I come in."

Nodding, she smiled. "Yep. You can arrest them and turn them over to the proper authorities. Oh, that sounds good...just like in the movies."

Logan swallowed ineffectively, the bite of pizza stuck in his throat. *There would be no arrest, no trial. He was tasked with eliminating the threat, but no way in hell could Viv ever know that.*

Patting him on the back, she frowned in concern. "Hey, are you okay? Did you swallow it wrong?"

Choking down the bite, he took the drink she held out. Finally, clearing his throat, he nodded. "Thanks. Sorry about that."

"I suppose what we're talking about is hardly a topic for dinner conversation."

"My fault," he said. "I'm the one who asked. Let's take our drinks into the living room." Standing, he placed the pizza plates into the sink and grabbed another beer. Refilling her wineglass, he followed her to the sofa, sitting next to her.

She twisted her body so they were close, but she faced him. Taking a sip of wine, she smiled. "What else do you want to know?"

"Back to what they're cooking up. Right now, does it look like I would be safe going in soon?"

Leaning back, Vivian tapped her nail on her wineglass as she thought. Hesitating, she opened her mouth and then closed it.

"Come on, spit it out."

Looking down at her hands, she said, "It would be so much better if I could go in and—"

"Not happening," he growled. "Jesus, Viv. Don't you get how dangerous these people are?"

She rolled her eyes. "Of course I do. I didn't say I was going in. I'm just terrified of telling you the wrong thing and something happening to you—"

Pulling her closer, he said, "Not gonna happen. You'll keep watching until you have a better idea of what we might be dealing with. Then, and only then, will I go in and get what you need. And we won't do that until you instruct me on what to get and how to get it. Okay?"

"Okay," she agreed.

He stared into her chocolate eyes and knew he'd do anything to keep her safe. He just hoped he could keep her from finding out what his entire mission was tasked to be.

26

While Logan finished working on the helicopter, he watched as a couple climbed out of a small airplane and listened to them as they excitedly talked about the scenery they had viewed. They thanked the pilot, and he grinned, thinking of the number of trips he had flown with tourists. He recognized it wasn't a bad gig, but he could now look back and see it was just a career stopgap between being a SEAL and running LSIMT.

Turning the wrench, he tightened the last bolt and glanced at his watch, wondering how Vivian was doing. His thoughts turned to her often, and even with all his training, he seemed unable to call a halt to her entering his mind constantly.

Grinning, he thought of their new sleeping arrangement. They might have to contend with the dip where the two mattresses were pushed together, but they'd slept much more comfortably than when they were in the twin bed. Hell, the sex was better since they weren't afraid of breaking the bed. So far, they had spent the past few nights curled in each other's arms after making love long into the night. Sex with Vivian had surpassed anything he had ever encountered. Sweet sex. Fun sex. Adventurous sex. Wild sex paired with soft kisses. *Damn.*

"Hey, Preacher!"

Looking up, he saw Iggie walking toward him. Waving, he tossed his wrench and headed his way. Shaking hands, he asked, "What are you doing over here?"

"I promised Sally I'd take her on a trip for our anniversary and heard some folks in the bar talking about going up to a lodge in Nome that's supposed to be fuckin' gorgeous."

"Sounds nice."

Iggie dropped his chin and stared at his boots for a moment before adding, "We can't be away from the bar too long. I was just going to take her for a night…but, uh…it's kind of a long drive."

He grinned and crossed his arms over his chest. "You looking to fly?"

"Well, I was hoping you could take us in your helicopter."

"You don't want a plane—"

"Nah. Sally doesn't care much for flying, but I hoped that maybe you and Vivian would come with us. You two being newlyweds and all… I figured you'd like a nice night out."

"When are you thinking about going?"

"This weekend—"

"Hell, man. You don't plan too far ahead, do you?"

He laughed, shaking his head. Dropping his chin for a moment, he stared at his boots, the guilt of mixing work with pleasure having never occurred in his career. The chance to give Vivian a night in a nice lodge, on a real bed that didn't separate when they turned over. It would make a perfect way for Viv to have a real chance to get away for a break. *It's just one night.*

He uncrossed his arms, placing his hands on his hips. Glancing at his boss, he caught the man's nod and stuck out his hand toward Iggie. "Well, all right. It looks like we're taking a trip this weekend."

The relief on Iggie's face was palpable as he shook his hand. "Oh, man, you've just made me and Sally so happy. I thought we'd leave early Sunday morning, get there, and get checked in. There are hot springs nearby, and we'd have most of that day and then that night. Sally's brother can watch the bar on Sunday night since we close early, and then we'll be back on Monday."

Chuckling, he said, "Sounds like you've got it planned."

Turning to walk away, Iggie said, "Uh, do you think Vivian will want to go?"

For a moment, he thought of her during the past week, each day bent over the laptop, observing the neighbors and taking meticulous notes. Nodding, he said, "Oh yeah. Viv'll be up for the trip."

"Are you crazy?"

Logan looked on as Vivian stood in the middle of

the living room, her hands on her hips, her eyes wide, and her mouth definitely not in a smile. Not knowing how to answer her rhetorical questions, he said, "Uh..."

"Logan! Spending the weekend, in close contact, with another married couple who thinks we're married? How the hell are we going to pull that off?"

His shoulders relaxed as his mouth quirked up. "Viv, we got this. It's easy. Fly there, spend time by ourselves, have a great night in a lodge in a bed that isn't on the floor with a dip in the middle, and fly back. Babe, it's no problem." Thinking his words would soothe, he stepped back a half foot when she rounded on him, her hands now waving in the air.

"No problem? Logan, this isn't about sex! How can you even think about sex when most of the weekend we'll be trying not to screw up our cover?"

Wisely deciding not to tell her how he could be thinking about sex, he remained quiet as she began to pace across the floor, her hands once more waving about.

"This isn't about us having a wonderful weekend, Logan. We'll be stuck in your helicopter for about four hours each way. What will we talk about? Huh? How do we sound like a married couple?"

Walking toward her, he reached out to place his hands on her shoulders to still her pacing, but she ducked away and continued her rant.

"I don't know you! I don't even know where you're from. I don't know your parents' names, much less anything about them. Or if they're even alive..."

Swirling around suddenly, she scrunched her face as a frown settled on her features. "Oh…are they alive?"

"Yeah, babe. They're alive—"

Relief flooded her face as she said, "Thank God. But see? I didn't even know that!"

"We can pull this off. We don't leave for another two days. We've got time to learn about each other," he cajoled. Grinning as he stepped forward, he added, "We've spent a lot of time together in the past two weeks."

She stepped backward, the back of her knees hitting the coffee table and her body stiffening. "You're kidding, right? Logan, I hate to break it to you, but a week of phenomenal sex hardly makes us a couple. It takes a helluva lot more than a lot of great sex to be able to be a couple."

"What the fuck are you saying, Viv? That what we have isn't real? That it doesn't mean something?"

Letting out a shaky breath, she shook her head slightly. "I don't know what we have. We haven't exactly talked about what's going on between us. We talk about the job. We talk about the neighbors. We talk about what we're going to fix for dinner. And we have sex." Wrapping her arms around her middle, she sucked in her lips.

Reaching out, Logan pulled her gently to him, feeling the tension in her body. Saying nothing, he hoped his body would offer her the solace she needed. After several minutes, he felt her relax slightly, her breath leaving her chest in a long sigh.

"I'm sorry," she mumbled, her face buried in his T-shirt.

"I'm the one who's sorry," he admitted. "First, for leaving you here in the house for so long. And second, for not realizing you...well, we need more."

"More what?"

"More understanding of what we are."

She leaned her head back and asked, "When you're typically on jobs, do you have to spend days or weeks cooped up, planning, analyzing, and being bored until the mission finally comes to fruition?"

Chuckling, he nodded. "You just described being a SEAL perfectly. Everyone thinks we ran around with special weapons all the time, raiding buildings, rescuing whoever the fuck needed it. Taking down the enemy, whoever the fuck it was at the time."

His gaze moved from hers to someplace over her head. "But no one ever saw the endless days of planning, or sometimes just waiting...desert, jungle, mountains. Wherever. Just waiting until we could strike."

"And what about now? Now that you have your own company?" she asked.

His brows knit as he pondered her questions. "It's a bit new to tell. I'll be more involved in the planning and take on missions that are right for me. The people who are like the SEAL support team are now working with those of us who will go out into the field. We'll plan and then execute the assignments together."

His answer seemed simple when, in truth, his business was complex. He could have sent any one of his Keepers to do this job. That thought hit him in the gut—

the idea that one of the men under him could be here with Vivian. *Would she have made the same decisions? Slept with one of them? Would they be falling for her?*

"Sometimes I feel so out of my element here," she confessed.

He jerked his attention back to her, knowing his thoughts would have no answers. *I'm the one who came. I'm the one who's here.* "You and me both, Viv," he said. "This isn't like any mission I've been on before."

A rueful snort slipped from her, and she offered a little smile. "I'm used to a desk job in the lab. Get samples, run tests, and analyze the results. Wash, rinse, repeat. I thought I'd like an assignment working in the field, but…" Uncertainty filled her words.

"But you didn't count on us." He supplied the words for her but they also were his words.

She nodded against his broad chest, and he loved the way her body fit so perfectly to his.

"Listen, we'll work on getting to know each other better, which isn't just for the trip. I want to know more about you. I'm interested in everything there is to know. We just have to focus on what we're doing here so much that it doesn't leave a lot of time for anything else." He watched her eyes narrow and quickly amended, "Well, okay. We did have time for sex." Breathing a sigh of relief as her lips curved slightly, he added, "But, Viv, I thought I'd made it clear that this wasn't just a fling."

Nodding, she said, "I know. You did. I guess I just can't quite wrap my head around what it is."

"Let's not worry about labels right now. Let's get to

know each other. Kind of a crash course in Logan and Viv."

Barking a laugh, she asked, "Crash course?" Sighing, she nodded, "Yeah, you're right. That should do to get us through the weekend."

"You know a day in a lodge with a hot spring isn't the worst way to spend the weekend."

Her smile was her only response, but as he squeezed her and walked back into the kitchen, he hoped his words were true.

Once they cleaned the kitchen, he reached for her hand and tugged her down the hall. Deciding to get comfortable while learning about each other, Logan lay sprawled on the bed, his back on the pillows piled against the wall. Vivian sat cross-legged, her feet tucked up underneath her, and, with her back against the other wall, she twisted to face him.

"Where do you want to start?"

She tilted her head as she tapped her forefinger on her chin. "I guess with basics."

"Thirty-five."

"What is thirty-five?"

Chuckling, he gently tapped his toes on her knees. "How old I am…thirty-five."

"Oh. Right. Uh, I'm twenty-nine."

Nodding, he watched her lips quirk as she stifled a grin. Pursing his lips, he narrowed his eyes. "Now what?"

"Sorry." She chuckled again. "I'm living with an old man."

Arching an eyebrow, he repeated, "Old man?"

"At least you're not a dirty old man!"

Lifting his toes, he dug them into her waist, searching for a tickle spot. She grabbed his foot, then jerked it away while lifting it as high as she could.

"Hah, got you," she declared proudly.

With a deft flip, he twisted his body so that his foot was no longer in her hand, and he straddled her body. Her legs were trapped by his much larger ones on either side, and her hand was held tight above her head.

"Who's got who?" He grinned, leaning down to place a kiss on her nose.

Vivian struggled to knock him off but only managed to become more entrapped. His free hand snuck down toward her stomach, his fingers wiggling. "Who's an old man?"

"I'm not ticklish, so you can't make me talk!"

Moving his mouth to hers, Logan kissed her hard and fast, knowing anything more would have them getting to know each other naked with him inside her. And as much as he wanted that, he also knew they needed this time. Swinging one leg over, he helped her sit up, but this time, he settled her closer to him so that they were still facing each other, but her body was much nearer.

"I guess it wouldn't take much torture to get me to talk, would it?"

"'Fraid you wouldn't make it as a SEAL, babe, but I like you just the way you are."

They sat silent for a moment before he asked, "Why don't you tell me about your family?"

The immediate smile on her face let him know he had chosen wisely.

"You already know about my grandparents. My mom grew up in tiny Tanana and attended the University of Alaska in Fairbanks. There, she met my dad. He was a geologist working for an oil company. He firmly believed in preserving all of Alaska's beauty, and his job was to find ways to mine it without damaging the landscape. Mom was an education major. It was her passion to teach. Once they met, they never dated anyone else. It was love for them…right away."

Smiling at her recounting, he asked, "Did they stay in Alaska long?"

"For a while. I was actually born in Fairbanks about two years after they married. But, much to my grandparents' sadness, Dad got transferred to the Redding office in California. I don't have any brothers or sisters, so it was just me and my parents. I finished school there and went to get my undergraduate degree in biochemistry close by at California State University, Chico. From there, I got hired by the Department of Homeland Security. That was fabulous because they paid for me to continue my education with Dr. Kendall Rhodes—the woman you rescued when her plane crashed."

"Well, she was truly rescued by a friend, Marc Jenkins, who works for a security company in Virginia. When they got caught in a storm, I managed to get a helicopter in to rescue them both, along with some of the other men from the Saints."

"Saints?"

"That's the name of the company he worked for. Saints Protection and Investigations."

"What's your company's name, or is that still on a need-to-know basis?"

He spied the interest in her eyes, as well as the dare. She wanted more than his company's name—she wanted his trust.

"I'm a partner with the Lighthouse Security Investigations." He started to tell her more but hesitated. He trusted her with the truth, but it was hard to explain LSIMT without giving her the whole story of him. And that could wait for another time.

She held his gaze. "Thank you," she whispered. Shaking her head, she sighed. "I keep wondering why on earth I took this assignment since I don't know how to do any of this kind of work."

"I think you were right when you said you were chosen because you have the training for the substance analysis and the heritage that allows you to fit in easily."

Vivian focused on his eyes, the color holding her captive once again. "You've got the prettiest eyes I've ever seen on anyone." She blushed, then moaned. "God, I can't believe I just said that. I sounded more like fifteen than twenty-nine—"

"No way, babe," Logan said, leaning forward to take her hand in his, rubbing his thumb over her delicate fingers. "That was…nice." Wishing he could have come up with a better description, he realized how out of practice he was with dating…flirting…hell, just having a heart-to-heart with a beautiful woman. And he wanted it all with her.

27

"Tell me about California."

Vivian thought about what was happening. She and Logan were sharing stories, histories, and information that a couple should know about each other. But it was still for the cover to make sure Iggie and Sally thought they were a true couple. Yet, in some ways, they were a couple. The lines between real and pretend had blurred. And in that blurred area between true and fake was the place where her heart could get broken. She looked into his gray-green eyes that were staring straight into her soul and was lost. Lost in all that was Logan, both real and not. But the possible heartbreak was very real.

She looked down at her hand in his. "Um… yeah… California."

"Hey," he said, drawing her eyes back to his. "You okay?"

"Just gathering my thoughts." She smiled, thinking about where she'd grown up. "I know this sounds so typical, but I love sunshine. That's why Alaska would never work for me…the change in sunrises and sunsets would kill me. Part of the year, they have only four hours of daylight, and others, only four hours of darkness. I could handle the daylight."

She pointed up to the curtain. "That's why most places have room-darkening shades or curtains. If it's light outside, you can make it dark inside. But if it's dark outside…ugh. Lamps just don't seem like sunlight."

She watched him lean back, the grin on his face warming her as she realized she had slid off topic again. "Sorry, I got sidetracked by talk of sunshine. Anyway, I've been working out of the Sacramento office for the past four years."

"Waiting for things to get exciting?"

Nodding, she dipped her chin, staring at her hand still clasped in his. "I told my supervisor I wanted more responsibility and was willing to travel." Snorting ruefully, she said, "And I landed right back in Alaska."

"You landed right into my lap," he said, giving her a little tug to pull her closer.

"It was a nice landing," she admitted and watched as his eyes seemed a little brighter.

"What's your favorite food?"

"Wow, quick change of topic," she responded with a laugh, "The answer is everything, but I love Asian food…Chinese, Thai, Japanese."

"Biggest fear?"

Twisting her head around, she looked up at him quizzically. She thought for a moment, then said, "Driving on snow. I hate driving on snow." Suddenly changing her mind, she leaned away from him and exclaimed, "No, no. Not driving on snow. That's second. It would be thin ice."

Blinking at her unexpected response, he shook his head as his brow furrowed. "Thin ice?"

Nodding rapidly, she said, "When I was a kid, a bunch of us went ice skating. I thought it was fun and had no idea how dangerous it was. One kid skated over some thin ice and fell through. He almost died, and it scared me to death! I learned my lesson that day. Never go skating by yourself because you might be on thin ice and not even know it. So if someone is with you and you fall through, then you can be saved."

Sitting quietly for another moment, she leaned her head on his shoulder as he wrapped his arm around her. "I guess that's kind of my story in a nutshell." Looking into his eyes, she said, "Do you want to start on you?"

Shaking his head, a gleam appeared in his eye. "Nah. I'd rather start on you." With that, he captured her mouth, this time taking the kiss soft and slow, as though savoring every nuance of her lips. The electricity slid through her nerves, awakening her senses until he thrust his tongue into her mouth, and then the jolts between her mouth, her nipples, and her core exploded.

Barely aware he was shifting them down onto the bed, she focused on the way he kissed her neck, nuzzling her wildly beating pulse point as his fingers unbuttoned her shirt. She wiggled, allowing him to remove both the flannel and her bra. With that accomplished, he glided his lips over her chest to latch onto a taut bud. Suckling one nipple after the other, he moved his hand over her stomach before his mouth trailed kisses in his hand's wake.

As her pants slid down her legs, she moaned in pleasure as he left her stomach to continue his trail of kisses down to her slick folds. Her legs fell naturally apart to accommodate him, and he took every advantage she offered as he licked her wetness. As his tongue dove for deeper access in her channel, her fingers ran through his hair, her breath catching in her lungs.

His tongue thrust in and out of her sex, and he reached up with one hand to fondle her breast as her hips rotated upward, pushing into his face.

Vivian could feel the delicious pressure building in her core and smell the scent of sex in the air, desperately needing her release. He moved his mouth up to her swollen clit, sucking it into his mouth, allowing his tongue to swirl around it. At the same time, he pinched her nipple, and she convulsed against his face.

Her hips bucked as she begged for more. He added a finger deep into her sex, and she exploded as waves of bliss pounded over and over. Throwing her head back, she allowed the sensations to carry her away to a place where there was no mission. No terrorists. No worry. Just Logan and her.

He watched her face carefully as the pleasure shone in her expression. Her eyes fluttered open just before she smiled at him. She raised her arms, beckoning him, and he acquiesced, kissing his way up her body. Spending time sucking each breast, he nibbled kisses over her neck and jaw, finally settling on her lips again.

She wound her arms around his shoulders, pulling him close. Although, with his body lying on hers, he wasn't sure they could get any closer. Then the tip of his cock settled at her entrance, and the rush of knowing how much closer they could be filled him.

Reaching over to the nightstand, he grabbed a condom from the new stash he'd bought from the store. Shifting to his knees, he rolled it on quickly, noting the way her gaze roamed over his body. He'd never been a man to care much about how he looked as long as he was clean and presentable. But now, he was glad for the weightlifting, the runs, and the hard work he'd put into building LSIMT. Her fingers trailed along his muscular chest and abs, following the path of her gaze.

He slowly lowered himself over her, keeping his weight off her chest with his hands planted on either side of her. Now, his gaze roamed slowly over her body, and he carefully shifted his hips between her legs, positioning his cock at her opening. Sliding his hand between them, he guided himself in and was fully seated with one thrust.

"Babe, I want you to feel every inch," he whispered, the words as strangled as his cock in her tight sex.

"I do," she rasped, her eyes wide and her lips curving.

He began slow thrusting, pulling almost all the way out before pushing back in again. Desiring to go deeper, he shifted to a kneel before pulling her hips upward toward his cock, gently pushing her legs apart as wide as she was comfortable. Keeping his gaze on her face to ensure she was relaxed, he began slow thrusts again.

She began to moan at the deeper friction, and her eyes clamped tight as her hands clenched his biceps. He leaned down to palm her breasts, his gaze darting from her face to where their bodies were joined. With one hand tweaking a nipple and the other sliding down to thumb the taut bud of nerves, he knew he'd never seen a more beautiful sight.

"Babe, open your eyes and come for me," he begged.

As though on cue, her inner walls grabbed his cock tightly. He felt her waves of pleasure as they crashed through her to him. Losing control, he pistoned the last few thrusts deep inside, allowing her contracting muscles to milk him. Leaning up with her hips tightly held in his firm grip, he threw his head back, neck straining as his release poured deeply inside. Continuing to pump until the last drop was gone, he then slowly pulled out. Gently moving to her side, he lay down beside her, pulling her into his embrace.

They lay together, sated, and he pushed her hair from her face. After a moment, he untangled himself from her, rising from the bed to dispose of the condom. A moment later, he stalked back, and her exhausted smile greeted him. He pulled her close as she snuggled into his side.

"Can I admit that I'm really excited about the upcoming trip to the hot springs? I love the idea of getting away from the world of spies, espionage, and terrorists."

He chuckled and squeezed her tighter. "You can

admit anything you want, babe. And for the record, I feel the same way."

Hearing her breathing slow, Logan knew zombie Viv was already peacefully slumbering. Sliding from underneath her, he moved through the house, checking the doors. Standing in the dark living room, he pulled the curtain back slightly, seeing the darkened house next door. Heaving a sigh, he wondered how much longer the mission would take, finding that he did not want to end his time with Vivian.

Walking quietly back into the bedroom, he slipped under the covers, pulling her close, tangling their legs. Kissing the top of her head, he followed her into sleep.

28

Stumbling into the kitchen, taking the proffered cup of perfectly creamed and sugared coffee, Vivian managed to smile at Logan as he looked her up and down.

"I've told my boss that I'm not working the next couple of days, so we've got today for you to do some more digging into what the neighbors are cooking up and some digging into what you want to learn about me."

"Hmm. Sounds like you've got the day planned."

"Come on, zombie Viv. Have a seat, and let me get some food in you. You're always a nicer zombie when your belly is full."

Attempting to cast a glare in his direction, he had already turned his back, so she shuffled over and plopped down in a chair. She'd barely sat when Sakari jumped into her lap. Seeing Logan plate scrambled eggs, sausage, and pancakes perked her up.

"Pancakes? I love pancakes." Her smile, wider now, beamed up at him.

"See what I mean? Get you interested in food, and my girl's smile comes out of hiding."

She felt the butterflies in her stomach as his words, *my girl*, slid over her. She watched as he laughed before sitting down next to her, and Sakari moved from her lap to his. He ate with one hand while petting the sweet cat with the other. Sucking in a deep breath, she turned her attention to her pancakes, finding them fluffy and light, just the way she liked them.

"How about we talk about you first before I start checking into next door," she suggested as she trailed the last bite of pancake through the syrup before closing her lips over the fork in ecstasy. When he didn't reply, she turned to look at him. His eyes were locked on her mouth as she licked the syrup off. "Logan?"

He blinked slowly before his gaze drifted back to hers. Letting his breath out slowly, he said, "Damn. That was sexy."

"Me eating pancakes?"

"You. Your mouth around that fork. That syrup on your lips. And where I'd like to put that syrup on you so I can lick it off myself."

She leaned forward until she was a breath away from his lips. "Talk first, sex later."

Kissing her quickly, he shook his head as he took the plates to the sink. "You drive a hard bargain, woman."

Having determined that the lab work was being accomplished when Malik, Rashad, or Nafisa were next door, they settled in the living room so they could talk while keeping an eye on the neighbor's driveway.

"I feel like I should be taking notes on you."

"So what do you need to know to feel like you're a Logan expert?"

"I guess the same things we went over about me. Your family. Your career. And how you ended up here as a mechanic known as Logan Preacher."

"Grew up in the middle of nowhere Kansas on a farm."

"I can imagine you as a dark-headed little boy running around a farm."

Chuckling, he said, "The farm has been in my family since my great-grandfather." His voice softened as he shifted his eyes, focusing on a distant point on the wall. "Clean air. Crops. Cows. Hard work from sunup to sundown."

She watched the play of emotions flit over his face. Understanding dawned, and she didn't need to ask, instead stating, "And it wasn't what you wanted to do."

His gaze moved back to her, and his lips curved gently. "First time I saw a Navy commercial on TV, I was totally gone—gone off the farm in the middle of the country. I wanted water, boats, submarines… if it had to do with the Navy, I wanted it. By the time I graduated from high school, I had spent more time at the recruiter's office than I had anywhere else. When I found out about SEALs, I knew." The intensity in his stare seared through her. "Have you ever wanted something so bad it was all you thought about?"

Shifting on the sofa to get more comfortable, she felt a pang of envy—she loved her job but had never felt about it the way Logan described the Navy. She shook her head slowly. "I wish…but no…not so far."

"My recruiter wanted me to join right away, but I wanted a college degree so I could be an officer. I went to Kansas State on an ROTC scholarship. I did four years, finished, and then headed to the Navy. I did basic training and officer school before being accepted for SEAL training."

She sat, entranced at the emotion pouring from him in a way she'd never heard before.

"I still remember the first time I was out on a ship. I stood on deck and watched the shore recede into the background. Thought about what it must have been like for those sailors of centuries ago, not knowing what or who was out there."

They were quiet for a moment as she gave him time for his memories to slide over him. Finally, with a head jerk, he said, "Anyway, I was accepted and made it through each level. Special Warfare Prep School, Basic Underwater Demolition, Parachute Jump, and SEAL Qualification. Hard as shit, but had the best team. I'd been flying my family's crop-dusting plane since I was a teen, so I also did pilot training."

"What happened?"

"I fuckin' loved my job… best job and the greatest friends. But on the last mission, things got fucked. One of my team was shot and had gone down. Our rescue helicopter had arrived, and we had to get out of there. It was too hot…too much firepower getting rained down on us. The whole mission was fucked if we didn't get out. I heard him shout and turned back to get him. Managed to pick him up and jog toward the bird."

He was silent, his eyes stormy as they settled on the

wall opposite him. "Almost fuckin' made it." He shook his head, almost in disbelief. "Managed to get close but then went down as an explosion hit nearby. We got into the bird, but I tore my knee to hell. Damn near shredded it."

She winced in sympathy as she watched him rub his left knee absentmindedly. Reaching toward him, she placed her hand on his leg gently so as not to disturb his memories but to remind him that he was alive.

He looked over and smiled, placing his large hand over hers and squeezing. "It's all good, Viv. No one can be a SEAL forever."

"Did you have to get out?"

"Even after surgery, my knee was never going to be strong enough for me to jump outta planes anymore or even swim as long as I needed."

"They kicked you out?" she cried with indignity.

"No, babe. I got out. I could have stayed in the Navy and worked a desk job. Even trained new SEALs. But the more I thought about it, the less I liked the idea."

"And the farm?"

Shaking his head while chuckling, he said, "It was never for me. When I left for SEAL training, I told my parents that it needed to go to someone who loved it as much as they did. I have a younger sister, and she stayed there. She married a good man whose dad owned a farm nearby. They've got both farms now and kids, two boys and two girls. They'll have someone to keep it going."

"But it was your legacy—"

"Nah," he countered, conviction in his voice. "It was

never my legacy. I loved the farm, loved growing up there, but farming's not in my blood. It's got to be inside you every second, and for me, that was being a SEAL."

"Where did you go?"

Leaning back with a grin, he replied, "Montana. Cut Bank, Montana. Out in the boonies. I got acres out in the middle of nowhere. I built a house and a large hangar for my helicopters. I made a business out of flying tourists around and doing rescues."

She heard all the words he spoke, but her mind was stuck back on Montana. Blinking, she tried to understand his reasoning. "Montana?"

Throwing his head back, he laughed. "Yeah, Viv. Montana."

Kicking him softly with her leg, she said, "But why Montana? It's not near the water...it's not near anything."

His mirth slowly faded, and his eyes held hers. She nodded slowly as understanding dawned. "You didn't want to be near the water. You didn't want to be near people." She knew she'd hit the nail on the head when he nodded slowly.

"I was never very sociable. Figured seeing the ocean every day would always remind me of what I lost. So Bumfuck, Montana, seemed like a good idea."

Sitting in silence, she considered his words. His downward turn of lips and dullness in his eyes made it obvious that flying tourists wasn't his passion. "What about your company now? Where did you move to?"

"Still Montana. The original Lighthouse team is in

Maine, and one is in California. That's the West Coast group. And mine is in Montana."

She remained quiet, wanting to know more but unsure if he would give her anything but the basics. A yearning deep inside grew, consuming her, but she forced the words to stay unspoken. Barely breathing, she felt the air leave her lungs when he finally continued.

"A man who had served in the Army Special Forces and then as a CIA special operator got out and started his own business. That's the original Lighthouse Security Investigations. Located in Maine, they grew a respected reputation and work with the government and private requests for security work as well as taking on the investigations that stymied or overtaxed law enforcement. They're known as Keepers, for the old lighthouse keepers who guided people to safety."

She watched as the shine returned to his eyes, and his voice held pride. She leaned forward, eagerly awaiting more.

"Then he partnered with a fellow special forces man who had a security-to-the-stars business in California but was destined for so much more. He made the change to the LSI kind of security and investigations and built a team."

"That's the West Coast group, right?"

He grinned. "You remember."

She just smiled and nodded. His smile slowly ended, a look of indecision crossing his face. She held her breath again, hoping whatever he was thinking, he would voice.

"While running tourists and doing rescues, I also took on a few covert jobs for DHS. Worked solo." He shrugged. "I liked the planning. I liked just relying on myself, not having to worry if a teammate was injured or going to be killed on a mission."

"As physically unsafe as it might be, you felt emotionally safe."

His eyes widened as his gaze shot to hers, and he exhaled forcefully. "Damn, Viv. That's exactly what it felt like."

She tilted her head slightly, curiosity about the *now* Logan since she understood more of his past. "So your new company has people working with you, right? The ones you've been talking to. The one who flew here with your equipment."

A deep chuckle erupted as he nodded. "Yeah... completely different change for me... again."

"But more like the SEALs?"

"Yeah. Instead of solo, I'm leading a team again. But not constrained by the military brass above. We can take the assignments we want. We can run them how we want. We choose what to do, when to plan, and when to go, and then step back. Our investigations can get turned over to the FBI or Interpol, and we go home knowing we did our jobs."

"If you're the company leader, why did you take this job? Why not send one of your employees?"

When he grew quiet and his gaze dropped, she wondered if she had pushed too hard or in the wrong direction. "It's okay, Logan. You don't have to—"

His head lifted his intense gaze on her. "This job is different. It came from the source who used to send me on solo missions. And my team is still new. We're still learning about each other's skills. This mission asked for something that I wouldn't ask of my other employees. Something that I won't do in the future. But the source who asked me to take it on thought I could handle it." He hesitated, a battle of emotions crossing his normally stoic face.

Blowing out a breath, he said, "I talked to the other partners and told them what I was doing. They weren't going to tell me not to take this assignment, but they understood why I chose to take it on myself."

There was much she didn't understand about his cryptic explanation, but knew he'd given what he could about the assignment. It also explained why he thought he was working solo and would just interact peripherally with the biologist. "And when it's over?" Her words were spoken casually, but the air hung heavy between them as their gazes held.

Swallowing deeply, he said, "I guess I'll go back to Montana."

Her trembling lips curved tightly, the slight smile forced. He reached out and linked his fingers with hers. Vivian blinked, battling the desire to cry at how his fingers entangled with hers made her feel.

"I figure I'll take a trip to Kansas first, though," he added.

Her head nodded in jerks, her heart aching with an unknown pain. She felt his thumb caressing her palm and swallowed deeply.

"Figured I'd want to introduce you to my folks," he continued, his eyes never leaving hers.

She blinked, but his words barely registered.

"Viv. Breathe," Logan ordered gently but firmly, his fingers giving hers a squeeze.

Her breath left her in a whoosh, but she continued to stare. Swallowing deeply, she whispered, "You want me to meet your family?"

"I still don't know what we've got here, Viv. But I know it feels like something real. Something that has fuckin' roots that can grow. Fuckin' wings that can fly."

His words, so badass and poetic at the same time, caused her smile to slip through despite the enormity of his confession.

"I may be kinda out of practice, but I know what I feel," he continued.

Licking her lips, she said, "We never even talked about any past…relationships."

Sighing, he said, "A girl like you—gorgeous and smart. I know you've had men crawl over you since you were probably fourteen."

Barking out a laugh, she shook her head. "Hardly. I had a high school boyfriend. In college, I dated a few guys, but no one ever sparked my interest. Since then, I've gone on dates… blind dates, men I met online. But other than a few relationships that lasted a couple of months at most, no one made the cut to something more substantive. Most of the men I work with are married or, if they're single, we'd go out and talk about lab stuff. I work with it all day, so why the hell would I want to spend a date talking about it?"

She clutched his fingers, admitting, "I'd never met anyone who made me want more. Until you walked through that door, barking orders and being all pissy. You were larger than life. So handsome, it almost hurts my eyes to look at you. A body that wraps around me and makes me forget everything but you, protecting me from whatever is out there. It's like I was waiting for some kind of a hero. I didn't know it, but I was waiting for you."

"I didn't know it, but I was waiting for you."

Those words scored straight through Logan's heart and mind, stealing the oxygen from the room. It took a moment for his heart to settle to a less frantic pace, and as she continued to hold his gaze, he realized she was waiting for him to speak.

"I... I barely dated in high school...maybe one girl. Dated a few in college, and had one girlfriend who lasted a couple of months. She was too jealous of the time I spent on my studies and getting ready for my Navy commission, so it ended. I'll admit, I'd occasionally go to the bars during my years as a SEAL, but that was nothing more than a scratch to an itch."

Logan caught her minuscule wince and inwardly cursed his crude confession. "Babe," he called, waiting until she lifted her eyes to his. "Honest to God, I rarely did that. Hence the name."

Her brows furrowed. "Name?"

"Preacher."

Biting the corner of her lip in concentration, she shook her head slowly. "I'm sorry, Logan. I don't understand."

"My call sign. We rarely used our real ones. Sometimes it was based on a physical characteristic or personality trait. My last name is Bishop, so someone initially called me Preacher as a play on the religious title of Bishop. But, as they got to know me, especially the way I stayed more sober than drunk, more alone than banging a FrogHog... Preacher stuck. When I took this mission, I decided to take that as my last name for our cover."

The important conversation was halted by the sound of cars in the driveway. Looking out, they viewed Milak, Rashad, and Nafisa alighting from their vehicles and moving into the house.

"I'm sorry, Viv," he began, "we're having an important discussion and get interrupted."

Smiling, she nodded as she patted his leg. Standing to walk over to the computers, she stopped and looked over her shoulder, grinning. "For the record, Logan, when this is over... I'd really like to meet your family. I still think I was just waiting to meet you. There's nothing you've told me that's changed that."

He watched her sit down at the table, open the laptops and begin searching the views as she picked up a pen and scribbled notes. Scrubbing his hand over his face, his heart lurched, knowing the full mission. He wondered if she would feel the same if she knew what he was tasked to do once her part of the job was complete and he was left to eliminate the threat.

29

"Okay, something's changed today."

Logan looked up from his computer to Vivan's scrunched face as she fiddled with the camera angle on her laptop. "What's happening?"

"Up until now, they've been cautious in the lab, but I'd determined that what they had was not highly contagious. They wore masks, but only after they had walked into the room without them. They put on their gloves in there as well. From the chemicals I've seen, my guess is they've been working with growing bacteria, but nothing airborne and certainly not lethal. Maybe they've been practicing. Maybe they're looking for the best solution to increase growth productivity."

"And today?"

"Overnight, someone sealed the outside of the closed doorway with plastic. The three donned gloves, booties, lab suits, and masks before entering. They worked for about thirty minutes, then left again. See?"

She turned the laptop toward Logan and he

observed Malik, Rashad, and Nafisa pulling off their protective lab garb and equipment and placing it in a plastic bag. Sealing the plastic covering around the door again, Malik took the bag and walked down the hall toward Akram, handing it off to him.

"Fuck," Vivian breathed. "I wish I could get ahold of that bag."

"Let me see what I can do," Logan said. He quickly stepped out the front door and moved to Vivian's car sitting in the driveway. Popping the hood, he puttered around inside for a few minutes. Soon, Akram walked outside carrying the garbage bag, and Logan waved before turning his attention back to Vivian's car. Planning on following Akram, he growled as he watched the man place it in a metal drum and toss a match onto the contents. *Fuckin' hell!*

Slamming the hood down, he turned as Vivian walked out onto the small porch. He was pissed about not being able to get to the bag, but seeing her put a smile on his face. He stalked over, stopping at the bottom step as she moved to the top.

Placing her hands on his shoulders, she gave a little hop, wrapping her legs around his waist. Heedless of anything else going on, he kissed her hard and wet. His tongue dove in, tangling with hers as their noses bumped.

She pulled away, giggling, as she encircled his neck with her arms. "I was going to come tell you I saw something else, but you looked like a man who needed a kiss."

"You got that right," he replied. "As long as I'm the only one you kiss like that."

Shrugging, she said glibly, "Well, I don't know about anyone else. I guess we'll have to see who else I'm with on my next crazy assignment—"

With a growl, he kissed her again as his hand smacked her ass. Climbing the steps, he carried her back through the house. Before he could get too far, she reached up and placed her hand over his lips as they moved in for another kiss.

"Hate to interrupt this, but I need to tell you what I saw when Akram went outside with the bag."

"Right," he agreed, setting her feet on the floor, steadying her as she regained her balance. He followed her to the table again, where he sat next to her, looking at where she pointed on the screen.

"Look there. They take off their compromised lab suits and give them to Akram. Now watch."

He stared at the screen as Malik, Rashad, and Nafisa went into the kitchen. Taking two bottles out of one of the kitchen cabinets, Malik shook out several pills. Handing them to Rashad and Nafisa, he took two and then placed the bottle back into the kitchen cabinet. Farrah was standing to the side, pouring glasses of water for each of them. All three swallowed the pills before handing the glasses back to Farrah.

Hearing a car door slam, he and Vivian shared a look before he checked the outside camera, seeing the three climb back into their cars and drive down the road.

Shifting his gaze back to her, he said, "Viv, you've gotta break this down for me. What's happening?"

"I can't see what's in those bottles, but my guess is that they're some kind of antibiotic taken as a prophylaxis—as a preventive. If they were dealing with a virus, there would be no need. So my guess, at this time, is they are working with bacteria. Now, which one, I have no clue."

"If you knew what antibiotic they were taking, would that narrow it down?"

Scrunching her face, she nodded slowly. "Yeah, but you've got to understand that it won't tell me what it is, just maybe tell me what it isn't."

"Tomorrow, they don't work since it's Friday. But today, Akram and Farrah usually go to the grocery store. I can get in and find out for you."

"Logan," she said, her eyes wide with fear. "You can't go in that sealed room. Not now—"

"No, no," he assured, "I mean, find out what pills they are taking."

She nodded slowly. "Okay," she said, dragging out the word.

"What is it, Viv?"

She let out a long breath. "Up till now, it's been play-acting—watching a computer screen or out the window—pretending to be something we're not—even setting up my lab in the shed. But this"—she pointed at Zaman's house—"you going in, hoping you don't get caught—actually going into the bad guys' lair." She swallowed audibly. "Now this seems real. And scary."

Turning toward her, he placed his hands on her face, his warmth surrounding her cold cheeks. "Babe, I got this. This is nothing compared to what I used to do.

This is easy, and honest to God, I promise nothing will happen to you."

"I'm not worried about me," she whispered, her dark eyes still wide as they stayed pinned on his.

"Then you got nothing to worry about," he promised, pulling her in for a kiss.

Cakewalk. A fuckin' cakewalk.

Logan slipped into the back door of the Zamans' house ten minutes after they left. The grocery was only a few minutes away, so if they had forgotten anything, they would have already returned. With Vivian casually hanging out on the front porch as the lookout, he knew she would call if needed. She had insisted on taking a cup of tea out on the porch and sitting in the dilapidated chair with her e-reader in her lap, keeping watch with her phone in her hand.

He wasted no time as he entered the kitchen, going directly to the cabinet. Opening it, he found two bottles and cataloged the location of them in his mind before turning them to face the front. Snapping pictures, he then opened each one and photographed the pills, knowing a different drug could be contained in the prescription bottle.

Replacing them exactly the way he found them, he made a cursory check through the bathrooms and bedrooms. He had cameras in every room—*fuck privacy when dealing with terrorists.*

Seeing nothing else untoward, he moved back

through the kitchen and out the back door. Rounding the corner, he observed Vivian on the porch, her eyes never leaving the driveway. Sunglasses covered them, but he knew they would be filled with worry. It struck him how he already knew so much about her—not just the facts they'd shared but also her moods, emotions, and expressions. He jogged over, making it to the porch, and she let out a long sigh of relief.

Leaning over her chair, with his hands on the arms of the wobbly, wooden structure, he kissed her faster than he wanted. "Jesus, babe, is this thing strong enough to hold up?"

"Barely for me, and I'm not sure with your weight on it."

He grinned long and slow, loving the blush that danced across her cheeks.

With his face still so close, she whispered, "Did you get anything?"

"Yeah."

"I was scared."

"I know. But I'm fine. Gonna stay fine. Come on, let's go see what I have." He stood and offered her hand, loving that she didn't hesitate to allow him to pull her from the chair. Once inside the house, they moved to the laptops, where he uploaded the pictures he'd taken. Soon, she studied the bottle labels and matched them to the pills inside.

"Okay, they match the labels. We've got doxycycline and ciprofloxacin. Both are antibiotics, but I'll have to do some research to see how they are possibly being used."

"Right. I'm going to keep working here this afternoon, as well. Let me know what you find, and then we'll get ready for tomorrow's trip."

When the trip was mentioned, her gaze jumped back to his. "Do you think we know enough about each other to pull off our cover with Iggie and Sally?"

"First of all, I think they'll be so excited about their mini-vacation they won't give a fuck what we know about each other. Second, for newlyweds, all we have to do is keep kissing, and our cover is complete."

"You are such a man," she quipped, rolling her eyes.

"You know it, Viv." Lifting her chin with his fingers, he kissed her, moving his mouth over hers, reveling in her sweet taste.

He then stalked into the kitchen to grab a leftover slice of pizza, and when he turned to offer Vivian a slice, she was ogling his ass. Catching her, he grinned, and as her gaze jumped to his face, she smiled in return. He carried the pizza and beer over to the table where they worked as they ate.

An hour later, she stretched her arms above her head, her neck and back aching from her inactivity.

"You got something, babe?"

Nodding, she waited until he leaned over before she began her dissertation. "Okay, doxycycline is an antibiotic that fights bacteria in the body. It belongs to the class of tetracycline drugs. It's common and is often used to treat many different bacterial infections, such as acne, urinary tract infections, and even venereal diseases. Dentists use it to treat gum disease. Since it was in Farrah's name, I have a feeling it was used for a minor infection. How she's managed to get so much...I have no idea."

"Go on," Logan said, focusing on her discoveries, knowing there was little a terrorist could not get their hands on.

"Doxycycline is also used as a prophylaxis and can be used by researchers working with tularemia, among other bacteria. I even used it when doing some of my studies. It's FDA approved and safe. Now, ciprofloxacin is completely different. It is also an antibiotic, but it is used to treat people exposed to anthrax or even certain types of plague."

"Fuckin' hell," he growled.

"It's a fluoroquinolone. It can have serious side effects and should only be used for infections that can't be treated with a safer antibiotic. And it's not FDA approved as a prophylaxis for tularemia, but if someone can't take doxycycline..."

"Then they might have to take the harsher drug."

"Exactly."

"Can you tell who is taking what from the earlier video?"

"It's funny you should ask that. I went back and reviewed it. Malik and Rashad both took the doxycycline. Nafisa took the ciprofloxacin."

"Any ideas?"

Shaking her head, she scrunched her nose in thought. "Not really. We know that antibiotics can lose their effectiveness if taken over time. Could be she used doxycycline a lot as a teen for something like acne. There's no way of knowing, but for some reason, she's determined that it's safer for her to use the harsher drug."

Sitting silently for a moment, her curiosity finally spilled over, and she asked, "So where are we in all this?"

He studied her face for a moment, recognizing her worried expression. "You're doing great, Viv. You're figuring out that they are quite possibly working with bacteria, and you're narrowing down the possibilities by using nothing more than visual clues. My people will monitor them tomorrow so we can take our trip with Iggie and Sadie and have a nice break at a hot springs resort."

"You think it will be our last break, don't you?"

Nodding slowly, he replied, "Yeah. I think things are heating up, and I'll be able to get in there soon with your assistance. Once I do that, you'll be busy figuring out what they have while I keep working on their plan."

"How?"

"My people are patched into all their computers and phones."

"And then you can arrest them—"

"I'm not law enforcement, babe."

"Oh, I know. I meant you can turn them over to the FBI or whoever as soon as we get the evidence as to what they're up to?"

"I'll take care of it all."

Smiling, she leaned back in her chair. "Good. Then we can get on with our lives."

30

"Oh my God, this is amazing!"

Vivian looked over at Sally, sitting next to her in the back seats of the helicopter, and grinned at the other woman's exuberance. "I was a nervous wreck when Logan first took me up, but I love it now."

While Sally continued to peer out of the window, exclaiming over the landscape, Vivian looked toward the front, where Iggie was in conversation with Logan. Smiling, she settled back in her seat, enjoying the vista below. So far, her fears about trying to convince Iggie and Sally they were truly married had been for nothing. Grinning, she remembered how, when they arrived at the little airfield, Logan made sure he had his arm around her. He had kissed her as he buckled her in, too. She had just rolled her eyes at him, receiving a grin from him in return.

The Zamans came to mind, but she tried to push them out. Logan told her there was nothing they could do today, so she needed just to enjoy the weekend.

Sally's hand suddenly grabbed her arm, shaking her out of her thoughts.

"Oh my God. Did you see that? Lived here my whole life but never saw it from the air."

Turning her attention back out the window, she watched the snow-capped mountains in the distance pass by and the crystal-blue waters of the lake below. "It's gorgeous."

"Preacher, you're gonna love the lodge," Iggie said, loud enough for them to hear in the back. "They got hot springs you can soak in that's gonna feel like a sauna. Good food in the restaurant, and I was looking at the rooms on their website, and they look nice. Got balconies that overlook the springs with the mountains in the background."

"Sounds good, man," Logan said. Vivian caught his eyes staring at her in the mirror that allowed the pilot to see in the back seats.

Grinning, she ducked her head. She was now excited to spend time with Logan that didn't involve terrorists or sleeping on twin mattresses pushed together on the floor. Logan called in his codes to the Nome Airport, and she felt them descend. Soon, he eased them to the ground.

Watching Logan alight, talking to the helicopter manager, and then turning back to give a thumbs-up to Iggie, Vivian followed Sally out the door. Iggie grabbed their bags, and as she reached into the back to get hers, a long, muscular arm came from the side and snagged it.

Logan whispered near her ear, "Babe, I cannot wait

to get to the lodge with you. Don't expect to come up for air the whole time we're there."

Twisting her neck, she looked up at him, her face near his neck. Lifting on her toes, she planted her lips there, right on his pulse, causing a swift intake of air.

"Oh hell, Viv, you just got me hard as a rock."

Giggling, she slid to the side, settling under his arm, with their bags on his other shoulder. "Then lead on. I'm yours to command for the night."

"Can't ask for more than that, woman. Let's go."

Iggie had taken care of the rental SUV, and with Sally in the passenger side, she and Logan shared the back seat as they made the short drive to the huge log cabin lodge. Once they'd checked in, he almost dragged her along the passage to their room. With Iggie's laughter and Sally calling out the time to meet for dinner, he unlocked the door, swinging it open. Stepping inside first, she noted he stopped as his eyes scanned the room. Not willing to wait, Vivian ducked underneath his arm and gasped.

"This is gorgeous," she cried out, twirling in the middle of the room. It was paneled with one wall containing a sliding glass door leading out to the balcony. The heavy, wooden furniture included a king-sized bed, and its posters were made of logs. The bedspread in blues and greens added color to the dark, cozy room. She peeked into the bathroom, her breath leaving her in a rush. "Oh my God, Logan. Come look."

He stepped behind her, his hands on her shoulders as they viewed the private toilet, long counter, large shower, and, in the corner, a huge, kick-ass jetted tub.

"I don't have a bathing suit, but we don't have to leave the room—umph!" she grunted as he scooped her up and stalked back to the bed, laying them both down.

"I've been hard since we got here, babe. We can explore the merits of the jetted tub later."

Laughing, she planted her hand on the bed and sat up. Standing, she grinned as she said, "Allow me." Bending, she grabbed one of his boots and undid the laces, pulling on the sides before sliding it from his foot.

Logan stared wide-eyed as she removed his second boot, dropping it on the floor next to the first one. Kicking off her shoes, she continued to grin as she grabbed the bottom of her shirt and pulled it slowly over her head.

"Man, babe, you're making it hard to breathe," he said, his hand on his chest.

Sliding her jeans down her legs, she stood in a simple bra and panty set. Nothing too fancy. Just light pink, with a little bow between her breasts. "Oh, yeah? What else is hard?"

He sat up quickly, reaching for her, but she skirted back. Waggling her finger in front, she said, "No, no. This time, I'm in charge." She climbed back up onto the tall bed and straddled his thighs, running her palm over his hard cock.

He groaned. "Babe, I'm totally in your hands."

She laughed as she leaned over to kiss him, her breasts teasing his chest. "I hope I don't disappoint."

An hour later, as they lay naked and tangled in the sheets, he kissed her forehead. "You most certainly didn't disappoint. Now, how about we check out that Jacuzzi?"

Hours later, Vivian sat on the deep, comfortable cushion on one side of the tall, wooden booth of the lodge's restaurant. Logan sat next to her or, rather, so close that his thigh pressed against hers from ass to knee. His arm was slung casually around the back of her shoulders, his thumb occasionally rubbing her neck.

Across from them were Iggie and Sally—their positions were similar. The seafood and steaks were excellent. Even now, their conversations never lagged over wine and dessert.

After she and Logan had come up for air from their afternoon tryst, Iggie called and told them to get to the hot springs. Neither of them had bathing suits, but a quick trip to the lodge's store solved that issue, and they soon met their friends in the hot springs. Lounging in the warm water, her tension was released as all her muscles relaxed. And now, sitting in the restaurant, she felt as much of a couple as Iggie and Sally.

She knew it was only half pretending— after all, she and Logan had become a real couple, but pretending to be married no longer felt adventurous. It felt disingenuous. She was falling, and Logan had even said he wanted her to meet his family. Yet there was so much more to do with the mission. And so much more she didn't know about him. The sex was phenomenal, and when he held her during the night, it all felt so real. *But there's a look in his eye sometimes when we're planning our work...a look I don't understand.* It takes a lot more than just great sex to become a real couple in the real world.

Feeling his fingers squeeze her shoulder slightly, she jumped, cutting her eyes to him.

"Viv? You okay, babe?"

His voice rumbled gently next to her ear, the look in his eyes one of concern.

Smiling, she nodded. "Yeah, I'm great." Glancing back to the empty plates and glasses, she said, "I think I'm just full and getting sleepy."

His lips curved at her answer, his fingers tightening once more. "Gotta get you outta here and back to bed. You'll have sweet dreams in that big, comfortable bed."

"I swear, this is our anniversary, but seeing you two so much in love makes my heart happy," Sally said, leaning against Iggie.

Vivian's eyes shifted quickly across the table, her smile still in place, but a tremor ran through her lips. Logan must have noticed because his hand returned to her neck, and he rubbed his thumb in long, slow movements to ease her tension.

Logan felt the change in Vivian the instant Sally mentioned the word love, and her body stiffened. His feelings for her had grown, but the middle of a mission was the worst time to start a relationship. It didn't matter that many of Mace and Carson's Keepers, as well as the two iconic leaders themselves, had found love during a mission, but Logan wasn't sure how they managed it. But one thing was for sure: he wasn't going to make Vivian feel better sitting here despite the excellent company.

Looking over at the other couple, he said, "Guys, this has been a great evening and a great meal. But my girl is about to drop, so I'm going to get the check and get her tucked in for the night." Before he could take the check, Iggie's hand snapped out, grabbing it first.

"No way, Preacher. You took time off from work and flew us here without charging for fuel—this meal's on us."

He opened his mouth to protest, but Iggie leaned in closer. "I know you're the kind of man who doesn't like others to pay. But Preacher, what you've gotta understand is, by doing this, you've allowed me to do something nice for my woman. She never asks for much, works harder than anyone I know, and loves me in spite of my craziness. This is me expressing my gratitude. Because of you and Vivian, my woman got a weekend full of good memories with good people in a nice as fuck place."

Logan moved his hand back and nodded, understanding exactly what Iggie was saying. He looked over at Sally, who stared at Iggie like he hung the moon. And to her, he did.

Feeling the pressure of Vivian's fingers on his leg, he turned to see her smiling up at him. Her expression was so similar to Sally's that it almost hurt.

"Come on, babe." He slid out of the booth, his hand holding tightly to hers as he assisted her up. "See you tomorrow," he called to the others as he tucked her underneath his shoulder, and they walked out of the restaurant side by side.

Back in their room, Vivian plopped down in one of the heavy chairs padded with a deep green cushion that, like the bed, was crafted from logs. Pulling off her shoes, she wiggled her toes as she leaned back and groaned. "I ate so much… drank so much. I can't move."

Chuckling, Logan disappeared into the bathroom and turned on the bathtub faucets. Her curiosity must have gotten the better of her because, in a few minutes, she padded into the bathroom on bare feet.

"Oh!" She smiled as she regarded the deep tub almost full of steamy water. He flipped the switch, turning off all the lights except for the candle sconces on the walls that circled the tub. Looking at the scene, she smiled, her hand going to the belt on her dress.

Stepping directly in front of her, he shook his head as his hands moved hers away. "Nuh-uh," he said, untying her belt before moving to the zipper at the back of her dress. "You stripped for me earlier…now it's my turn."

Slowly, he peeled her dress, bra, and panties away, then held her hand as he assisted her into the tub. She sank into the water and leaned back, another smile lighting her face. He stripped quickly and said, "Slide up just a bit, babe."

She obeyed, and soon the water rose even higher as his body slid in behind hers, his muscular thighs on either side of her hips, her back now resting against his chest. Wrapping his powerful arms around her, he held her…engulfed her, wanting to give her all of himself.

"I said what I meant back there in the restaurant," he said, his voice low as he kissed the side of her neck. "You need a hot bath, someone to take care of you, and then a good night's sleep curled up next to me in a bed that doesn't separate when you roll over."

A light bark of laughter erupted from her as she nodded. "I like sleeping next to you, even if the bed moves when we roll over."

"I kind of got that, Viv."

She twisted her head around, but he kept his arms tightly around her.

"Every morning, I wake up with your leg over mine or tangled up in mine. Your hand is on my chest or my stomach. Your face is on my shoulder, and your body is smooshed next to mine. From the first night we slept together, I got that you like being next to me."

"That's irritating, you know," she huffed. His chuckle caused her body to move with the vibrations, and she sighed. "And for the record, Logan, you laughing at me is irritating also."

"I've never woken up wrapped around a woman before. Hell, it's been over a decade since I even woke up to a woman in my bed."

He was uncertain of her reaction to his proclamation, but her breathing halted and he squeezed her lightly before she inhaled deeply.

"Never wanted to. I might have been called Preacher, but I wasn't a monk. Either I left, or they did. Never took anyone to my apartments when I had them. Never took anyone back to my house in Montana. Sure as hell never took anyone to meet my family... not even the girl I dated in college." Leaning down so his mouth was right next to her ear, he continued, "So do you get why waking up with you all tangled up with me, knowing you want that as much as I do, is so important to me? I'm not making fun of you, Viv. I fuckin' love it."

She moved so quickly he barely had time to brace. She twisted her body around and grabbed his cheeks in her hands while straddling his legs. Some water sloshed over the side, but he didn't care. All that mattered was this woman pulling him in for a kiss. They battled for dominance, devouring each other's mouths, taking and giving at the same time.

Logan felt a change in her, as though any lingering doubts about his feelings for her had melted away. Taking charge, he tilted her head so he could maximize the kiss. Soon, she rooted herself on his cock, her hands on his shoulders, riding him with her breasts lightly bouncing as the waves of surrounding water sloshed even more over the side of the tub.

Later, they made it to the huge bed, legs tangled, her head resting on his chest where his arms pulled her in tight. Sweet dreams followed.

31

"Looks like everyone's busy next door. Guess the weekend is over."

Logan followed Vivian's gaze toward the Zamans' house as they drove into the driveway. He heard her sigh and matched it with one of his own. The weekend had been more than he could have hoped for, including room service breakfast in bed—along with other activities in bed—before having to leave. He knew they'd turned a corner in the relationship over the weekend. Her doubts seemed to melt away, hopefully realizing that, while their marriage might be a cover, his feelings for her were not. Meeting up with Iggie and Sally for the uneventful flight back home had been the perfect end to a perfect weekend.

Now, parking behind Vivian's little car in the driveway, his mind jumped to the inevitable—stepping up the mission and getting his hands on what was cooking in their neighbors' makeshift lab.

Moving inside, he could barely walk with Sakari

protesting loudly at having been left alone overnight. There was still food and water in her dishes, so he knew she was fine, but scooped her up to pet. As Vivian came up behind him, he transferred the cat to her arms and picked up the bags again before he walked to the bedroom and dumped them onto the floor.

As he came back into the living room, he saw her already firing up the laptops. Her eyes met his, and she nodded, saying, "I know. We've got to get back to work."

He walked over and kissed the top of her head. "I need you to give me as much as you can, Viv, 'cause I have to get inside to find out what they're working on. We have to have hard evidence that what they're working on is illegal and dangerous and needs to be taken out."

"Can't they just be arrested on suspicion alone, and then we can search the area?"

Shaking his head, he said, "That's not how it works. We need to know specifically what they're working on. For all we know, this might not be their first batch of substances, and they might have tried them out somewhere."

At that, Vivian gasped, her eyes widening in fear. "I never thought of that. They would have to test it out, wouldn't they?"

"That's why my people and DHS are searching their correspondence and emails, monitoring their phone calls, studying their talks in the house, and checking on their visitors. You name it, we're on it. Until we know for sure what they're working on, going in could set off a firestorm if we're not right."

"Okay." She nodded, a look of determination settling on her face. "I realize my inexperience gives me no idea what all you need to do. So I'll figure out what you can take from their lab the instant I can do so safely. And then, I'll pray I can analyze it before the Zamans decide to test it on humans somewhere."

Logan knew Vivian was at her wit's end after a couple of long days sitting in the house, staring at the screen on one laptop, researching on another, and all the while agonizing over making a mistake.

Logan walked into the house after keeping up his cover by going to the airfield. When he'd accepted the assignment, he'd hoped it would last a couple of weeks at most. They were now almost into their third week with no end in sight. He'd talked to his Keepers that day, telling them he was going to stop the cover so he could spend more time helping Viv go over the camera views. He knew it might be overkill but hated her worrying over the cameras. He wanted to get the mission done so that he could get back to his life in Montana and figure out how to convince Viv to come with him.

He observed Vivian hunched over the kitchen table, her hair pulled up into a messy bun, two pencils somehow holding it in place, and her fingers tapping on her keyboard. It was the same position she had maintained for days, so he was stunned when she twisted around, her eyes bright as they landed on his.

Her smile illuminated her face as she pronounced, "I have it."

Hurrying over, he gripped her shoulders as he peered over them, staring at the screen. She took a pen and pointed at Nafisa sitting at a table. "She's the one. She's the key. Malik and Rashad are there, but for the most part, they seem to be creating different solutions for her to actually do the experimenting. Everything, over here"—she pointed to one area of the room—"is just what they are working on. Basic solutions, basic compounds. There is nothing of interest there. But here," she said, pointing at where Nafisa was sitting in the back corner, "is where the real work is going on. These vials contain different solutions, but they also hold whatever she's working on. She is now taking what they have created and is using it. When she's done, she sets everything here."

He watched as she pointed one last time to the area of interest. He nodded slowly, memorizing the room and her explanation. "So when I get in, this is what I need to get."

She sucked in a deep breath, letting it out slowly before she spoke. "Logan, we need to talk."

He looked down at her, his eyes narrowing at her tone. "About what?"

She moved her chair slightly, indicating her intention, and he stepped back, his hands staying on her shoulders as she stood. She turned in his arms and said, "Can we sit down? Get comfortable first?"

After allowing her what she needed, he moved to the refrigerator and grabbed two beers before following her into the living room. He sat on one end of the sofa, but she was facing him with her legs tucked up underneath her.

"Okay, Viv, you're making me nervous. What is this about?"

She played with the beer bottle label for a moment before she lifted her gaze to him. "Were you ever on missions where you had to change your perfect plans because things didn't play out exactly the way you thought?"

Her question caught him off guard, and he stared at her for a moment, recognizing her nervous fiddling and the pleading for understanding in her eyes. Nodding, he said, "Yeah. Lots of times. Sometimes there were things we hadn't planned on, other people around that we hadn't anticipated, and incomplete or even inaccurate intel."

She seemed to take this in as she thought for a moment before asking, "What about with personnel? Did you ever have to change up duties or responsibilities in the middle of a mission?"

Now, he was quiet as understanding dawned, and it hurt like a bitch. She was trying to tell him that she wasn't able to handle the stress and needed to get out of the mission. The only thing he wondered about was if she also wanted away from him.

Sucking in a deep breath, he knew he owed her honesty. "Yes. Sometimes we had to change up personnel mid-mission for many different reasons. If someone became incapacitated and unable to complete their part of the task, others would step in to take over."

He watched as she mulled over his answer, his heart pounding in a way he hadn't felt in...well, he couldn't think of a time he felt this way. Other than his family, his team, and now his Keepers, no one had ever meant something to him—not like this. "What are you thinking, Viv? You want out?"

He watched as she blinked twice—slowly—before scrunching her face in surprise. "Out? Out of what?"

Now, it was his turn to be surprised. Lifting his chin, he said, "I thought you were asking about new personnel because you wanted out."

Shaking her head quickly, she threw her hands up and barked, "No! Why on earth would I want out?"

"I don't know," he responded in defense. "I know this isn't exactly what you signed up for. I know Alaska's not your favorite place to be. I know things have moved fast with us, and I know for a while that flipped you out. I know this is far more dangerous than you ever expected—"

"Good grief, Logan. Stop with all the excuses for why you think I want out," she argued, huffing before taking a long swig of her beer. "Geez, I can't believe you thought that."

Uncertain how to proceed given her obvious pique, he scrubbed his hand over his face before joining her, downing half his beer. Setting the bottle on the coffee table, he twisted his body back toward her. "Okay, babe, you've got to spell this out for me. Why the questions about changing missions midstream and changing personnel?"

Her face softened as her shoulders slumped. "Oh.

Okay, wow. Hearing you put it that way, I can see why you thought I might want out. I'm sorry." Heaving a huge sigh, she said, "The reason I wondered those things is because I want to present something to you... a change in how we make our next move. And I have compelling reasons, but I'm afraid you'll shut me down before you even hear me out. So I wanted to know if you had any experiences you could fall back on."

He almost laughed but kept his face neutral. *If she only knew how SEALs were trained to change in an instant. Alter plans. Rethink missions. Step in when someone else is better suited or in proximity to do something. Hence, the reason the LSI branches almost always hired former special forces.* Clearing his throat, he said, "Okay, good. I can work with this."

"Promise you'll listen to everything?"

"Viv."

"I suppose that one utterance of my name is to indicate that you will," she quipped, pursing her lips. "Okay, here it goes in a nutshell. I need to be the one to go inside the Zamans' house—"

"Abso-fucking-lutely not!"

"Logan! You promised!"

"Viv, if you think for one minute—"

"You promised to hear me out! You owe me that," she pleaded, plunking her bottle on the table next to his.

Not one to renege on a promise, he dropped his chin to his chest, silent for a moment as he tried to tamp down the irritation. Lifting his gaze, he saw her staring at him, her focus not wavering. "You're right. I promised. It won't change my mind, but go ahead. I'm listening."

"Listen and *absorb* what I'm saying, okay?"

"Okay," he agreed, but he already knew his answer would not change.

"In order to create the samples I need, I have to have a certain amount of the solutions in certain combinations. I need them to be marked carefully, or I won't be able to tell anything about what I'm looking at, or it will take a lot longer to determine what they are. By studying the cameras of them working in their lab, I understand what they're working on and how their space is utilized. They have codes on the labels that won't mean anything to you but will to me."

Vivian eyed him warily, but he was listening. His expression might be all hard lines, stormy eyes, and frowns, but he was listening.

Continuing, she said, "If I send you in, I will have to give explicit, step-by-step instructions, and since biochemistry isn't your thing, it will be much harder for you to know what you're looking at instinctively. Yes, I could be watching, and I'm assuming you'll have some kind of camera on you and an ear thingy so I can talk to you, but that'll take time. Precious time."

Leaning forward, she placed her hand on his leg. "And honey, you can't make a mistake. That's what scares me… there is no room for error. If they come back before we expect them, and you're still inside, you can't just rush out, jiggling the samples. Too much is at stake. And I sure as hell don't know how to create a diversion…unless I set the grill on fire."

His lips twinged, but he fought to remain stoic.

"You, on the other hand, would make a much better outside person." Seeing him about to speak, she said, "I'm not finished. You've got to give me this." When he settled back on the sofa, his eyes still on her, she continued, "You could get me in, then stay on watch outside. I go in, quickly and efficiently get what I need and label in a scientific shorthand, while leaving enough solution that they don't suspect anything... hopefully. Then I come back out to you. You do your super-spy lock up, and they'll never know. Or, God forbid, they come back early, you'd know what to do to give me time to get out."

Sitting on the worn sofa in a little, somewhat shitty house in the middle of nowhere Alaska, Logan stared at Vivian, his heart filled with everything she was. Smart. Funny. Daring. Beautiful. Resourceful. And he hated like hell to admit it, but she had a point. A really fuckin' good point.

Logan sat with his arms crossed, filled with the fear that comes from the unknown. He'd agreed to present Vivian's plan to his Keepers and now wondered if he'd lost his damn mind. Vivian sat next to him in front of the laptop screen, where they used the secure connection to the Keepers at the compound. The screen just held the LSIMT logo so she couldn't see anyone, but they would be able to see him and Viv.

She had been nervous at first, but her voice was

steady as she laid out her plans to them, just as she had for him. When she was finished, he turned the laptop and nodded. Their faces around the compound table appeared. He cast off a hard stare. "So? Comments? Ideas? Discussions?"

"She sounds badass to have come up with the plan," Sadie said, lifting a brow as though to dare Logan to disagree.

Dalton's lips curved. "She's made it this far and managed to get the necessary information. She knows what's at stake."

"She's right about working faster than you being able to on this plan," Cory said. "The time it would take to instruct you as you go—"

"And the possibility that you don't get one of the right chemicals," Sisco interjected.

Cory nodded, then continued. "You're more likely to make an error."

"She would be safe with you on the outside," Tim added.

Logan's jaw tightened as he listened, but then slowly eased. He trusted these people. He'd made them Keepers and worked to instill how they needed to rely on each other. *What would it say if I didn't do that now?* Blowing out a breath, he moved his gaze to Landon and lifted a brow.

Landon nodded. "Her reasons are solid, boss. Her plan is sound. They'll be in the mosque in Fairbanks on Friday, giving you and her the most time to do what needs to be done. And it gives you tomorrow to practice. I think it has the most chance of success."

With that, he ignored the off-screen fist pump from Viv sitting close to him and simply nodded. "Okay. But I want every scrap of intel you can give me from when they leave, following the tracer on their vehicle, and eyes on the other three."

Murmurings of agreements sounded out. Disconnecting the video conference, he turned to Viv. Her eyes were on him, guarded but bright. "Looks like we've got a lot to get ready for because the day after tomorrow, you'll be in the middle of the mission."

He'd said the words but wished they could have made the ache in his gut ease.

32

Vivian stopped outside the plastic-covered door, sucking in a deep breath before her hand reached up to gently pull the tape from the doorframe.

She and Logan had spent yesterday working on their plans, practicing them in their house, and modifying them as needed until he was satisfied. He had his team back in Montana watch her as he videoed her practice, a tactic that made her so anxious she thought she might throw up. Finally someone named Sadie told him to stop acting like a nervous ninny and just to let Vivian do what she needed to do.

He had continued to grouse and grumble every step of the way, but she knew it was because he was worried. And the last few nights, he'd held her long after they made love, even in his sleep. It was as though his fears penetrated his dreams, and she would wake with his arms tighter around her.

He had planned her steps exactly. They had carefully watched and, on schedule, the Zamans left on Friday morning for their time at the mosque in Fairbanks, and none of the others showed up either. The Keepers had tracked them before on Friday mornings and reported to Logan that all five attended the same mosque. It was the only time they were all gone. And now, Friday morning, she was inside.

She noted her gloved hand shook slightly as she peeled the tape back slowly, not wanting to tear any of the setups in the Zaman's house. Wearing a full chemical hazmat suit, complete with a mask, she finished peeling back the plastic. Knowing time was of the essence, she opened the door carefully and stepped inside. Having familiarized herself for weeks with the inside of the room, she moved with determination to the table on the left wall, ignoring the ones in the middle of the room.

Setting her tray on the floor, she took out the first test tube and dropper. The work was repetitive as she removed a few drops from one of the vials on the table, noted the label before depositing the drops to her tube, placed the stopper in, and then marked it with the chemical shorthand. Next, she replaced their vial back in its exact position, having noted it before she moved it the first time. Over and over, she moved down the table, taking the ones she was certain she needed.

"Babe, are you okay?" Logan's voice came through her earpiece, causing her to jump but comforting her at the same time.

"Yeah. Just finished the table where Malik and Rashad work. I'm heading to Nafisa's work now."

She knew Logan's team would watch for the group's

return, but he'd added a small camera at the end of the road to let them know if anyone else approached. He couldn't trust that they would use the vehicle with the tracker.

Vivian, battling the urge to keep talking to him, kept quiet, determined to focus on the job at hand. Moving to Nafisa's lab table, she sucked in a deep breath, noting the difference in the vials and dishes she had. Not recognizing the labeling language, she returned to her task, taking drops of the liquids and depositing them in her vials, where she had to copy the labels onto her labels. A drop of sweat dripped down the side of her forehead, but she ignored it.

By the time an hour had passed, she stood, knowing she had all she had come for. Jumping when Logan spoke again, she bent to pick up her test tube tray. "Logan, I'm finished. I'm getting ready to leave now."

"Okay, babe. I'm right outside."

Stepping through the lab door, she gently set the tray on the floor and turned back to the door. Shutting it, she carefully taped the plastic back in place, making sure to fix it exactly the way it was found. Looking at her handiwork, she nodded in satisfaction. Her eye for detail helped, and she was certain they wouldn't be able to see a difference.

Taking her tray, she walked down the hall and turned right into the kitchen. Their house was like the one she and Logan shared, only flip-flopped. Walking carefully, she was aware her booties were slick on the floor, so as she approached the counter, she set the tray down before pulling them from her feet. Stuffing them into her hazmat suit pocket, she picked up the tray and approached the back door.

Seeing Logan's frantic eyes on her, she smiled. "It's all good, honey," she said as she stepped outside, avoiding his hand, which naturally shot out to assist. "No, don't touch me. Not now."

Logan nodded in acknowledgment and turned back to the closed door behind her, making sure it was secured exactly the way it had been when they first came. "Sixty-seven," he muttered.

She threw him a questioning gaze.

"You were in there for sixty-seven minutes. I counted each one. I swear they were branded in my mind. Christ, I can't do this again."

Landon radioed, "The house looks good. She covered her tracks perfectly."

"Thanks, everyone," Logan managed to say. "We're heading to the makeshift lab."

He stepped back and viewed the area, and she carefully carried her tray around the back of their property. As soon as she could, she followed the path they had charted to give her the fastest way to the shed without being seen by anyone who might drive down the lane. She heard him jogging behind her, but she made each step as carefully as possible with her volatile chemicals.

Catching up to her, he said, "We're safe. Even if they come now, we're out of sight. She nodded but continued on the path into the woods, heading toward the shed. "You just focus on what you need, Viv, and I'm watching out from behind."

Approaching the shed, he reached his long arm

around her and opened the door. She lifted one foot, and he replaced her booties over her shoes, then they repeated the process for the other foot. Stepping past him, she entered the clean, plastic-lined interior. Turning, she said, "Close the door behind me, honey. You know you can't come in."

Grimacing, he stood with his fists on his hips, his unhappiness rolling off him. "I know, but I don't like it."

"We talked about this, Logan," she added, her gaze holding his.

"But what if something happens? I don't want to be back at the house with you out here alone."

"I have my radio earpiece. And we've got your people on the radio, as well. I need to start, and we don't have time to discuss this again."

"She's right, you know," Landon radioed.

Vivian battled a grin at the narrow-eyed expression on Logan's face. Blowing him a silent kiss, she watched as his facial muscles eased.

Nodding, he stepped back. His hand stayed on the doorknob, and he sucked in a deep breath before closing the door, leaving her to her task, all alone.

Vivian immediately got to work, almost positive she knew what Nafisa had been working on. Hours passed as she carefully analyzed the contents of the vials. Having set up her makeshift lab weeks prior, she moved efficiently from one table to the next. Logan had affixed a portable air conditioner inside, allowing her to keep a steady temperature.

Even a simple lab in an old shed was familiar to her. Finally able to complete the tasks she'd been trained to do, she found herself smiling slightly as she meticulously analyzed her data.

Back in the house, Logan waited impatiently, trying to keep from talking to her on their radio, afraid of startling her. Sitting down at the table, he propped his laptop in a position that allowed him to view the front window toward the Zamans' house, but he found he couldn't focus. Not knowing what the terrorists had been working on, his fears of what Vivian might be exposed to shook him to his core.

Akram and Farrah had returned from their Friday sojourn two hours ago. He anxiously monitored to see if anything appeared out of the ordinary, but they hadn't been outside, nor had Akram made any calls or sent any emails. Knowing that they hadn't been aware of Vivian in their home, at least on the outside of the lab, he breathed a sigh of relief.

"Honey?"

Smiling at the soft voice coming through his radio, he replied, "Right here, babe. How's it going?"

"Good, I'm good. As you know, I had an idea of what she was working on so that was my starting point."

"And..."

"And it looks like I was right. I've definitely discovered they are working with tularemia. The good news is, if you remember, it's not lethal—"

"I've gotta confess, I don't remember much about the different diseases. Sorry, but—"

"Don't apologize, Logan. Not with all you've got to keep up. I just didn't want to go into details about something you already knew."

"No worries. Tell me anything and everything," he assured, his mood lifting as he heard the excitement in her voice.

"Well, the low lethality is the good news. The bad news is that the bacteria can be stable for months and has a short incubation period."

"I know all this is important, but, Viv, what I really want is for you to get the fuck outta there and back here."

"I'll be there soon. Now that I know what it is and that it's stable, I can destroy what is here safely. I also need to dispose of my suit. Do you have the fire barrel ready?"

"All set for you, babe."

"I'm going to bleach the shed and take down some of the plastic sheets to put in the bleach tub in here."

Thirty long minutes later, he watched as she exited the woods. The evening sun had set, casting the yard in dark shadows as the sky above turned deep shades of blue. Her hair was still in a tight bun, exposing her tired face, but her smile was firmly in place. In her hands, she carried the tray of vials.

Bending, she said, "These chemicals are not dangerous, pointing at the ones near the back of the tray. I have added water to them to destroy them, and they can easily be added to the fire."

He took what she handed him and dropped them in, one at a time. Next, she bent to choose the last vial, the one she had been studying. "It can be safely burned," she assured. "The bacteria won't be airborne, so we're safe."

Nodding, he watched as she destroyed it as well.

Peeling her hazmat suit from her body, she dumped the armload into the metal drum. Within a few minutes, the flames turned the suit to ashes. Looking up, she said, "There's nothing left but the equipment."

"You need food, baby," he said, his voice full of concern.

She turned her gaze from the fire up to his eyes. "What I really want is a long shower. I feel gross."

Grinning, he reached for her hand, linking his fingers with hers. "Come on. The shower's small, but we'll make it work."

Wiggling her eyebrows, she laughed as he led her inside.

33

Standing in the kitchen the following morning, Logan poured a cup of coffee for himself, then pulled down another mug and filled it with coffee, creamer, and sweetener. Hearing the scuffing of footsteps coming down the hall, he hid his grin as he pushed the mug toward Vivian, still encased in her flannel pajamas.

"Umm," she grunted, taking a sip before moving around the counter straight into his arms.

Tucking her head under his chin, he closed his eyes for a moment, allowing the sweet floral scent of her shampoo to tease his nostrils, finding it eased his stress. Her body fit perfectly next to his, and the feel of her arms around his waist and her cheek resting against his chest made his heart pound with joy.

"Is zombie Viv awake yet?"

"Maybe after a few more sips," she grunted, hugging him tighter. Tipping her head back, she looked up at his face. "You still have the worry from yesterday etched on your face. Are you okay?"

"I never worried about a mission," he began. "My team...we worked as one. We could look at each other and know what the other was thinking. We could tell by the tone of each others' voices over the radio what the fuck was happening and what we needed to do. I don't have that with my Keepers yet, but I will. With their training, I know it'll come."

He dropped his gaze to hers, his arms tightening around her back. "But yesterday damn near took me over the edge, babe. You gotta know, though...I couldn't be prouder of you than anyone I've ever worked with."

He bent and took her lips, his mouth plundering, tasting, searching as his tongue tangled with hers. She responded in kind, desperate to join with him.

Walking her a step backward, he lifted her and planted her ass onto the counter. His hands were on her shoulders, pulling her top downward, when his buzzing phone halted them.

"Ughhhhh," she groaned. "I know you have to take that, but the timing sucks." Hopping down from the counter, she grabbed her mug on the way back to the bedroom.

He watched her walk away before he grabbed his phone. Seeing the caller, he watched her walk down the hall before he answered Donald's call.

"Ms. Sanders is certain it is tularemia?" Donald queried.

"Yes, she's sure. I'm not at my computer right now, so I can't give you the details, but she said it was a stable bacterium, and the incubation period is only two to fifteen days. It's rarely passed from human to human, but the cell's scientists may have done something with it."

"I have it pulled up now," Donald said. "Ingestion of contaminated food or water. So it could be simply added to a water supply. It says it can also be used in aerosols. Fuckin' hell, Preacher. Fever, chills, nausea, vomiting, muscle aches—"

"I remember Vivian telling me that many people could have it, and doctors wouldn't know to look for it until vast numbers showed up, draining the medical resources."

"Then destroy that house today."

Deciding he needed privacy, he walked outside and headed toward his truck. "I need to get Vivian out of here first."

"She's finished with her analysis and doesn't need anything from the Zamans."

"I'll take care of it, but I'd feel better if she were gone."

"Understood. You know what to do, Logan. Take them out—everyone."

"That's not what this is about, Donald."

"Do you really think that if you don't eliminate them, they won't go after her? They'll know who pointed the finger at them. They'll know who to blame. You can't protect her if they're still alive."

"Fuck!"

"I trust you, Preacher. Do what you need to do."

Donald disconnected, and Logan sat in the truck for a moment, trying to figure out his next move. Never, as a SEAL, had he been faced with such indecision. Now, he fully understood why Mace and Carson warned him about the risks associated with such an assignment. Keepers are protectors and investigators first and always. He let his past relationship with Donald influence him, but couldn't deny that Donald was right. *They could come after Viv.* Scrubbing his hand over his face, he sighed heavily.

He had to keep her from knowing how he would dispatch the cell members…*hell, she can't even know I am dispatching them.* But to send her home early might undermine the relationship they were building. *Christ, what the fuck am I going to do?* He sat for another minute, steeling his resolve, knowing that whatever happened when he went back inside would gut him, but he prayed when the mission was all over, she would let him explain—grovel if that was what it took.

Climbing out of his truck, he slammed the door harder than he meant to. Stalking to the kitchen door, he entered, seeing Vivian sitting at the dining room table, finishing a bowl of Lucky Charms. Despite his mood, a grin slipped over his face, seeing her turning her bowl up and slurping the milk.

Standing, she walked over to the sink and placed the bowl in it. " Are you okay? 'Cause you don't seem like that was a good phone call."

Rubbing the back of his neck, he ducked his head, staring at the counter instead of her. His mind warred with his heart.

"Now you're not looking at me."

His gaze jumped to hers as he steeled his spine.

"You've done your job, Viv. Thanks to you, we know what we're dealing with and how to move forward."

She narrowed her eyes, peering at him, but he managed to keep his face emotionless.

"Okay," she said, drawing out the word.

"It's just that now things will get hotter, and I have to be able to do my job. And that's not something that I need an audience for."

"An audience?"

"A distraction."

Her voice dropped slightly as she repeated, "A distraction? I've gone from a partner to an audience to a distraction. Wow, that's some kind of fast demotion. Do I dare ask how me as a *lover* fits into that?"

"Don't make this harder than it already is."

Her mouth dropped open as her expression became etched with incredulity. Her chest depressed with the air that forced its way from her lungs. "Harder?"

He worked to keep his voice steady, but his gut was clenching. "I needed you to tell me what they had so I'd know how to destroy it properly and safely. You've done that. Now, I need to finish the job I was hired to do."

"Turn over the information, right?" She stood with her arms crossed, her foot tapping a pattern on the floor. "Why do I need to leave for that? Won't I be needed to testify against them?"

"I need to take care of them and destroy the lab. Me...not you."

"Destroy how?"

"Fire," he responded. "Nothing there will explode, so everything can be destroyed in a fire."

Pinching her lips, she tried a different angle. "What about my makeshift lab in the shed?"

"I'll destroy that too."

She threw her arms out to the side. "I could help with that, Logan. Why are you pushing me out?"

"I'm not willing to risk your safety anymore. I can focus on what I need to do if I know you're safely away from here." Holding himself back from taking her in his arms, he clipped, "Your part in the mission is finished now, and you need to go home. That was what was always supposed to happen."

Time stood still, seeming longer with the agony that filled the air so completely that breathing was almost impossible without choking.

Vivian made no movement other than the slight quivering of her lips as tears gathered in her eyes. Her hand formed a fist that she beat softly against her chest. "Are you telling me to leave the job...or are you telling me to leave *you*?"

Sucking in a ragged breath, Logan hardened his voice as he repeated, "You need to head home."

Her head gave a short, jerky nod as she set her unfinished coffee cup in the sink and walked past him, rounding the counter. He swallowed deeply, his heart ripping in fear she would never give him another chance when the mission was over.

Ten minutes later, Vivian returned from the bedroom with her suitcase in hand. Bypassing him without speaking, she moved to the table and packed up her laptop. Glancing around the room, she snatched her e-reader from the coffee table and added it to her purse. Taking out the burner phone, she laid it on the counter before reaching into the drawer and snatching her personal phone from where he'd placed it weeks ago. "What about Sakari? I don't want to leave her here—"

"She'll be fine."

Scoffing, Vivian shook her head. "Oh yeah. The man who so easily shoves meaningful people away is going to assure that our... the cat is fine. Sorry if I don't believe you."

"I promise I won't leave her to her own defenses. I'll find a home for her. I promise no harm will come to her."

Pulling her purse up on her shoulder, she picked up her suitcase and moved toward the kitchen door. Stopping, she choked back a sob before swallowing it down. She turned to face him, staring as he kept up the stone-faced persona he managed to hold on to.

"I was in the bedroom packing and thinking of all the terrible things I wanted to call you...say to you. But I just can't. I told you I didn't do flings, but the truth is, I'm glad I was here. Glad I met you. Glad I got to work with you." She took another shuddering breath, and a lone tear ran down her cheek as she finished, "And I'm glad I..." Choking back a sob, she shook her head as though arguing with herself. "Good luck, Logan."

With those emotionless parting words, she walked out the door, threw her bags into the back of her little rental car, and backed out of the driveway. Logan watched her every movement, a weight heavy on his heart. Stalking out of the house, he headed toward the shed with destruction on his mind.

34

"You're leaving?"

Vivian stood at the bar, offering a strained smile toward Sally. "Just for a bit. I'm heading to Tanana to visit. I thought I'd like to see where I played as a child when my grandparents were still alive. I had planned on…uh…well, visiting sometime in the next few weeks, but it seems like this is a good time."

"Preacher goin' with you?"

Shaking her head at Iggie as he wiped down the bar, she said, "No. He's got work to do right now. So…I just wanted to stop by and let you know I would be away."

Sally walked over, pulling her into a hug as she softly said, "Honey, I've been working bars a long time… talked to a lot of people. And I get the feeling you and Logan are having a little spat." As Vivian was about to protest, Sally squeezed her arms tighter and added, "But all couples have that. Lord knows Iggie has made me nuts over the years."

She offered a watery smile as Sally continued, "But

seeing the two of you together...now that's love. He loves you, Vivian. So visit your grandparents' place, but know that man is crazy about you. And then the next time you see him, you'll jump right into his arms and forget about all this."

"Thanks, Sally," she said, giving a final hug before waving to Iggie and walking out into the sunlight. Climbing back into her car, she swallowed back the tears, knowing that Sally was wrong...she wouldn't see Logan again.

"Are you okay?"

Logan held his phone to his ear, glad to have Landon's voice on the other end. That was another new recent experience... knowing a team had his back.

"No, not really. Donald convinced me that she was in danger if I didn't take care of everything. I was a fucking fool for agreeing. You didn't uncover evidence that the neighbors suspected Vivian or me. I don't see the situation as having a long-lasting threat against her, but how can I take that chance?"

"You can't. You've got to do what you need to do, Logan. And we're still working back here to make sure you and Vivian are safe. Cole is flying Casper and Sisco to you for backup. We're monitoring the communication of the five terrorists involved, and so far, you're good to go with what you need to do."

"Yeah, right. Thanks, Landon. I have work to do, so I'll let you know when the first step is complete."

Disconnecting, he headed down the wooded path behind the house toward the shed. As he took one last look at the bare space, his heart ached. Grimacing, he knew he'd never had a problem focusing on a mission, and now, all he could think about was the mess he had made with Vivian.

With frustration pouring off him, he carefully destroyed the remaining contents of the shed, following the instructions he was given. He doused the shed with a special sulfuric acid compound before spraying it with water. It immediately began eating at the wood, a way to get rid of evidence and danger while not setting a fire that would alert others to what he was doing.

Walking back slowly toward the house, he tried to think of the next step, but the look on her face as she drove away filled his mind.

As he walked across the yard, a flash of light lit the sky, and an explosion rocked the ground. The roar and heat blasted him, and, reacting immediately, he threw himself down on the ground as flames shot into the air from beyond his house. Adrenaline pumping, he jumped up, running to the other side of his truck, halting at the sight. The Zamans' house was completely engulfed in flames.

Within seconds, he realized they had destroyed their own home, which meant they'd left. *How the fuckin' hell did I miss this?* Ignoring the blazing inferno, he raced inside to his computer, quickly searching the videos. His phone rang, and he hit connect as soon as he saw the caller ID.

"I'm fine," he barked. "At my computer now. What the fuck do you see?"

"Sadie is on it," Landon replied.

Goddammit! "Fuck! Akram and Farrah loaded the car with several boxes before driving away." Observing the time stamp, he cursed again. "It was while I was at the shed finishing the cleanup."

"I have Cory tracking their car—"

"Landon, if they've destroyed the house, they took the tularemia with them to use somewhere. Tell Cory to stay on them—"

The sound of a siren could be heard in the distance. "The firetrucks are approaching. I'm going back out to be seen as a spectator of his neighbor's house." Stepping onto the porch, he watched as the Ester Volunteer Fire Department rolled up in two fire trucks and an ambulance. He disconnected his call and jogged over to talk to them. Iggie climbed out of the first truck.

"Damn, Preacher," Iggie called. "What the hell happened?"

"Got no idea," he responded. "I was inside when the whole house shook. Thought the world was coming to an end."

The firefighters immediately went to work, hooking up the hoses to the truck with the water tank that pulled in behind the ambulance. As the streams of water hit the flames and soaked the surrounding area to keep the fire from spreading, Iggie turned back to him. "No one could live through that," he said.

"They weren't there," he said.

"Thank fuck," Iggie responded, relieved. "You see 'em leave?"

"Earlier. Akram and Farrah both left. In fact, I was just packing up for a little trip myself when this happened." Hoping that would satisfy Iggie's possible curiosity, he turned to go back into the house to check with his Keepers to see if they could find out where Akram was headed.

Calling out orders to the crew, Iggie shifted his gaze back to him. "So Preacher. You heading to Tanana?"

Confused, he halted and turned back. "Tanana?"

"Thought you might be checking on Vivian." Grinning, he added, "Figured you wouldn't be able to stand not being with her for even one night. Sally was surprised when Vivian stopped by this morning to say she was taking a few days to visit where her grandparents used to live. We figured you two wouldn't be able to be separated." Turning back to oversee the dying flames, Iggie missed Logan's anguished expression.

Five minutes later, he hurried inside to his computer with his radio earpiece bringing in the information coming from LSIMT.

"We've got their phone records. About the time the explosion occurred, Akram had sent a message to Rashad," Frazier said.

"Does it give his location?"

"It says 'testing in Tanana.' That's a small town. Perfect for trying out their bacteria contaminating water or food."

Tanana? "Goddammit, that's where Viv is heading!" He raced into the bedroom, grabbed his bag from the closet, and checked the content with hasty efficiency—weapons, Kevlar, ammunition, night vision goggles, and a variety of other necessities. Throwing in extra clothes, he hefted the bag on his shoulder before stalking back to gather his electronics. Seeing Sakari sitting on the floor, staring up at him with an accusing glare, he dropped his bags and raced to the closet, where he'd seen a cardboard box. With a few slices of his knife, he had poked air holes in the top and sides. Scooping the cat up, he placed her inside before securing the top. Grabbing some cat food, he thrust it into his duffel.

Three minutes later, he threw his hand up toward Iggie as he climbed into his truck. Tapping his earpiece, he said, "On my way to Tanana. Let Cole know of the different location to fly to. I can't get Viv to answer. Have someone there see if they have any luck getting ahold of her."

As he executed a three-point turn in the yard to leave, he passed the emergency vehicles still dealing with the Zamans' destruction. With the cul-de-sac in the rearview mirror, he steeled his mind. *You might have saved me the trouble of destroying your house and lab, assholes, but I'm coming for you.*

Small. That was the only word Vivian could think to describe Tanana as she drove through. *Why do things seem so much bigger when you're a kid?* She grinned as she spied the town sign listing the population as 308. Driving along the rough, partially paved roads, she passed stores, a few she remembered, some new, and some appearing to be long empty. A few restaurants. A bar. A couple of churches. And even a school, which she assumed housed kindergarten through high school in the one building.

Turning off the main street, she drove north for a mile, passing houses and a few subdivisions. The road was so familiar, she remembered summers of riding in the back of her grandfather's pickup truck, bouncing as he hit the invariable potholes. Looking back, she wondered if he hit them just to see her bounce and giggle.

Finally, pulling up to the small house, she parked on the street. The wooden siding appeared to have been recently stained, and it was nice to see her grandmother's flower gardens were still neatly tended. The plot of land next to the house had been wild, with trees flanking a meadow, but it now held a newer house. Looking up and down the street, she noted more houses, creating a neighborhood instead of just her grandparents' house standing alone.

When she climbed out of her car, she heard children playing in the backyard and could see a woman hanging laundry on a line tied between two poles set in the ground. The woman looked up at her and smiled.

"Hello," she called out as she walked up the front stone path. "I'm Vivian Sanders. I hope this doesn't seem presumptuous to stop by… it's just that my grandparents used to live here. My mom was born here, and I remember lots of summers spent here as well."

A wide, welcoming smile greeted her warmly as the

woman said, "Oh, the Panikaks were your grandparents? I knew them when I was younger. I'm Carly. It's nice to meet you." She jerked her head toward the house. "Would you like to see inside?"

"You wouldn't mind?"

"Not at all, come on."

She followed Carly inside, immediately engulfed in memories. While the furniture was newer and the walls painted a different color, the house resonated with the images of her grandfather sitting in his comfy chair in front of the TV and her grandmother bustling in the kitchen.

Turning down an offer of tea, she said, "No, I really have to be going, but this"—she waved her hand around—"has meant so much to me."

"Are you staying long?" Carly asked.

"I saw there's a hotel in town." Chuckling, she added, "It wasn't there when I was a kid."

"Oh, that horrible *Men of Alaska* show on TV that they filmed around here brought in tourists, and of course, the show's crew needed somewhere to stay. So they tore down the cute little single-room cabins that had been here for so long and built a new hotel that could house so many more. I have a feeling they'll have plenty of rooms now that the show is over. We still get tourists looking for the places the show exploited, but hey, it brought some money into the town."

"Sounds good, I'll check there. It was really nice to meet you. My grandparents loved this house, and it's nice to see that it's still housing a family." Smiling at Carly, she thanked her for the chance to revisit her family home. Stepping out into the sunshine, she slid her sunglasses on her face as she walked to her car.

A helicopter flying overhead caught her attention, and she leaned her head back, shading her face with her hand at her forehead. The reminder of Logan was painful, but she battled through, determined not to shed another tear. She had shed enough of them on the hour-long drive to Tanana.

Climbing back into her car, she took one last look at her grandparents' house and drove into town.

Stepping inside the warm interior of the Tanana Inn from the crowded parking lot, Vivian heaved a sigh, wondering if this stay was a bad idea. *I've seen my grandparents' house...maybe it's time just to go back to Fairbanks and catch a flight home.* The hotel was much busier than she anticipated, but seeing a large sign in the corner announcing a *"Men of Alaska* Tour Weekend," she grimaced, realizing the hotel might be full. Looking at her watch, she shook her head, knowing it was too late to arrange a flight today.

The desk clerk was on the phone but mouthed, *"Sorry, I'll just be a minute."* She nodded and walked to one of the windows overlooking the parking lot. A shawl-draped head caught her attention, and as she moved to the left to have a better line of vision, she recognized Akram and Farrah.

Her breath left her lungs in a rush as she tried to think of why they were here. She could only come up with one reason terrorists working with a known bacterial agent would come to a tiny, nowhere town on a weekend with a hotel full of guests from all over—*It can't be good, no matter what they're doing!* Reaching her hand into her purse, she grabbed her phone, then realized it was her personal phone, still turned off. The burner phone with Logan's number was back on the kitchen counter of the house in Ester, and she didn't have his number.

Sucking in a deep breath, she knew whatever happened, it was up to her to stop them. Smiling at the receptionist who had just hung up the phone, she said, "I...uh...see a friend. I'll be back." Moving to the door, she watched as the Zamans got into their car and backed out of the parking lot. Hurrying out the door and down the steps, she jumped into her car and began to follow them from a distance.

35

Having landed and loaded his equipment out of the helicopter and into another truck, Logan leaned down and stuck his finger through one of the holes in the box. "Hey, girl. I'll be back just as soon as I can." He unfolded the top and placed some food into one side of her dish and water in the other. Then he opened his bag and pulled out a T-shirt and tucked it inside as well.

A few minutes later found him churning down the road, finding it took only about three minutes to drive through the small town. No sign of Vivian or the terrorists. Gripping the steering wheel with white-knuckled intensity, he pulled to the side of the road.

Parking, he tapped his earpiece. "What have you got for me?"

"Her phone is turned off, and we never had it traced, so we don't know where she is. Devlin is on satellite tracking now since that town is so small, but he hasn't located her yet," Landon said.

Logan lowered his head and rubbed his eyes. "All

right, I'll go back into town, hit the bar and restaurant, and see if anyone has seen them."

Frazier jumped back on the line. "Logan. I'm tracking Akram's vehicle, and it's right next—"

Logan caught a glance of a woman wearing a hijab sitting on the passenger side of a car that passed him. Disbelieving his luck, he watched as the Zamans drove past.

"Next to me? I just saw them! I'm tailing them now!" As he started to pull out onto the road, another car came from the same direction as the Zamans. "Dammit, this town's got only a couple hundred residents. Are they all fuckin' out today?"

A small car drove past, and his disbelief took another jolt—Vivian was intently staring ahead at the Zamans' car, never looking over to see him staring at her. "Christ! I just spied Vivian following the Zamans." Realizing the danger she was exposing herself to, he jerked his truck onto the road, following her.

"Stay with them," Frazier said. "I have you on satellite now."

"It's like a fuckin' convoy on the road—not exactly incognito!" he groused while his heart hammered in his chest at the good luck of finding Vivian.

Vivian followed at a distance, noting when the Zamans turned onto a gravel driveway leading to a small house sitting on the side of a hill. Several cars were parked next to the house, the long drive visible to anyone inside. Frustrated, she continued down the road for another mile until she came to a widening where she could turn around. Turning to look behind her, she squeaked when an old truck pulled right in front of her, jamming on its brakes.

The driver hopped out of the truck and rounded the hood, jerking their sunglasses off. *Logan?*

Before she had a chance to roll down her window, his hand was on her door, opening it swiftly. Forcing her back against the seat as he leaned his large body in, he unclipped her seat belt before clamping his hand around her upper arm and pulling her gently but firmly out of the car.

"What are you doing?" she asked, jerking against his hold.

"The better question is what the fuck are you doing here?" he growled, maneuvering her to the far side of his truck, out of sight from the road.

"Logan, stop. I saw Akram and—"

"Jesus, Viv, do you have any idea how much danger you're in just by following them? How do I get it across to you that they are fuckin' terrorists who'd kill you for interfering?"

"I wasn't going to go up there and knock on their door, Logan. Give me some credit!"

Logan pinned her back against his truck with his arms on either side of her. With him so close, she breathed him in. She had only left him this morning, yet she had missed him already.

He shifted his gaze down the road and pinched his lips. Sucking in a deep breath, he let it out slowly before dropping his eyes down to hers. As much as she wanted to kiss him, she peered up to see his face unreadable. "What's happening, Logan?"

"Akram blew up their house."

At that announcement, her eyes bugged out, and her mouth fell open, but no sound came forth.

"I was finishing the cleanup on the shed when they left. I fuckin' missed it, and by the time I got back to the house to take the next step, the goddamn house blew to bits. The fire trucks showed up, but there was not a fuckin' piece of it left."

"How..." Her mind raced. "How did you know they were here?"

"Iggie showed up with the volunteer fire squad. He said you stopped by and told them you were going to take a trip here. 'Bout that time, my people checked their chatter. Akram sent a message to Rashad that they were coming here."

Vivian's shock at seeing him had worn off. The first flush of pleasure that he had come for her died as she realized he was all about the mission. Inwardly cursing, she realized she was a complete fool. Of course he was about the mission. That was what we were here for. *It was me who forgot and fell for him.*

Hiding her emotions, she said, "I just happened to see them when I was checking into the hotel. They didn't see me, but I knew it was important to find out where they were going. I wasn't going in guns blazing or anything. Trust me, I don't have a hero complex." She tilted her head and peered at him more closely. "How did you find me?"

"I landed in town and happened to see them drive by. It was pure fuckin' luck. But then I saw you right behind them and couldn't believe my eyes."

Fixing a tight smile on her face, she said, "Well, okay then. You…uh…know where they are. I suppose you saw the other car there. I think it might be Malik's, but I'm not sure."

A short jerk of his head was the only response. His arms stayed in place, and she wondered if he even realized he had her pinned in.

He dropped his gaze back to hers, asking, "How will they test it?"

Knitting her brow, she shook her head for a second, replying, "I…I don't know. I…" She stopped and began carefully analyzing the situation. "They didn't have a lot of the solution with the bacteria in it. I suppose direct contact would be the quickest. Um…shops, restaurants, public places where people touch things… shit! The hotel."

She looked up quickly. "The hotel is full right now with some tour groups. The Zamans might be there planning or even staying, but Logan, the hotel must be the key. It would be so easy to spread the bacteria around. People from all over the country who are up there for the event wouldn't realize they'd been infected until a week or so later."

He glanced up the road toward the house the Zamans had gone into. "I'll take care of them, but I need you to get out of here." He reached into his pocket and pulled out her burner phone, tucking it into the front pocket of her jeans.

She tried to ignore the feel of his fingers pressing so intimately on her hips, but his warm breath across her face could definitely not be ignored. Swallowing deeply, she asked, "Do you have backup...or whatever they call it, for going in to arrest them?"

His eyes grew stormy, and he leaned his face closer. "I have to see what they've brought with them and destroy it, too. At least, I know I can burn it."

"But you can use me for that! I can help!"

"No, I need you gone."

She jerked her chin back, his words coming as a blow. "But..."

"Vivian, we're wasting time. I have a job to do. No arrest. Just termination."

Blinking, Vivian tilted her head slightly, staring as she processed his words until her eyes widened with understanding. Her voice was shaky, and she opened her mouth, but the only word that formed was, "Oh." Her head jerked back, hitting the side of his truck, but she ignored the pain. "Not just destroy the chemicals, but... you...you're...you're going to—"

Standing to his full height, Logan pulled his hands back and placed them on his hips. "Yeah, Viv. That's my mission. That's my job. Your job was to figure out what they had and how best to destroy it. You did that, and now it's my turn to do my fuckin' job. Destroy and then terminate." He watched as her face registered shock, but her dark eyes accused.

Her breath came in a spastic pant as she shook her head. "But surely...this can't be the right thing to do...to just..."

"You think who hired me is going to take a chance that the legal procedures would put these terrorists in jail? That justice would be served? They're to be dealt with one way and one way only. And if you think for one second that those terrorists would spare your life if you got in their way, then you're way too naive."

Blinking at the sting of his words, Vivian grappled with what he was saying. Sucking in a shaky breath, she simply nodded, unable to process what he was going to do. But one thing stuck in her mind. Looking back up into his face, she asked, "You're going alone?"

"Do you see my team here with me? I have men coming, but this is what I'm here to do, Viv. Terminate the terrorists before they have a chance to spread their destruction. What I don't have time for is to stand here and argue with you."

She reached out to touch his arm but stopped short. "Thin ice," she said, her words soft and laced with pain.

He jerked back, his brows drawn down. "What?"

"You're skating on thin ice, Logan. Out there all alone. But you don't have to because I'm here. There's safety in numbers."

Logan dropped his chin as a long, slow sigh left his chest. Finally, he lifted his head, his eyes now on hers. "I appreciate that...more than you know. But this isn't skating we're talking about. This is my job. What I'm trained to do. I can't focus on the job if you're a distraction." Blowing out a long breath, he added, "I need you to go."

Swallowing deeply, Vivian slipped underneath his arm and walked over to her car, her whole body shaking. Opening the door, she paused, looking over her shoulder. "Will I see you again?"

His face, set in granite, seared straight through her, saying nothing. But telling her everything at the same time.

36

Crossing through the woods, Logan made his way toward the house on the hill. He'd grabbed items from his truck, including one of his weapons. Only two cars remained in the driveway, and he recognized both of them—Akram's and Malik's. He eyed a tree near the back corner and slipped closer. He radioed his location and plan but hated that he'd felt such a sense of urgency when he left that he didn't take the time to locate the video camera he could attach to his shirt, leaving him hands free. At least he had a snake camera to aid him, even if it was handheld.

After a quick assessment, he climbed the tree to the second level. Using the snake camera to peek into a window, he observed a room empty of furniture. The dust on the floor indicated no evidence of human contact for a while.

Using a glass cutter, he quickly cut a circle out of the window directly above the old flip lock. Reaching in, he unlatched the window and opened it with practiced ease. Sliding through silently, he stepped carefully onto the wooden floor.

Stealthily moving around the edge of the walls where the floor would be more supported and less likely to creak, he once again used the camera to peer out the door into an empty hall. Scanning the other open doors, it appeared the entire upstairs was devoid of any signs of life. They'd found an abandoned house outside town, making it the perfect hideout.

He heard voices below, raised in argument, recognizing Akram and Malik.

"It makes no sense for you to send them!" Malik yelled. "Farrah is a weak link. You know that."

"She might be, but Nafisa certainly is not. She will keep an eye on Farrah and make sure she does what she is supposed to do. Once it is done, then Farrah will have no choice but to keep doing as she's told. She'll be afraid of being caught, and that will keep her in line."

"Nafisa shouldn't have to worry about Farrah on top of what she is doing—"

"Why do you think I sent Rashad with them? Your feelings for Nafisa are too close to the surface. You would fail where Rashad will succeed. Nothing will deter him from his great jihad."

Listening carefully at the top of the stairs, he remembered Vivian telling him that Malik had feelings for Nafisa but that Nafisa had feelings for Rashad, who appeared not to reciprocate those emotions. Silently thanking Vivian for that tidbit of information, he hesitated before slipping downstairs, wanting to hear where the women had gone.

Akram's voice came from the right of the stairs, which, from what he could ascertain, was where the dining room would be. He heard the keyboard clicking, probably Akram on his computer, as well as Malik's pacing.

Wanting them to be in the same room, he waited patiently until he heard Malik's footsteps move close to where Akram and the computer were.

Slipping down the stairs with his weapon drawn, he rounded the corner, catching the two men unaware. Their eyes widened, first at him and then at his weapon. Malik stood perfectly still, his hands raised by his side, his mouth open in surprise.

But Akram's lips slowly curved upward as he stood, one hand slightly behind his back. "Well, well. Mr. Preacher." He chuckled. "I should have known that name was false. I congratulate you on your charade."

"Hands where I can see them."

Akram's smile dipped slightly as he slowly raised his hands, a gun held loosely in one of them.

"Drop the weapon," he ordered as Malik began to babble.

"What are you going to do? Arrest us? You can't do this. You can't stop us. It's already started—"

"Our neighbor has no intention of arresting us, do you?" Akram's dark eyes remained locked onto Logan. "He has to get through us to get to the women."

Malik looked between the two men, understanding

dawning on him. "Nafisa!" he cried as he whirled, darting for the front door.

Logan fired, and Malik dropped onto the floor, a pool of blood spreading out from underneath him.

Akram fired a wide shot, hitting the wall next to Logan as he ducked, then fired another shot toward Akram. The bullet hit the man in the arm, sending his gun skittering down the hall. Standing, Logan stalked forward and leaned over the bleeding man, surprised the smile was still on Akram's face.

"You cannot stop us. You take down one, and a hundred more will rise to take our place."

"Your particular jihad stops here," he growled.

Grinning, Akram reached his hand to press against his bleeding arm when he suddenly slammed it against his chest instead.

A beeping began, and Logan yelled, "Fuck!" knowing the sound of a timer on a bomb. Whirling around, he snatched the laptop off the table and sprinted toward the door to the screams of Akram.

"Noooo!" Akram wailed.

Racing through the front yard, he was unable to discern the voices of the Keepers in his earpiece as the ground shook when the explosion behind him rocked the land. Throwing himself face down onto the grass, Logan covered his head as pieces of wood flew past him. Turning back to observe the blazing inferno, he pushed himself up and ran into the woods by the side of the driveway. Having parked down the street, he raced to his truck, throwing open the door. Once started, he gunned it, churning up the gravel. He put distance between him and the destroyed house, assuming the Tanana fire station would respond, just like they had in Ester.

Two miles down the road, he pulled into a parking lot at the edge of town, desperate to find where Farrah, Nafisa, and Rashad were.

"Tell me what you've got!"

"The last message Akram sent before the explosion was in code. We've just got it," Sadie radioed in return.

Arriving at the Tanana Inn again, Vivian retraced her earlier steps and returned to the reception desk. The same man looked at her, his head tilted in question.

Offering a smile that was as fake as she felt, she shrugged. "I thought I saw some friends, but…uh…"

"Oh." He nodded. "Didn't find who you were looking for?"

"No…no, I didn't. He…uh, they weren't who I thought they were… at all." Looking around the lobby, she said, "I know you've got the show tour…um… thing going on. Do you have a room for the night?"

"Looks like you're in luck, but it's not my best room. We're at capacity in the main building, but we've got one of the original cabin rooms toward the back that's rarely used."

She scrunched her nose in distaste, saying, "What kind of shape is it in?"

He threw his hands up in defense and quickly explained. "Oh no, ma'am, don't worry. It's a perfectly fine room. It's just behind the inn. Two of the original cabins were left when they tore the others down to build this building. They were the ones closest to the woods. One is for overflow guests, and the other is used as the housekeepers' storage room and hotel laundry."

She cocked her head to the side, searching her memory. "I used to spend my summers here with my grandparents when I was little. I remember this inn… it was tiny, individual cabins."

A smile spread across his face as he nodded. "Yeah, I always loved those cabins. They were torn down when new owners decided to make this a hotel to get more rooms and more money. We usually rent it last since a lot of customers don't like the distance or the laundry noise, but other than that, it's a perfectly good room. And anyway, the housekeepers are gone for the day and the laundry's all done. So there won't be any noise. You should be good for the night."

"It'll be fine," she replied, her gratitude real in the face of overwhelming exhaustion. "I'll be leaving early tomorrow morning anyway."

Leaning forward, he smiled and said, "I'll give you a discount since you're being so nice about it."

Smiling her thanks, she handed him her credit card. A few minutes later, she walked past his desk and down the hall to a door that opened to a path toward the cabin. The mulched path led her to the door of a tiny log cabin. The front faced the back of the hotel, and to the side, farther in the woods, was an identical cabin with an engraved wooden sign over the door indicating the laundry.

Her room key was just that—an old-fashioned key on a key ring with a white plastic tag and the cabin number engraved on it. Entering, she flipped the light switch and breathed a sigh of relief. The room was old but perfectly clean. The window facing the direction of the laundry had been boarded over, probably to attempt to keep out the noise and possible prying eyes of the housekeepers. Shutting the door behind her, she dropped her overnight bag on the floor.

Walking over to the only other window, she pulled back the curtain and stared out over the back of the hotel and parking lot in the distance. Not worrying about the view, she turned and moved to the bed, jerking the covers down. Seeing the clean sheets, she flopped onto the bed, her body finally giving in to the day's exhaustion.

Thoughts of Logan and the mission filled her mind. Angry with herself that she agreed to the job without finding out the entire facts first, she had to admit that her supervisor probably did not know the extent of the *security specialist's* job description.

Rolling to her side, she thought of Logan's deception but knew he was right when he said he never mentioned arresting anyone. That was her expectation. *So he didn't lie...he just let me keep my false assumption.*

The faces of their neighbors and visitors drifted through her mind. She knew they were terrorists... she knew they were working on biological warfare... and they had to be stopped. *It's so much easier being just a civilian who wants terrorism to stop, yet we sit in our safe houses and never know what others endure to make that happen.* She thought of Logan's SEAL team and the injury that forced him to find another way to earn money and then serve again. *He has the guts to do what it takes to make us safe. How can I sit in judgment of that?*

37

When her mind refused to stop swirling, Vivian climbed off the bed and, listening to her stomach growl, walked over to her purse. Checking her wallet, she pulled out some cash, deciding to hit the vending machines she'd seen in the lobby. Not in the mood for a meal, she thought a soda and some chips would work. *And maybe a candy bar...yeah, definitely chocolate.* The thought that vending machines should stock wine ran through her mind, but she'd settle for chocolate.

Walking to the door, she hesitated when she heard voices just outside her room. Knowing there were no other guest cabins and the receptionist had said the housekeepers were gone for the day, she leaned closer, placing her ear to the wood. Whoever was outside talking, their voices moved farther down the path.

Frowning, she stood on her tiptoes to look out the peephole in the door. The viewer was old, but wiping it on her side, she stared at the pathway, seeing nothing.

Setting her heels back to the floor, she shoved the

cash into her pocket, still intent on getting a snack. Not wanting to startle the housekeepers if they'd returned, and having no desire to draw unwanted attention to herself, she opened the door quietly and slipped outside. Male and female voices were coming from inside the laundry, but she wasn't sure how many. The door was partially open, but she was unable to see inside.

Assuming the housekeepers hadn't finished their work, she turned and hurried quietly to the back door of the inn. Once inside, she trudged along the carpeted hallway before rounding the corner into the lobby. Fatigue had settled deep inside, and each step was harder than the one before.

Seeing the receptionist's eyes pinned to the small TV on his counter, she headed to the vending machines. Grinning at the low prices compared to California, she soon had a caffeine-free soda, a bag of chips, and a chocolate candy bar.

She turned to ask the receptionist if the returning housekeepers would be in the laundry area for long, but a crowd of people came from the main hall and into the lobby. They were talking loudly and, from their conversations, were from the tour group. As they passed her, chatting about the bar they were going to for dinner and how it was part of the *Men of Alaska* film set, she stepped to the side and made her way back to the hallway opposite the lobby.

Returning down the old, worn, multi-patterned carpet toward the back door, her hands were now full of her snack booty. As she neared her cabin, she shuffled the chips and soda to one hand to snag her room key out of her pocket. She could still hear low voices from inside the laundry cabin as she stuck her key in the lock.

Opening her door, she looked over her shoulder. With the laundry door now fully open, she could see two female housekeepers filling spray bottles with liquid from a large plastic container. Leaning slightly, she could now see the housekeepers' heads were covered in hijabs. Gasping, she started to turn back toward her room when one of them stepped outside. *Farrah.* She jolted just as the other woman stepped outside. *Nafisa.*

Her mouth opened to scream when a large hand from behind clamped over her face. She rolled her eyes to the side and saw Rashad, his jaw set and lips turned down in a frown.

Struggling as he wrapped his arms around hers, he easily dragged her down the path and into the laundry room.

"Damn," Nafisa bit out, her eyes blazing with fury. "Why is she here spying on us?"

"I don't know," Rashad said, still trying to subdue Vivian as she struggled. His hand stayed in place, firmly shutting off any chance she had of screaming.

Stepping forward, Nafisa stood directly in front of her and, pulling out a long knife, ordered, "Kill the bitch."

Vivian immediately stopped struggling, and Rashad moved them backward. "Are you stupid? Kill her with that...here? We have work to do, and you want to bring the police and feds here to investigate the dead body of a woman left in the laundry room?"

Nafisa's eyes narrowed as she stared up at him. "Do not call me stupid. I'm the one who developed what we needed—me, not you, and certainly not that fool, Malik."

Rashad towered over the woman, using his height to his advantage, and smirked. "You? The great Nafisa? Do you think you'll live to see our plan in action if you spread her blood all over the room? You're a fool."

Eyes wide, Vivian attempted to follow their bickering, but her mind stayed firmly on the words *Kill the bitch*. Her gaze lingered on the knife in Nafisa's hand, her heart pounding as she watched it slowly lowered.

"What are you going to do?" Nafisa asked, her words hard and angry.

"Tie her up for now. We finish what we came to do here, and then she comes with us. We go out into the woods and kill her, where the wild animals will easily destroy any evidence. Get what you need and bring it along."

"No, no," Farrah moaned, her body visibly shaking as she rocked back and forth.

Nafisa whirled, and a resounding slap sounded as her hand contacted Farrah's cheek, leaving a red print. "Shut up, you weak, worthless bitch!"

Rashad roared, "Stop!" Stalking back to the women with Vivian still dangling in his arms, he lifted his hand from her mouth to grab Nafisa's arm, swinging her around. "Touch her again, and I'll use that knife you're so fond of carrying around on you."

Vivian opened her mouth to scream, but his hand clamped her mouth shut again. This time, the grip partially covered her nose, and she fought to breathe.

Nafisa's eyes widened as she stared up at Rashad and then back to Farrah, her chest heaving. "Well, well. You and her? Akram's supposed wife? You choose her over me?"

"It was never a choice between the two of you," he ground out.

With the two distracted, Vivian managed to move her head enough to clear her nose from his hand, pulling in much-needed air.

Rashad looked down at her before lifting his gaze back to Nafisa. "Enough of this. Use your knife to cut some strips to bind her with. Then do your job. Fill those bottles. Now." Having given his curt orders, he grabbed at the bindings handed to him and pulled Vivian outside and farther down the path into the woods.

Taking a long strip, he tied Vivian's wrists together before tying one around her head and over her mouth. Pushing her against a tree, he forced her to sit.

His eyes narrowed on hers as he growled, "Stay there. Stay quiet, and when I kill you, I'll be merciful and do so quickly."

Her eyes darted everywhere, but the setting sun cast the woods in shadows. Rashad had placed her where they could keep an eye on her as they worked inside, giving her the chance to watch them working as well. Grateful he'd at least tied her hands in front of her, she felt around to see what she could use as a weapon but soon came up empty-handed.

The strip of sheet cut into her wrists as she wiggled them in an attempt to loosen the bindings. Grateful the cotton material was old and somewhat worn, she found the knot might be solid, but the cotton binding had some stretch to it. As she continued to move her wrists, she still had not come up with a plan or a weapon to use, nor could she dislodge the gag. *But if I can get my hands free, at least that's something*, she thought over her panic, trying to ease the pounding in her chest.

"I can't get Akram or Malik to answer," Rashad growled, his pacing now stilled, his phone to his ear. "Something's not right." Looking at her, he stalked over and stood over her, his face full of rage. "If she's here, I wonder where her husband is."

Nafisa walked over and grinned. "If he shows up to Akram, he'll get a surprise. That house is set to go, just like the other one."

Vivian forced her eyes not to widen at the thought of Logan in danger, not wanting to give away her emotions.

Rashad stood, his hands on his hips, for a moment before he looked back at Nafisa and Farrah. "I'm going to the house to see what's happening. It'll only take me ten minutes to drive there. Stay here and watch her. Finish what you need to, and I'll be back within a half hour. Don't fuck this up. Just leave her tied until I get back."

As he stalked away, she watched Farrah and Nafisa

come out of the laundry room and caught a sly grin cross Nafisa's face.

Logan pulled into a lone space at the Tanana Inn, stunned to see the almost full parking lot. Jumping out, he hustled toward the front steps leading to the rustic inn. Approaching the porch, his eyes caught a small black car tucked next to the pickup trucks, vans, and SUVs. Rushing to the parked vehicle, his gaze sought the license plate, and his heart dropped.

Sadie had reported Vivian's car was there, and she'd used her credit card, but the inn didn't have a room assigned to her. "She's not at her car, so she must be inside somewhere," he radioed.

Turning, he ran to the entrance and hurried inside, his plans for finding the terrorists now gone awry. All he cared about was making sure Vivian was safe.

After a quick glance at the small, empty lobby, he stalked to the receptionist's desk. The young man sitting behind the counter was talking on his cell phone, but his eyes widened at the sight of him standing in front of him, angry vibes filling the room.

"My wife just called and said she's not feeling well, so I brought her medicine," Logan lied. "What room is Vivian Pr...Sanders in?"

The receptionist hesitated. "Uh...we're not supposed to give out room—"

Leaning forward, menace in his eyes, he growled, "If

my wife gets sick 'cause she can't get her medicine in time, I'm coming for you."

"Uh…yes, sir. Uh, we were full in the regular rooms, but I had an older cabin room behind the inn that I put her in. It's clean and perfectly fine, but—"

"Where?" he bit out.

The receptionist pointed to his right. "Down the hall…at the end is a door…it's the only cabin next to the laundry—"

The boy's words were cut off as Logan stalked around the corner, his determined footsteps softened by the carpet. Opening the door carefully, he peered out, seeing two cabins farther down a path, one with a laundry sign over the door. Nearing the first, he viewed the open door, observing a drink, a bag of chips, and a candy bar lying on the floor. A quick search showed him Vivian had been here, her still packed bag sitting near the turned-down bed, but she wasn't in the room or bathroom.

Heading out, he noted a light shining from the laundry cabin's doorway. He glanced down, and his heart plunged as he saw the evidence of a scuffle, one where someone with small feet was dragged down the mulched path toward the door of the laundry room. "Someone's got her," he radioed. Logan knew he needed backup and tossed up a grateful prayer that Cole had flown to Ester and then was on his way to Tanana. "Get Cole and Casper here."

"They're close and on their way."

38

The side window of the laundry room, closest to Vivian's cabin, was boarded with wood, so Logan slipped around to the other side, some of the tension leaving his body when he saw that window only covered with a light curtain over the panes. Leaning his ear next to the glass, he heard a commotion inside. A female's voice was close, saying, "Get what you can. We'll take it out so we can keep an eye on the bitch. With Rashad gone, she'll have to deal with me now, and he's not the only one with a gun… although carving her with my knife might be fun."

Recognizing Nafisa's voice, he knew she was talking about Vivian. Bending slightly, he breathed a sigh of relief as his gaze found a slit at the bottom of the curtain, allowing him limited vision into the room. He spied Nafisa and Farrah working on the far side of the small room but was unable to see what was in their hands. Nafisa occasionally glanced out the door in the direction of the woods. *Viv must be outside.*

Wishing he could let her know he was close, he shook his head, clearing out all thoughts but what he needed to do. Cataloging the room, he noted two large industrial-sized washing machines on the far wall next to two equally large dryers. Shelves holding sheets, towels, and extra blankets lined the back wall. The two women worked near the washing machines, and as Farrah bent low to pick something up from the floor, he saw plastic bottles used for hotel cleaning.

Understanding filled him, and he realized how easy their plan was. The Inn's housekeepers would spray liquid with the bacteria all over sinks, showers, toilets, and counters, thinking it was their cleaning product. *Fuck, this would be devastating in restaurants, stores, hospitals.* The terrorists would not even be in the area by the time innocent people were exposed to the bacteria. *And they wouldn't have to use a non-lethal bacterial agent... lethal ones could be developed to use with the fake solutions.*

Seeing Nafisa and Farrah start to walk outside together, he leaned around and saw them stop just down the path where Vivian was seated, bound, and gagged with her back against a tree.

Calculating his options carefully, he knew he could easily kill both women. Stealthily moving to the front of the laundry cabin while staying in the shadows, he made his way forward, his footsteps silent on the forest floor, hoping to catch Vivian's eye.

Nafisa was on Vivian's far side, behind the tree, watching Farrah gather their supplies. Just then, Vivian happened to look his way, her widened eyes indicating she realized he was there. With a nod, he burst into action.

Logan rushed forward, easily disabling Farrah and drawing Nafisa's attention away from Vivian. Farrah screamed, dropping as he kicked her legs out from under her. Her hands flew into the air as his booted foot pressed on her back, keeping her on the ground.

Nafisa, with her gun in hand, scrambled to the side. Vivian's hands were still bound, but she grappled with the other woman, fighting for the weapon between them.

With his foot still on Farrah and his gun now pointed at Nafisa, he shouted, "Give it up, Nafisa. You're finished."

Vivian was still grappling with the gun as a loud shot rang out, and Nafisa's body jerked before going limp on top of her.

With his heart in his throat, he pressed his boot harder on a shaking Farrah and growled out the order, "Stay."

Vivian managed to roll the bleeding Nafisa off her just as he knelt at her side. Assisting her to sit, he scanned her for injuries. "Christ, Jesus, Viv. Are you okay?"

She jerked her head up and down as her eyes latched onto his. He reached behind her head to untie the gag. "I'm okay, I'm okay," she blurted.

She lifted her left hand, the torn rag hanging from

her wrist, bruising already, turning the injured area a dark purple, still holding Nafisa's gun in her right. His gaze moved over her body, searching as though to make sure she was not bleeding before coming back to land on her face.

When she heard a noise from behind Logan, her eyes widened, and before he had time to turn, she jerked her right hand up, pulling the trigger of Nafisa's gun.

"Fuck!" Logan shouted, whirling around, his attention having been so riveted on Vivian's well-being he'd ignored the threat still behind him.

The blast sent Vivian's arm flying backward, but her aim had been true... or, more likely, pure luck. Farrah fell to her knees, blood running from her chest with an unfired gun in her hand. She dropped to the ground and lay motionless.

He vaulted over, ascertaining the two terrorists were indeed dead, before rushing back to Vivian. He noted the glazed look of shock in her eyes, her cold hands shaking. "Viv—"

"Is she dead?" her hoarse voice whispered.

Bending, he got directly in her face, his hands clutching her bruised cheeks. "Viv, baby, look at me."

Her blank eyes lifted to his.

"I'm so sorry, so fuckin' sorry you had to do that—"

Shaking her head as she stared over at Farrah's body for a moment, she spoke so softly he had to strain to hear her. "I had...no...no choice. She was aiming at... you."

His heart ached as he pulled her against his chest, one hand cradling the back of her head and the other wrapped tightly around her middle. He closed his eyes, willing his heart to cease its erratic pounding, but he was unsuccessful. *Never...not once did I feel this out of control in the SEALs.*

"Baby, I have to know that you're okay," he said softly, his mouth moving against the top of her head.

She leaned back against the tree trunk, her face still registering shock as she looked around at the bodies. Her voice, as emotionless as her blank gaze, said, "We need to clean up."

"Listen to me. There's nothing you need to do. Akran and Malik are dead. I'll handle—"

Her eyes widened as understanding seemed to slip through the cracks in her shock. "No. No, you've got to go after Rashad. I know that." Each word seemed forced from deep within her chest and dragged over dry lips.

Standing with his help, her body quivering, she gazed around the ground again, shaking her head. "I...I have no idea..." She looked up at him. "You'll have to tell me what to do. I don't know how to fix this."

His heart wanted to shelter her from this horror but warred with this head, knowing she was right. The longer it took for him to begin looking for Rashad, the more time it gave him to get away. Sighing, he said, "I'll carry the two bodies away from here. I just need you to check the laundry room to make sure whatever they were pouring into bottles is gone."

Vivian avoided his eyes and staggered toward the laundry cabin, his arms supporting her. Her movements were uncoordinated, almost automatic, rather than purposeful. Finally, she nodded and looked at him. "I have to focus. I have to get rid of any traces of the bacteria."

"I'll help—"

"No," she said, shaking her head. "I don't want to take a chance on your becoming contaminated. I know what to do."

He stayed at the door, grabbing his phone while she moved to the shelves next to the washing machine. She picked up an industrial-sized bottle of bleach. Opening the lid, she sniffed, then nodded. Taking a towel from the shelf, she soaked it in bleach and began wiping down the surfaces, including the floors.

"Cole? Are you close? I need Sisco and Casper at the inn. There's a path and a cabin. I need a disposal for two." With Cole's agreement, he called Landon. "Vivian is okay. All are eliminated except Rashad. Sisco and Casper will help me clean the area. Disposing two. I need Sadie to erase all security footage in the area. Viv is working on disarming the contaminants."

Disconnecting, he watched as she bleached every surface Farrah and Nafisa might have touched. She found plastic garbage bags and dumped all the soiled towels inside. Looking up at him, she shook her head. "You can't touch this, Logan."

Sisco and Casper approached from the back, and he greeted them silently. Their gazes swept the area, landing on Vivian, but this was not the time for introductions. She glanced at the men, her eyes widening. "They're with me, Viv."

She turned her gaze to him, but her thoughts were

hidden. Nodding, she walked out of the laundry room and over to where the bodies were.

Sisco and Casper quickly moved the bodies after ensuring they were protected from contamination, and Logan noted she turned her head away. The air in her rushed out, and she held on to the nearest tree for a few seconds. Then, straightening, she walked toward the plastic spray bottles still on the ground. Breathing deeply for a moment, she shook her head and bent to her task. Without gloves, she improvised with the bleach-soaked cloths, using them to hold the bottles. Pouring pure bleach into each one, she gave them a shake. "This will kill all the bacteria."

Logan nodded, then headed into the woods after Casper and Sisco, making sure they were handling the remains. "You got this?"

"No worries," Casper said. "We'll carry them a few miles away, farther into the woo."

"We'll come back and head to the airport. Give us about an hour," Sisco added. "I'm checking to see that Sadie erased any security footage the hotel has. It'll be like none of us were ever here."

Casper inclined his head back where Logan had come from. "Go take care of your girl."

Snorting, Logan shook his head. "I'm afraid after all this, the last thing she'd ever want to be is *my* girl."

Sisco held his gaze. "You can always talk—"

"It's done," Logan said, his voice definitive. "Probably better this way."

"If you believe that, you're wrong," Casper added. He

turned away and hoisted one of the bodies over his shoulder before walking away.

Logan offered a chin lift to Sisco, then headed back toward the cabin. When he walked in, she squeaked in fright, so intent on what she was doing she hadn't noticed him approaching.

"Did you—"

"All done," he clipped. His gaze drifted to what she was doing, his eyes darting around.

"I've wiped down the entire inside of the laundry cabin with bleach. I have the towels in there." She pointed at the large plastic bag. "I've poured bleach in all of these bottles to kill the bacteria."

"I have gloves. I'll dispose of them," Logan said, his eyes finally lifting to hers. Feeling uncertain, he gentled his voice, his heart aching, as he asked, "Babe, how are you doing?" As soon as the words left his mouth, he hated the question, guilt eating at him. *She should have never fucking had to have dealt with any of this.*

Swallowing audibly, she blinked away the sting in her eyes and licked her dry lips. "I…I killed someone, Logan."

He immediately stepped forward, enveloping her in his arms. Holding her close, he murmured soft words as his lips pressed to the top of her head, wondering how he could ever make things right for her.

39

At the knock on the door of Vivian's cabin an hour later, she lifted her head as Logan entered. She sat in the lone chair, her packed bag at her feet. Staring at him in the doorway, she felt like she should speak, but no words came forth. She was blank inside, devoid of all feelings, and was sure her face was cemented in a blank expression.

"What did you tell the front desk?" he asked softly.

"I called to say that my husband brought my medication but that I still didn't feel better, so I was checking out early."

Nodding, he stood with his hands on his hips. "Okay, good. You're doing good." He winced before continuing. "I've arranged a flight for you from the little airfield here all the way to California."

She nodded, or at least thought she did. Having looked in the bathroom mirror to make sure she had no spatters of blood on her, she knew her face was pale with dark circles under her eyes.

Logan moved toward her, moving as though he were approaching a wild animal. Kneeling in front of her, he placed his hands on her knees. "I can't imagine what you're going through or what you're thinking. You did everything that was asked of you on this mission and did it to the best of your abilities. I couldn't have asked for a better partner."

His eyes searched hers, but she kept her emotions locked down.

Continuing, he squeezed her thighs for emphasis, saying, "You saved my life, Viv. I know you're battling with that, but you did the right thing—"

Shaking her head, she stopped him. "You don't have to convince me of that." Sighing heavily, she said, "You were right...they were going to harm a lot of people. And it wouldn't have stopped with this little hotel in the middle of nowhere." Giving an unladylike snort, she added, "As a bioterrorism scientist, I know what they could have done. I just... well, you said it best... I was incredibly naive."

"I've talked to Donald. He knows how everything went down. Your supervisor will talk to you when you get back...he'll know certain things happened."

Her eyes widened, and she gasped at the fear of others knowing she'd killed someone.

"All he'll know is that we were successful, and you were forced to do some things beyond your training. He'll have the number of a therapist who works with former military... someone who can help you as you deal with everything."

Vivian nodded once more, fatigue pulling at her very

core. Wanting to get off the emotional roller coaster and on to more practical matters, she asked, "What about my car?"

"I've already taken it to the little rental place here, and they were glad to get it with all the film buffs in town. I got your stuff out of it and into my truck."

Standing, he assisted her to her feet. She leaned her head back and said, "And you? You're going to go after Rashad?"

"Yeah… I have to get him before he leaves the country. As soon as we leave here, one of my men will set fire to the laundry cabin. It'll look like an electrical fire, but it will help get rid of any lingering traces of the contaminant."

Letting out another deep sigh, she nodded wearily as he picked up her bags, and they walked out of the little cabin. Without looking toward the woods, she allowed him to lead her around the outside of the hotel to where his truck was parked. Sliding into the passenger seat, she leaned back against the headrest, her exhausted mind ready to shut down.

Once at the airfield, he stowed her luggage in the small plane. The pilot approached, and she blinked in recognition. The pilot was one of the men who'd come to help Logan deal with the bodies. Her insides quaked as she locked her knees together to keep from sinking onto the tarmac in exhaustion.

"Viv, you've met our pilot, Cole, before. He will be taking you back. I'll stay here with my other Keepers as we try to find Rashad. He's also a paramedic and will be able to check your injuries."

Cole leaned forward and offered his hand as well as a small smile. He, too, appeared to be approaching a frightened animal. Steeling her spine, she shook his hand. "Thank you for flying me home."

"My pleasure, ma'am."

She lifted her arms, showing the abraded skin, as she shook her head slowly. "I'm fine. I'd just like to get home."

Cole climbed into the cockpit while Logan stood with her at the passenger door to the small plane.

Determined to face their goodbye with a modicum of control, she looked up at his rugged, handsome face, her heart skipping a beat for the millionth time since meeting him. Drawing in a shaky breath, she said, "Thank you for everything, Logan."

Logan stood statue still, his gaze searching hers, before growling, "Oh, fuck it," and pulled her in for a close embrace. Her body shivered against his, and she battled back the sob that threatened to explode from her lungs, even though she wrapped her arms around his waist.

Leaning back, she stared in silence at the moisture that had gathered in his stormy gray-green eyes. A tiny ounce of hope filled her chest that maybe, one day, she'd see him again. But he offered no promises, and the flare of hope died in her heart.

"Thank you, Viv. You kept me from skating on thin ice by myself."

At those words, a sob rushed out, and she let go of him, her hand reaching up to cup his face. "Godspeed, Logan." Inhaling a shuddering breath that filled her senses with his outdoor essence, she turned and climbed into the seat of the plane. Logan shut the door, and Cole made sure she was buckled safely. As the aircraft revved down the runway, she kept her eyes on Logan even though a tear slid down her cheek.

It was hours before they landed in California, and thankfully, Cole had remained quiet for the trip, allowing her the dignity to grieve the loss of Logan, as well as her naivety. It was only when they landed in California and had taxied to the hangar that Cole turned to her, his gaze soft.

"Ms. Sanders, I want to thank you for all you did back there. Logan told us how you handled your job perfectly, and we all saw how you got rid of the contaminants and saved his life with quick action."

Uncertain what to say, she looked down at her clasped hands resting in her lap. "It was my pleasure to work with him." She lifted her gaze back to Cole. "As we got to know each other, he talked about being a SEAL and then the accident that stole his career and his identity. I know he landed on his feet, working by himself for a while. But you should know it was easy to see that starting LSIMT and having the opportunity to work with his new team gave him a renewed purpose. He's prouder of the new team you all are forming than anything he's done in the past." She looked back down and snorted. "I have no idea why I just said all that, but I guess I just wanted you to know."

"That's mighty kind of you, Ms. Sanders. But it's been obvious to the rest of us during the past weeks that you've brought something special into his life, and I'd hate to see it end."

Her emotions jumbled inside her heart, and unable to think of anything to say to him with that revelation, she simply nodded.

Cole climbed down and soon retrieved her luggage, making sure she was safely ensconced in the limousine Logan had arranged to take her home. Sitting in the back seat, she offered a wave to Cole, then leaned her head back and closed her eyes, bone weary and heart sick. It had been a journey she'd never expected, yet strangely, she didn't regret it.

Logan had watched the plane lift into the sky, taking Vivian away from him. His heart had ached more than he'd ever experienced, and that included living through his career-changing injury and the long rehab afterward. As he stared into the night sky, he'd stayed rooted in place until the lights of the plane mingled with the stars and faded from view, taking the woman he'd fallen in love with away from him.

Finally turning, he spied Sisco standing next to the truck with Casper leaning against the door. He walked over and was grateful he didn't say anything. Climbing inside, he turned the ignition, and the engine rumbled to life. It was time to finish the mission. The first major mission of LSIMT. And even if it would go down on the books as a success, it would always be remembered by him as his great failure.

40

TWO MONTHS LATER

Logan tried not to think about her too often, but she was always on his mind. When he'd fix his *unsullied* morning coffee and found that he wanted to fix another cup full of sweetener and cream. Even in his home, where she'd never been, he would almost expect her to stumble into the kitchen...*my zombie Viv*. And every time Sakari jumped into his lap, he'd see Viv in his mind as she'd stroke the cat while sitting at the computer.

Late at night was the worst, when the loneliness of his bed would threaten to choke him. The sunsets that painted the sky and the sunrises that shook off the night, all brought her right back to him—and the reminder that they were never meant to be.

It was crazy, considering they had only known each other a couple of weeks before they separated. He'd never believed in the notion that love could come so quickly, but now, with an emptiness in his heart, he knew it was possible.

After returning from Alaska, he'd called Donald.

"Logan, I got your report about Rashad. You tracked him to where he caught a ride on a Russian tanker just leaving the country. Interpol will handle him now. And you managed to destroy the contaminants that were developed. Congratulations on a successful mission. The country owes you and LSI a debt of gratitude."

He'd wanted to tell Donald where he could shove the gratitude but just grunted instead. Since returning from Alaska, he'd thrown himself into the leadership role at LSIMT, ensuring they had vendors and suppliers they could rely on, going through their contracts more carefully before sending any of his Keepers out into the field, and not taking any more assignments like the one he'd agreed to for Donald. He'd stayed in close contact with Mace and Carson, forming an even closer bond with the other leaders. He'd added more runs to his training, each footstep pounding the earth unable to stop the memories of her face when they'd said goodbye.

His Keepers had avoided the topic of Vivian once he was home, although he knew they were curious. Landon had tried to talk to him, but Logan had just shaken his head and said, "I know you mean well, but I'm not talking about her. She's better off without me, anyway." Landon had just held his gaze and then sighed heavily but nodded.

Alone at night, he tried to imagine what she was doing and how she was getting along. There were times his fingers would hover over the keys on his phone, wanting to call or to text, just to see how she was. But each time, he shoved the phone back into his pocket. If she was getting over the events in Alaska, he didn't want to bring them back up for her. Checking in with her would be a particular torture for him, and he needed to respect her privacy

At the end of another long week, Mary wheeled over and said, "Logan, I just received notification from Mr. Markham that he wanted a video conference with you. Only you."

Jerking slightly, he started to ask why but knew that Donald would never have given that information to anyone but himself. His jaw tightened in anger as he wondered if Donald had forgotten that Logan had told him, in no uncertain terms, that they would not take another termination contract. "Thanks, Mary. I'll take it in my office." He walked into the small office he maintained just outside the large workroom the other Keepers used. He preferred to be out there when possible, but sometimes, the chance to work in quiet still reigned.

Moving to his desk, he sat and logged on to his computer. In a few seconds, Donald's face came on the screen. "Donald."

"Good to see you, Logan. It's been a couple of months since we last debriefed."

"Two months, four days, and about twelve hours."

Donald's gaze remained steady as he slowly nodded.

"Any particular reason you called…other than to check to see if I'm functioning? You've got no worries. Once a SEAL, always a SEAL. You know that. And now, once a Keeper, always a Keeper. What happened up there… how it ended… that was fucked up." Sighing,

Logan added, "She shouldn't have had to deal with that."

"Bottom line, Logan... you completed the mission. What Ms. Sanders went through, especially getting sick, was unfortunate."

Logan's eyes widened, and his body jolted. "What...sick...what are you talking about?"

Donald grimaced. "Ms. Sanders became ill upon her return to California. She was exposed to the bacteria, but it appears she wasn't a carrier. She was the only one ill."

His breath left him in a rush, and Logan leaned forward, his gaze anguished. "Is she all right? Is she—"

"She's fine; she's fine," Donald assured, his gaze assessing. "She was treated in a hospital with antibiotics. I talked to her DHS supervisor, who was in constant contact with her and the hospital staff." Donald stared at him intently, his eyes showing understanding that Logan didn't bother to hide. "So as I said, her supervisor says she's fine... she got debriefed... she got counseling. I'd say she handled things very well."

Logan's jaw hardened as his eyes narrowed. "Seriously? You seriously think that? She had no fuckin' clue—"

"If she had left when her part of the mission was over, she wouldn't have ended up in the thick of things at the end—"

Slapping his hand down on the worn table, he growled, "I told you what happened. She just happened to be in the wrong place at the wrong time."

Donald nodded slowly. "Or perhaps she was in the

right place at the right time." Not giving Logan time to respond, he continued, "She did her part of the mission without fail and then, at the end, worked with you instead of against you when she realized what you had to do. From what you said, it seems she saved your life."

Silence descended as Logan's mind shifted back to Alaska. "Thin ice," he mumbled under his breath.

"What was that?" Donald asked, his head cocked to the side.

"Nothing," he responded. "Just a saying I heard from someone."

"I also wanted you to know that I understand what LSI will and won't do from now on. There may be more cases I'd like help with, but I get your hard line."

"You have something for LSIMT, send it my way, and we'll consider it. We might not be able to take it, but we'll consider it."

"Understood," Donald said with a nod. "Then, good-bye, for now."

Logan stared at the blank screen, his body not moving. He finally lifted his hand to rub his chest, right over his heart. The pain was real, and the ache was heavy for the suffering Vivian had to endure, as well as the loss of her in his life.

Finally, he walked out of his office and headed upstairs. Alone. And destined to be alone.

41

ONE WEEK LATER

"Boss," Sisco called. "You've got a visitor at the gate. Do you want me to let her through?"

Logan sat with Sadie, Cole, Landon, Casper, and Cory. "A visitor?"

"Yeah, and I think you'll want to meet with her."

Logan glanced at the video surveillance, and his heart started pounding a rhythm he thought was lost to him. Standing outside the lane in a rental energy-efficient car was Vivian. Taking to his feet, he scooted his chair back, nearly hitting the table behind him. The others turned to him, but no one spoke. He'd told everyone of Donald's call... all of it. At first, he'd thought to keep what happened to Vivian to himself but found that it was a story that needed to be told—a warning not to take anything for granted when on a mission.

"Let her in," he replied to Sisco. "I'll meet her at the house." Without another word to his Keepers, he hastened upstairs. By the time he made it to the front porch, Sisco was waving her off as she pulled up to the side.

Stepping out of her vehicle, she looked up at him. Long, dark, silky hair, gently blowing in the breeze. Navy corduroy pants curved over her hips and thighs, paired with a light blue sweater. Black boots. Petite body that he knew fit perfectly with his. She was pale and appeared thinner than when he'd last seen her. But she was so fucking beautiful, his breath caught in his throat.

As he closed the distance, his heart began to pound, and he wasn't sure there was enough air in the Montana skies to fill his lungs at the moment. As he approached, he noted the forced smile darting about her lips and her hands twisting together. He gazed into her eyes, and her nervousness was palpable. Stopping a few feet away, he drank her in, but not knowing why she was here, he held back from pulling her into his arms.

They stood, silent, as though both were afraid to speak. Finally, he simply breathed, "Viv."

She immediately pressed her lips together tightly before sucking in a deep breath and letting it out slowly. "I thought this would be easier," she said, blinking several times as she breathed in and out.

His brow furrowed in silent questioning.

"Seeing you again, that is."

"I'm really glad to see you." Seeing her uncertain smile again, he wondered about her motive. "Uh...did you want to talk...or uh...?"

"Yes, very much. I'd like some... um... I need some closure."

"Oh. Yeah…sure." The idea of her forever goodbye hitting him while in his home gutted him, but he also knew he'd want the memory of just having her be in his space. He offered his hand, grateful when she took it. The electricity from her fingertips had them both staring at their clasped hands for a moment before their gazes jumped back up.

Knowing this would be the last time her hand would be in his, he entwined his fingers with hers and led her up his front porch steps. He felt a gentle tug and looked down, relieved she was not trying to disengage his hand but was instead staring off into the distance, a smile curving her lips.

"Oh, my," Vivian whispered, her voice filled with awe at the Montana vista. "This is breathtaking. To think that you look at this every day. Every sunrise and sunset. Wow." Giving her head a small shake, she blushed as she quickly continued up the steps.

Throwing open the door, Logan led her inside, giving her the view of his open but warm living space and the minimal, comfortable furnishings. Offering her a seat on the sofa, he reluctantly let go of her hand as he headed to the kitchen, grabbing two beers before walking back to her.

Poncho was already sitting at her feet, purring loudly as his head was being scratched. The cat stared up at her, loving the ministrations, and for the first time, Logan was jealous of a cat. A tiny meow sounded out from in front of the fireplace, and Vivian's gaze shot to the other side of the room.

"Sakari! You kept Sakari?" Vivian slipped off the sofa

and knelt on the floor with her hand extended. Sakari rose from her cushion and glided on delicate paws to offer her head for petting. Not to be ignored, Poncho moved in closer, and soon, Vivian's face was awash with a sweet smile as she rubbed both cats. She finally looked over and then moved to resettle on the sofa.

Choosing to stay close, no matter how much her words were going to hurt, he chose to sit on the sofa, twisting his body to face her. "I had to bring Sakari back. And that's Poncho, by the way. He's become rather enamored and protective of her."

Vivian's eyes widened, and he hastened to add, "I had them both neutered. There are other strays around, but for them, I didn't want him to go after her when she was in heat."

"Good thinking," she said softly, nodding. Taking a long swig of her beer, she looked down for a moment, seeming to gather her courage.

"Viv, you came a long way to talk to me… or to tell me something. I'm going to let you take your time to say whatever you need. You can call the shots." He steeled himself for her anger, and his stomach clenched.

"I… um… I became sick when I got back from Alaska," she began, looking up to hold his gaze. "It must have happened when I was cleaning up, although with so much bleach, I have no idea how. I handled the plastic bag afterward, so that must have been it."

"I am so sorry—"

"No, no. I mean, it's not your fault. It certainly proved what we knew could happen as far as biological terrorism." Snorting, she added, "I was very mildly sick, and in fact, they used me to study what drugs worked best and how to contain contamination." Hefting her delicate shoulders in a slight shrug, she said, "I became another DHS biological test."

"Oh shit, Viv…"

Unable to hold back a rueful chuckle, she smiled, and he felt the punch to his gut. He had woken up to that smile for weeks and had missed it for the past couple of months.

"Anyway, I'm all better… no lasting side effects or anything, other than a little lingering fatigue." They sat in silence again for a few minutes as she stared at her beer bottle again. "I'm also in counseling. For… well, for everything." She lifted her gaze back to his and said, "My supervisor said it was mandatory for me to keep my job, and let's face it, I needed it. So I've been seeing someone who works with former military personnel. They understand PTSD."

His heart ached at her words. He knew what she went through, but hearing her speak of it pierced straight through him.

"I'm actually doing really well," she admitted with a small smile. "I don't have nightmares anymore. Well, at least only rarely, and when I do, I know several techniques for calming myself."

"I'm glad," he said, sincerity filling his voice. "I never meant for any of that to happen, Viv. None of it—"

She leaned forward and placed her hand on his arm, giving a little squeeze. "Oh, Logan, I know. None of it was your fault. You had a job to do, and I know that." Swallowing deeply, she said, "I'm not here to make you feel guilty. I'm here because my therapist told me I had one more thing I needed to take care of and that was to face you. The way things ended... I had no closure."

"And that's why you're here? Closure?" He wasn't sure his heart could take any more pain but was determined to let her have what she needed.

She nodded slowly. "I need you to hear me out, please." Seeing him give a quick nod, she sucked in a deep breath, then let it out slowly. "I'm not sorry at all that I took the assignment. The truth of the matter is, I was bored just working in a lab, and even as scary as the situation became, I needed to see how my work had meaning when faced with how terrorists can use biological warfare. It opened my eyes."

She blew out another long breath. "But on a personal level with the way things ended... it was all so..." Huffing, she grimaced. "I've practiced what I was going to say so much, and now that I'm here facing you, my words all seem so stupid."

Reaching over to take her hand, he rubbed his thumb over her soft skin. "Just say whatever it is, Viv. I know I deserve whatever you've got to get off your chest."

She startled, and confusion filled her eyes. "I was going to say that I felt so connected to you. It wasn't like we had to play the part of being a couple. Honestly, I fell for you. Truly, honestly, fell for you."

His hand stilled as he jerked his head to the side, but before he could speak, she continued. "It's just that at the end, when you had to do your job and then everything went crazy, I felt like we didn't get our chance to tell each other how we really felt. It was all so much about the mission, and I know it needed to be, but I've felt for months like so many things went unsaid."

Pushing her shoulders back, she steeled her spine, holding his gaze. "So that's what I came to say. I fell in love with you in Alaska, and I'm not sorry at all. I just didn't get a chance to tell you how I felt. I once told you I was waiting for a hero, and that hero was you. That's still true. My counselor said that I need to face the fact that I was grieving lost love as much as the PTSD, and I should come face you so at least I will have said it instead of holding it all in." Her voice was etched with sadness, and her shoulders now hunched slightly as though her energy was spent.

She smiled gently, reaching up to cup his stubbled cheek. "Please don't feel the need to say anything. I don't want anything from you other than the chance to have seen you one last time. Thank you for letting me get my feelings out." Standing, she slid her purse strap on her shoulder and started toward the door.

Dizzy with emotions, he stood quickly, calling out, "You loved me?"

She turned. Her gaze sought his, and she nodded slowly. "Yes. That's why I needed to come see you. To know for sure that I told you how I felt, and then hopefully, I'll be able to move on from this."

"Why do you want to move on?"

Her brow furrowed as she tilted her head. "I need to move on, Logan. What happened in Alaska happened. But I know it's over. The mission... us... it's over.

Staying in love with a man who doesn't reciprocate that love isn't healthy."

"But you only just told me how you felt," he accused gently. "You didn't ask me how I felt."

Pinching her lips together, she stared without saying anything.

"I went to Alaska to do a mission. Find the terrorist cell. Work with a biologist to determine what they were up to. And when I had the evidence, destroy it. Then eliminate. That was it. That last part isn't what being a Keeper is all about, and I'll never take a mission like that again. But I did what I was sent to do because when it was all over, leaving them alive would only leave you exposed if they figured out who was after them. I did what I needed to do, but it gutted me to push you away to keep you safe." Spreading his hand out from his body, he said, "But I never counted on falling in love with you."

She gasped as her eyes widened, but she remained silent.

"Living with you... laughing with you... hell, just being with you was more than I ever expected. And came to be all I wanted." He let out a shaky breath. "But when it came right down to it, I was afraid. I hated to think of you knowing what I had to do. I hated to think of how you would look at me. And so, I took the chickenshit way out. I pushed you away instead of telling you the truth and then letting you figure out if you could still care for me."

Vivian faced him fully now, her purse dropping to the floor as she wrapped her arms protectively around her middle. "I was scared. Never scared of you, but I admit, knowing what you had to do unnerved me. I didn't stop loving you," she admitted. "But I wish we'd had time to talk about us. Everything went to hell so quickly, and I didn't know how to cope."

Shaking his head sadly, he said, "Me neither. I pushed you away to protect you, but all I did was make you feel rejected. I'm sorry, Viv. So fuckin' sorry."

Her chin dropped, and she stared at her boots for a moment, then lifted her head, her eyes full of determination. "So what now?"

"Do you still love me?" The question slipped out, and once the words were spoken, his gut clenched once more in fear of her response.

Her mouth opened and closed several times.

Steeling his spine, he prodded, "Simple question, Viv. Do you still love me?"

She nodded, slowly at first. "Yes. I never stopped loving you."

"Then why are you on the other side of the room?"

"Wondering about you," she said, her words barely above a whisper.

"I never stopped loving you either," he said. He opened his arms wide, and she darted forward, jumping into his embrace. The feel of her body pressed against his and his arms wrapped around her was achingly familiar and unconditionally needed.

As she leaned back, their gazes met just an instant before their lips. The kiss was filled with promises made and the certainty they'd be kept.

Separating, he said, "I have some people downstairs I'd like you to meet… tomorrow."

42

FOUR MONTHS LATER

Logan stood on the porch, his smile wide as he watched Vivian drive up, her eyes bright when they landed on him. He'd anxiously waited for her to return, his surprise burning a hole in his pocket. As she walked to the steps, he rushed down, picking her up, swinging her around, his lips on hers.

Finally setting her down, he grabbed her laptop bag from her shoulder and carried it toward the front door before taking her hand and leading her to the porch swing. He had gladly added it to the porch when she moved to Montana so she could enjoy the sunrises from their bedroom and the sunsets from their porch. Sitting down, he settled her next to him, tucking her in closely.

"Have a good day?"

Smiling, she replied, "Got the exams graded, and all semester grades are in. So I'm a free bird until next fall."

Taking a job with a university less than two hours away, she made the drive three days a week, teaching biology classes and working with the Public Administration degree program as a Homeland Security Adviser.

"How was your day?"

"Two security system jobs came in, and the governor is requesting a security specialist to travel with his daughter on a scholarly trip."

She looked around, her brow furrowing. "Where's everyone else?"

"Most headed to the bar in Cut Bank. It's Friday night, and no one is away on an assignment right now, so I gave them all the evening off." He leaned over, unable to stay away from her lips a second longer. He mumbled against her soft skin, "You're officially on vacation?"

"Mmm," she muttered in reply, her eyes closing.

He leaned back, chuckling at her pout when the kiss ended. "Sorry, babe, but I have something to do, and I can't really do it justice when my lips are on yours."

He reached into his shirt pocket and pulled out a ring... a beautiful solitaire, simple and elegant. She gasped, her eyes filling with tears as he slipped the ring on her finger.

"I want you to be my wife, Vivian. I promise to always be by your side and never want to skate on thin ice by myself again."

The tears sliding down her cheeks were gently wiped away, and she smiled. "Absolutely yes!"

Her arms encircled his neck as he pulled her close, his lips finding hers once more.

LOGAN

Two Months Later

Logan stood underneath the white party tent erected at the edge of his deck. He had no idea what a party tent was until Mary had insisted that he and Vivian would need one when they held the wedding ceremony. Vivian had protested, saying she didn't need a large wedding, but by the time they'd planned the invitations, it appeared the wedding would be larger than they'd initially envisioned. And that was fine by him.

And with Mary planning with Vivian, and Bert eagerly adding in his logistic expertise, they were now all under the tent massive enough to cover them all.

He stood at the front and looked out over the gathering seated, his lips curving at the sight while his stomach fluttered with unaccustomed nerves. Most he knew well, and those he didn't—the family, and former and present coworkers of Vivian's—he'd met at the gathering last night. They'd shunned the traditional bachelorette and bachelor parties and invited guests to the town bar for a get-together. His parents had insisted on helping with the costs since there was no rehearsal dinner. He had wanted to refuse until his sister pulled him to the side and told him, in no uncertain terms, to stop being stubborn and to let them have their moment.

After seeing his parents mingling with the guests last night, he was glad he'd listened to his sister. His dad had pulled him to the side and clapped him on the shoulder.

"Your granddad would be proud of you, son. Lord knows your mom and I are."

Now, standing before the gathering, his gaze swept over the guests he knew well and was proud to call friends. Former SEAL buddy Bart Taggart and his wife, Faith, had made the trip from Virginia, along with Bart's boss and leader of the Saints Protection Investigation group, Jack Bryant and his wife, Bethany.

Mace and Sylvie Hanover flew in from Maine, along with Marc Jenkins and his wife, Kendall. He'd met the two of them when they needed a rescue from the Canadian wilderness during a storm. Vivian had been thrilled to see Kendall again, and the two biologists spent time the night before catching up. He had a feeling that he'd be seeing more of them in the future.

The West Coast Keepers also made an appearance, led by Carson and his wife, Jeannie. Jeb Torres and his wife, Skylar, who Logan met when he assisted with her rescue were also in attendance.

Then his gaze landed on the men and women in the front rows. Landon, Cole, Frazier, Dalton, Cory, Casper, Todd, Timothy, Sadie, Bert, and Mary.

And standing by his side were Sisco and Devil. They'd been through fire and hell, only to have risen again in triumph. The night before, Devil had taken him aside at the bar to once again thank him for saving his life. He'd gripped his friend on the shoulder and was ready to tell him that no thanks were needed. But then Sisco joined them, and he knew he needed to do the same— after all, Sisco had saved them both.

In the past couple of years, his life had changed

irrevocably... and for the better. His life, which had felt halted when he was injured and left the SEALs, was now reborn into a new world of camaraderie and purpose. He'd gotten to know each of his Keepers, certain down to his very marrow that he had the best crew he could ever work with.

But all those thoughts faded away when Vivian appeared at the back of the tent in a white dress that trailed her. She was a vision of lace and silk, and his breath halted on its way to filling his lungs. Her lush black hair was pulled back from her face with a clip that held a lacy veil. And in her hands was a bouquet of native wildflowers that complemented her more than a mass of roses would have. She was gorgeous, and feeling lightheaded, he remembered to let the air out and suck it in again. He never knew the act of breathing could be so difficult to remember and perform.

By the time she made it to him, he had reached out and took her hand in his, guiding her to his side, now feeling whole as their linked fingers joined them. When he turned to face the minister, his gaze lifted to the mountains in the background. The light tower was prominent, the tangible evidence of its ability to guide others to safety. The same motto he and his fellow Keepers had taken and adhered to. Theirs wasn't a job or even a career... it was a calling.

Turning back to Vivian, he shared her smile before they began their vows. The ceremony was simple, and while he would like to say he remembered each word, it mostly passed quickly, and before he knew it, the minister declared them husband and wife.

As he pulled her into his arms, he kissed her deeply. It wasn't their first kiss, nor would it be their last. But it was the one he would remember for the rest of his life.

Don't miss the next LSI MT story!
Sisco

ALSO BY MARYANN JORDAN

Don't miss other Maryann Jordan books!

Baytown Boys (small town, military romantic suspense)

Coming Home

Just One More Chance

Clues of the Heart

Finding Peace

Picking Up the Pieces

Sunset Flames

Waiting for Sunrise

Hear My Heart

Guarding Your Heart

Sweet Rose

Our Time

Count On Me

Shielding You

To Love Someone

Sea Glass Hearts

Protecting Her Heart

Sunset Kiss

Baytown Heroes - A Baytown Boys subseries

A Hero's Chance

Finding a Hero

A Hero for Her

Needing A Hero

Hopeful Hero

Always a Hero

In the Arms of Hero

Holding Out for a Hero

For all of Miss Ethel's boys:

Heroes at Heart (Military Romance)

Zander

Rafe

Cael

Jaxon

Jayden

Asher

Zeke

Cas

Lighthouse Security Investigations

Mace

Rank

Walker

Drew

Blake

Tate

Levi

Clay

Cobb

Bray

Josh

Knox

Lighthouse Security Investigations West Coast

Carson

Leo

Rick

Hop

Dolby

Bennett

Poole

Adam

Jeb

Chris's story: Home Port (an LSI West Coast crossover novel)

Ian's story: Thinking of Home (LSIWC crossover novel)

Oliver's story: Time for Home (LSIWC crossover novel)

Lighthouse Security Investigations Montana

Logan

Sisco

Hope City (romantic suspense series co-developed with Kris Michaels

Brock book 1

Sean book 2

Carter book 3

Brody book 4

Kyle book 5

Ryker book 6

Rory book 7

Killian book 8

Torin book 9

Blayze book 10

Griffin book 11

Saints Protection & Investigations

(an elite group, assigned to the cases no one else wants…or can solve)

Serial Love

Healing Love

Revealing Love

Seeing Love

Honor Love

Sacrifice Love

Protecting Love

Remember Love

Discover Love

Surviving Love

Celebrating Love

Searching Love

Follow the exciting spin-off series:

Alvarez Security (military romantic suspense)

Gabe

Tony

Vinny

Jobe

SEALs

SEAL Together (Silver SEAL)

Undercover Groom (Hot SEAL)

Also for a Hope City Crossover Novel / Hot SEAL…

A Forever Dad

Long Road Home

Military Romantic Suspense

Home to Stay (a Lighthouse Security Investigation crossover novel)

Home Port (an LSI West Coast crossover novel)

Thinking of Home (LSIWC crossover novel)

Time for Home (LSIWC crossover novel)

Letters From Home (military romance)

Class of Love

Freedom of Love

Bond of Love

The Love's Series (detectives)

Love's Taming

Love's Tempting

Love's Trusting

The Fairfield Series (small town detectives)

Emma's Home

Laurie's Time

Carol's Image

Fireworks Over Fairfield

Please take the time to leave a review of this book. Feel free to contact me, especially if you enjoyed my book. I love to hear from readers!

Facebook

Email

Website

Made in the USA
Las Vegas, NV
20 October 2024